LOVE
ON
THE
LINE

ANABELLE BRYANT

OLIVERHEBERBOOKS

PUBLISHER'S NOTE: This is a work of fiction. Names, characters, places, and incidents either are the product of the author's imagination or are used fictitiously. Any resemblance to actual persons, living or dead, business establishments, events, or locales is entirely coincidental.

Published by Oliver-Heber Books

0 9 8 7 6 5 4 3 2 1

One

LONDON 1817

The glint of his knife caught her attention. Perched high above Vauxhall Gardens, balanced on a tightrope less than two inches wide, Lola York witnessed a murder. Captivated by the brutal act and unable to scream, she remained trapped between the surety of her steps and a death fall to the ground below.

Usually, her nightly performances suspended her above the cruelties of reality. Walking the rope was the only time she felt completely safe and utterly free. As though she could finally breathe once she rose above London, unfettered by the sins of the past and uncertainty of her future.

But now halfway across, poised between two wooden stanchions, the unexpected flash of moonlight on metal drew her eyes to the violent scene as it unfolded on a shadowy path beyond the grandstand. Horrified and transfixed, she stayed motionless while below multitudes of gathered spectators and excitement seekers waited breathlessly for her next step.

Still, she couldn't move. Not while two dark figures fought, one with malice, the other in defense. The attacker wore a long black greatcoat and came at the other person in a silent rush that took the victim unaware. There wasn't much else to see. It was over in the length of a few exhales.

Someone in the stands yelled an obscenity, impatient with her immobility. She blinked several times in succession and fixed her eyes on the rope, moving forward with rote memory and unerring balance until she reached the other side. An oblivious burst of applause swelled upward into the air around her as she waved numbly to the blurred faces of the crowd. She was a mistress of grace and balance. Nothing was more important than the show.

Shaken, she glanced over her shoulder, beyond the grandstand to the darkened path where she'd witnessed someone's life stolen in a matter of seconds. Now only darkness met her eyes aside from the slumped form of a body left behind.

Pickpockets, swindlers, prostitutes and the like, were common to Vauxhall. In fact, many visitors thrived on the danger and illicit juxtaposition the pleasure gardens offered.

But murder, *murder* was unsettling.

She had no time to reconcile her thoughts as the grandstand emptied, the show having ended. A heartbeat later a high-pitched scream pierced the air. Several more followed. Male voices barked orders. Crowds dispersed. Others gathered along the path periphery, seeking a bit of morbid gawking. The shrill whistle of the watch sounded. On that isolated path, things were becoming known.

Far above the chaos, Lola waited on the wooden platform.

"Lola."

She recognized Marco's voice and glanced to the rope ladder dangling over the side of the platform and down to the ground. Marco DeLeon was a fellow performer and good friend. He climbed halfway and paused when their eyes met.

"Are you all right?"

He began to climb higher and she stalled him by holding up her flattened palm. Noticing how her fingers trembled, she dropped her hand just as quickly. "Yes. I'm fine."

She wasn't ready to talk about what she'd seen. Not even with Marco, the one person at Vauxhall who knew about her past. Someone she'd grown close to and shared a brief relationship. Even though they'd separated over a year ago, he continued to be protective and she didn't want to answer his questions or ignite his concern. The less she told him, the better it would be all around.

"A man was killed." He'd reached the platform, having climbed up anyway. "Did you know?"

"No." She lied and leaned over to adjust her slipper, avoiding his eyes. "Did you see it?"

"I saw nothing." He answered. "I don't think anyone did. All eyes were on you, on the rope. Everyone else was busy performing or preparing. I was inside the pavilion. I only came out when I heard someone scream."

"What have you learned?" She stepped toward the rope ladder, knowing he would have to descend so she could follow.

"Not much." He spoke as he moved. "A man was stabbed. He's dead. But it hurts us all. The last thing we need is Bow Street nosing around here. It cuts into the profits."

Marco didn't exaggerate. The more nobs and cits who sought respite from life's tedium by visiting the infamous pleasure grounds, the more money there was to be made. Crowds were important. Size definitely mattered.

Lola and the other performers were a misfit collection of outcasts and drifters who looked out for their own and shared a common dislike of Runners and lawmen. The entertainers were loyal to each other and rarely asked questions, more interested in their present than another's history. Lola had come into her occupation on the tightrope by accident, but it suited this new version of her life. Perhaps it was only what she deserved. Past decisions were better left unexamined at the moment and like Marco, everyone in employ at Vauxhall had secrets of their own to protect.

. . .

Theodore Michael Coventry, third Earl of Essex, awoke to the sound of loud pounding. Fighting off the weight of interrupted sleep, he glanced at the clock on the mantel and startled to awareness. At this hour? Who the hell knew he was in house anyway?

With a breath composed of annoyance and impatience, he left the comfort of his chair near the fire and answered the door. Having only just returned to London the day before, he hadn't secured the staff needed for his town house in Mayfair.

From what he could tell, little had changed in the city of his birth since he'd left two years ago to travel abroad. Perhaps he hadn't changed either, that same relentless restlessness in his blood persisted, even now at half past midnight. It could be nothing more than exhaustion. Sleep often escaped him and the deep slumber he'd experienced before the knocking began was ever elusive and rare.

Drawing a cleansing breath, he lifted the latch and opened the door. Two men stood on the front steps.

"We need to speak to the Earl of Essex," the taller man stated.

"I am Essex," Theodore replied, chagrin overriding his earlier annoyance. It wasn't every day he was mistaken for the butler.

"May we have a moment of your time, my lord?" This came from the shorter man. "We're from Bow Street. There's been an incident of which you should be informed."

The latter remark ignited curiosity instead of concern. He was an only child with deceased parents and distant, if any, extended family. Having been away for over two years, he couldn't imagine what the Runners sought at this ungodly hour.

He angled the door wider in a gesture meant to invite the men in. Perhaps if he could dispose of the issue quickly, he'd have the chance to reclaim some much-needed sleep tonight.

"What is this about?" Theodore asked as he led the Runners into the front drawing room. A modest fire still burned in the hearth keeping his chair warm until he could return. He walked to the decanter atop the mahogany console table and gestured to the crystal glasses. "Brandy?"

Both constables declined.

"I'm Frederickson and this is Johns," the taller man said, indicating the other. "We're here on official business."

"Ordinarily I would offer you tea and refreshments, but unfortunately I've just returned from travel in America. I haven't staffed the house yet."

"Thank you, my lord, but that isn't necessary," Fredrickson continued. "There's been an incident and we'd like to ask you a few questions in regard to the matter."

"So then, I'll need a brandy." Theodore turned, poured himself a drink and took a hearty swallow. "Obviously there's more to the story. What happened? And what does it have to do with me?"

"You returned yesterday?" Johns asked, glancing at the pad in his hand.

Theodore wasn't aware the man had taken notes. "Yes. By way of the packet ship *Esmeralda*. She docked two nights ago and I've since arrived in London."

"Are you acquainted with Stephen Blakely, Viscount Fremont?"

"Yes. Why do you ask?" Theodore hoped his closest friend and ally hadn't found his way into trouble.

Fremont was a devil-may-care type fellow who never failed to lighten the mood in a room with his entertaining antics. He was one of the few people Theodore trusted implicitly, having gone through university together and later maintained their relationship into adulthood. Despite Fremont's escapades, he possessed a heart of gold and unflappable character. They didn't share bloodlines, but in actuality the viscount was the closest thing to a brother Theodore would ever have. He valued their friendship immeasurably and looked forward to seeing Fremont now that he'd returned to London. An unexpected smile accompanied that thought.

"What has the wastrel done? Gotten foxed and waded bare arsed into the St. James fountain? Popped someone's cork over a pretty lady? Or has he raced his phaeton down Rotten Row? You must tell the buffoon I'll not pay his fines again."

A formidable silence permeated the room. Theodore turned from where he'd grinned at the fire and met the solemn stare of both constables. "What's happened?"

"We are sorry to inform you of Viscount Fremont's passing."

For a moment, Theodore couldn't breathe. Had he misheard? "What are you talking about? Stephen is my age, only nine and twenty. He's not dead. You're mistaken."

"With regret," Fredrickson shifted his stance, his shoulders straightening with the movement. "It is not a mistake."

Theodore downed the last of his brandy and set the glass on the mantel, anger quick to override all other emotion. "What happened? I've asked you three times. Tell me what happened." He paced across the room, wanting to separate himself from whatever the two officers meant to share and at the same time, needing to learn every detail. Fremont couldn't be dead. The son-of-a-bitch was too full of life. Had too much to live for. Something was very wrong here.

"He was the victim of a crime at Vauxhall Gardens earlier this evening," Johns said plainly. "We're working to understand exactly what occurred. At this point we know the viscount was overtaken on one of the private paths. He was stabbed and killed. It may have been a simple robbery."

"A simple robbery." Theodore repeated the words as he strode across the room, not stopping until he stood within a pace of the two Runners. His thunderous expression caused Johns to take a step back. "There's nothing simple about this."

"Of course not." Fredrickson was quick to amend. "But crime happens all the time at Vauxhall and while we work to investigate—"

"Crime, yes. Stolen watches and illegal dice. Not murder. Not murder of a nobleman. Not murder of my friend." His voice had grown louder with each statement until he'd shouted the last words. Drawing a deep breath, he waited, attempting to process the inconceivable idea Fremont was gone.

Fremont was gone.

"What do you know?" Theodore asked, impatience and rage coursing through him like repeated lightning strikes. "Tell me what you know."

"My lord, we've come tonight because Viscount Fremont had a letter from you in his coat pocket."

"Yes. I'd written to him. About my return. We'd planned to meet once I was settled." Theodore shook his head, still rejecting the truth. There would be no meeting now. He'd never hear his friend's jovial laughter. Never hear his voice again. "What have you learned about who did this? Stop wasting time. Shouldn't you be at Vauxhall questioning people?"

"Unfortunately, our information is limited," Johns answered more delicately, nodding for his partner to continue.

"By the time we arrived at Vauxhall, the visitors had already left. It appears the crime occurred while one of the entertainers performed her act. All eyes were on the tightrope. Most areas were busy with customers. Dinner boxes were full. The orchestra played for a large audience on the opposite side of the rotunda. The other main acts were already finished for the night and the employees had returned to the large tent or gone home." Fredrickson paused in the retelling, visibly uncomfortable with whatever he would say next. "Lord Fremont was found on a darkened path behind the grandstand. It is a remote and deserted area sometimes used for amorous assignations. We've spoken to Mr. Morland, the man in charge. Due to the loud music and typical goings-on, no one reported hearing anything untoward, mainly because a stabbing is silent in comparison to a gunshot. Considering the seclusion of the private paths, no one witnessed anything unusual. We have a plan to return tomorrow morning at nine o'clock to interview whoever was working at the time. Morland will arrange for all employees to be there."

"I will accompany you." Theodore stared at the officers. His heart had calmed enough now to ache with the pain of loss.

"With all due respect, Lord Essex, we came here tonight to inform you of Viscount Fremont's passing and ask about your relationship. Nothing more," Johns said. "Any further involvement is not necessary. We'll—"

"I said, I will accompany you." It could have been the note of finality in his voice or the dead seriousness of his stare, but both officers gave their agreement before Theodore promptly led them out.

Two

Almost everyone was already seated on the wooden benches inside the Turkish tent when Lola entered the next morning. Marco was quick to motion to the empty place beside him. She walked over slowly, skimming a glance over the makeshift family who'd adopted her since she'd found her way to Vauxhall two years ago. She greeted them with a slight smile.

Pockets of murmured conversation continued though concern was etched into everyone's expression, a stark contrast to the lively colors of the tent panels. Here with these talented people, opera singers, acrobats, dancers, and jugglers, she'd found acceptance. No one cared about the color of one's skin, manner of speech, level of education, or purse size. It was a cruel contradiction that by being born on the right side of the blanket, the upper ten thousand possessed all the betterments of society and yet rapaciously sought out the rare gifts of the people they regarded as beneath them. However, she was one of the guilty. Willing to exchange the risk of falling to her death from an unimaginable height for the thrill of walking the rope in front of a crowd.

The world she lived in rarely made sense.

"Morland just entered," Marco said as she approached. "When I didn't see you here, I thought you forgot."

How could she forget?

She'd hardly slept last night.

"I wasn't in a hurry," she answered, settling on the bench and making a process of smoothing her skirt where the hem brushed against her calves. She looked across the tent to where Morland waited. Word had spread that a few Runners would question everyone this morning.

"I almost came to get you. I wasn't sure."

"You needn't worry about me, Marco. We're no longer together." She stared straight ahead, watching Morland as he ushered three men into the tent.

"But we're still friends."

"Yes. Of course."

She watched the first two men as they spoke with the Vauxhall manager, but the third stranger stood apart from the conversation. His attention remained on the benches where the performers had assembled.

By comparison to the other officers, he was taller. Broader. His hair was dark as pitch, while the other two men were less intimidating somehow. But not this man. He wore a long black greatcoat in kind to the attacker. Seeing it unnerved her, no matter that type of coat was likely the preferred uniform of better society. Still, something unexpected alerted her to this man's presence and she didn't like the feeling.

She watched as he slowly assessed everyone seated across the back of the tent, waiting for his focus to move to her section. Her pulse raced as if by merely glancing in her direction he would be able to tell she'd witnessed the killing. Shaking her head to dismiss the idea, she dropped her gaze to her slippers.

"The Runners are here now," Marco muttered, seemingly just as uncomfortable as she. He indicated the men with a slight wag of his chin.

She didn't answer, not wanting to look in that direction again. Instead, she concentrated on Marco's profile outlined by the early light stealing through the gaps in the canvas panels. He hadn't shaved this morning. He looked tired. Perhaps he was more affected by the murder than he'd let on. Marco was a good man who, by being of mixed heritage, knew only injustice in his life. Dismissed by better society, he possessed finer qualities than many of the nobs who visited Vauxhall in search of drunkenness and debauchery. The current situation couldn't sit well with him either.

A prickle of awareness skittered up her spine and she bit into her lower lip, willing herself not to turn toward the Runners. When they were ready, they would address the crowd. There was no need to create unnecessary eye contact and yet her pulse ramped up another notch and her breathing grew stilted. Unable to stay focused, she shifted her attention to the right where her gaze collided with the dark-haired stranger. Their eyes held. The moment became unbearable.

"Listen, everyone."

Morland approached, clapping his hands to gain the performers' attention, not unlike a schoolmaster demanding his students take notice. A bittersweet memory from her childhood resurrected the image and she pushed it away as she brought her attention to the manager.

"As you're already aware, a tragedy occurred here last night. A man was killed."

A ripple of hushed conversation chased Morland's words across the tent until everyone quieted again.

"Bow Street has sent two of their finest Runners to speak with all of you in case anyone has seen or heard something unusual. Please give the officers your full cooperation. Remember, gossip about crime and heinous activity will keep visitors away. It's bad for business. I expect everyone to continue on as if nothing happened. Later tonight, things will proceed as always, but for now do your best to tell the officers everything you can recall from last night."

Without further comment, Morland stepped aside and the two men Lola had already assumed were Runners walked to the forefront. The other man, the one with the disturbing presence, lingered in the background, his eyes examining all of them as if specimens under glass. Marco must have noticed as well. He reached out and placed his hand over hers where it rested on the bench, but she was too agitated to accept his comfort. She slipped her hand free and leaned down to adjust her slippers, keeping her fingers busy.

When she glanced up again, the dark-haired gentleman had moved to the area directly across from the bench where she was seated. His penetrating gaze caused her heart to pound, yet unwilling to appear skittish, she didn't immediately look away.

He had sharp, chiseled features, similar to the marble statues near the garden's entry gate. By Morland's description, this man was not a Runner. Who was he then? She took in his expensive clothing, polished leather boots and arrogant stance. Was he a superior sent to oversee the investigation? Belatedly she noticed the black mourning band wrapped around his sleeve where it blended into the wool. So, he was a relation to the man who was killed. Since when did Runners involve family members in their work? Bloody nobs with their superior entitlement always got their way.

She raised her eyes to his face and found he watched her as well. She averted her gaze, not wanting to invite further interest.

THEODORE DIDN'T KNOW WHAT TO THINK OF THE collection of performers before him. He'd come to Vauxhall years ago and taken in a few shows, but to see so many unusual people assembled in one place when his mind spun with questions and heart ached with loss, was almost too much to comprehend. He scanned the group, searching for something, any indication that seemed unnatural. But there was the rub. These performers thrived on the unnatural. They purposely enhanced any quality considered untraditional, whether in their physical features, manner of dress, or eccentric skill. It was their trade, yet it made his task that much harder. So many of them gawked at him, as if *he* was the oddity. Others ignored him altogether. It was a peculiar situation.

Continuing his perusal, he noticed a young woman at the far-right side of the tent. She looked startled, for lack of a better description. As if she held her breath in wait. He'd observed how the man beside her had reached for her hand and she'd pulled it away abruptly. That man appeared equally troubled. He too was young and from another country if the color of his skin was any indication. Although, the audience before him consisted of every imaginable skin tone. Life at Vauxhall couldn't be more different from the world where Theodore lived. Not in appearances or the strict decorum of the earldom.

He brought his attention back to the woman at the same time she chose to glance in his direction. Their eyes met and held. An unexpected frisson of emotion coursed through him. Did he know her? That was an impossibility and yet something in her gaze felt familiar, as if they were connected somehow. His brow creased with the inane thought, though he didn't look away.

She was beautiful with delicate features and large, luminous eyes. Her dark, glossy hair fell nearly to her waist and the image was intimate for its evocative invitation. Ladies of the ton kept their hair pinned back, hidden under bonnets or braided into intricate designs. *Unseen.* He inhaled deeply, ignoring a misplaced pulse of lust.

Why hadn't she looked away? Did she feel the same invisible bond? The very idea was ludicrous. She likely challenged everyone in the same manner. Life in this atmosphere couldn't be easy.

When she suddenly turned away, he felt the loss of her attention and mentally cursed himself. His emotions were erratic, running high as he came to grips with Fremont's passing. Regardless of the early hour, he needed a drink. Probably more than one.

"Thank you for coming in early to meet with us." Fredrickson addressed the performers, his back to Theodore. "So that we can gather information in an orderly manner, Johns and I will speak to each of you individually and that may take some time. You are free to leave the tent briefly if absolutely necessary, although I ask that you return within the hour. Mr. Morland has supplied us with a list of employees, so failure to appear will cast you in an unfavorable light."

Theodore was impressed. Fredrickson knew how to enhance his preamble with subtle threats aimed to get exactly what he wanted. Compliance.

"If anyone was near the pleasure paths behind the grandstand area, your information could be especially helpful in apprehending the attacker," Fredrickson went on. "Anything unusual or suspicious should be shared."

"And it doesn't only have to be events you observed last evening," Johns interjected. "The assailant may have visited repeatedly, waiting for the right opportunity. Any instance or strange happening that seems odd, uncommon or inappropriate should be reported."

A loud snicker from the left side of the tent overrode the end of Johns' sentence.

"You'll be here to next Tuesday if you want us to tell you all that," a male voice called out.

Fredrickson began to organize the interview area and Theodore glanced to where the young woman with the beguiling eyes was seated, but her half of the bench was empty now. He turned toward the exit at the rear of the tent in time to see her leave through the flap. Without a moment's hesitation, he set out after her.

. . .

14

LOLA'S HEARTBEAT HAMMERED SO LOUDLY IN HER CHEST she wondered if it would be the death of her. She wanted to visit the spot where she'd witnessed the murder and then she'd return. Everyone was back at the tent. Now seemed a good time to slip away. Besides, if someone questioned her actions, she would claim curiosity. A desire to see the area in case it jarred a memory. Something like that. She didn't think more on it.

Hurrying, she rounded the back of the grandstand and walked toward the maze of hedgerows and flowering shrubs that composed the pleasure paths. In the bright morning sun, the gardens looked welcoming and innocuous but in her time at Vauxhall, all sorts of erotic acts and scandalous debauchery were reported to have happened within. Once inside, one could be assured of privacy. Even in daylight, it was easy to become lost in the labyrinth of green shrubbery lined with identical lanterns. She'd experienced it herself the few times she'd allowed Marco to take her inside.

Now she swallowed her indecision, glanced cautiously over her shoulder, and entered through the gate. Unless one had been inside the close walks at the exact time of the murder or accidently happened upon it, the act would have gone unseen. When she'd looked back a moment ago, the wooden stanchions and taut rope where she performed each evening rose high above the tent. The knowledge she might be the only person who'd witnessed the killing pressed on her chest. She could never confess such a thing. Not with her past. Not at the risk of discovery.

Besides, she'd seen nothing more than a man in a long black coat. It was hardly a useful description. She pressed her eyes closed not wanting to relive the experience though the memory showed itself nonetheless.

Several minutes later, she reached the area she sought. With tentative steps, she approached the small clearing and crouched down, running her fingertips over a patch of bloodstained dirt and crushed gravel.

What had happened? Why was a man killed in a place meant for amorous acts and titillating entertainment? Had he been lured here purposely or was he waiting for a loved one? Too many questions bombarded her at once.

"You there."

She jerked to her feet, thrusting her hand behind her back as if she hid something, even though her fingers held nothing more than the sensation of having touched death.

It was the same tall stranger from the tent. The man who'd stared at her until a sheen of sweat had coated her skin. She drew a breath and exhaled slowly. She hadn't done anything wrong. She shouldn't feel as though she had.

"Yes?"

"Do you work here?" He stepped closer and the sunlight glinted off his thick hair, black as a raven's wing, dark as the intention in his eyes.

"Yes." She moved her hands to her sides, uncomfortable and at the same time intrigued. She was graceful by nature, able to move silently through the world, but here in front of this man with her heart pounding and mind spinning, a strange combination of exhilaration and fear clashed inside her.

"Shouldn't you be with the others?"

He indicated the direction she'd come with a shallow wave of his hand. He didn't wear gloves which was curious indeed. He looked like a man who always kept his hands clean and mingling with Vauxhall performers would definitely be considered filthy business.

Three

S he looked guilty. Her wide eyes watched him as if she feared he meant her harm. Nothing could be further from the truth. If she knew something about Fremont's death, he wanted to hear what she had to share. And yet, he had no idea if she knew anything at all.

"Shouldn't *you* be with the others?" She threw his question back at him and her slender shoulders eased.

"Not necessarily," he replied, taking in the way she'd tilted her chin higher after she'd spoken.

"Are you a Runner?" She asked, her dark brows raised slightly.

"I am an earl."

"Of course, you are." Her tone was all disapproval.

"Does that bother you?" He stood only a few strides from her now. He hadn't been mistaken inside the tent. She possessed uncommon features, a delicate nose and fair skin, though her full, heart-shaped lips couldn't be labelled anything other than sensual. What could life possibly offer her here at Vauxhall?

"Should it, my lord?" She asked in that same tart tone.

"Not at all," he said, his eyes never leaving her face. Was she a singer? An acrobat? She moved with an elegant grace that belied her situation. She seemed out of place here, and yet, here she was.

"If you're not a Runner, why are you questioning me?"

He didn't answer at first, taking her in and noting her evasive answers. She was as clever as she was beautiful. *And bold.* He'd give her that. "I'm interested in what happened last night."

She seemed dissatisfied with his explanation, evidenced as one slender brow arched upward.

"The man who was killed was like a brother to me. Possibly the closest I'll get to family. He deserved better than what happened here." He accomplished the words without undue emotion thought his chest tightened reflexively. He moved his eyes to the same spot the woman had examined when he'd interrupted her. The place where Fremont was killed. Did he struggle? Was it over quickly? He clenched his jaw, impatient and angry, while in his periphery he saw her take a few silent steps toward the exit.

"I'm sorry for your loss." Her voice gained a softer quality. Gone was the defiance he'd heard earlier.

Intelligence showed in her eyes and another more elusive emotion he couldn't decipher. It was his own shortcoming he'd misjudged her earlier. Better he came to this awareness before he delved deeper into the cause of Fremont's death.

"What do you know?" He paced slowly to the right, intercepting her path were she to try to leave.

"Only what Fredrickson said." A bird crossed the sky and she followed its path with her eyes as she spoke. "You were standing there."

"Why are you here?"

"I was curious," she answered quickly. "Sad, but also curious."

"Curious about what you saw?" He asked pointedly, pressing for answers.

"I never said I saw something."

"But you did, didn't you?"

"I don't know what you want from me. I told you why I came

here." She glared at him and folded her arms across her chest, the action momentarily distracting.

"Is this a game to you? Because I assure you it is anything but a game for me. I will discover the truth and when I hunt down whomever is responsible, they will pay for what they've done."

"Because you are above the law."

"In this, my title has no bearing."

She didn't answer him though her eyes rolled heavenward in a flash of disgusted tolerance. Her blatant disregard of his title defused his anger. They lived in two entirely different worlds. "What is your name?"

"What does it matter?" She replied in a petulant tone, her gauzy dress floating after her as she paced a step to the side. "Although I suppose, with all your privilege and opportunity, you'll learn it anyway. I'm Lola."

"Thank you." He crossed the clearing until he stood within reach of her. She was petite, the top of her head barely met the bottom of his chin. Was she completely on her own? Without someone to protect her? It was an absurd thought and he blamed it on the recent events. "Will you help me, Lola?"

She startled. Whether from his question or the use of her name he couldn't know.

"In what way?" She said, suspicion and curiosity alive in her eyes.

"People will talk. They always do. Performers here at Vauxhall or other workers. Maybe a visitor or customer will share an interesting bit of gossip. Whenever you hear something about what happened here, whether it be a rumor, idea or recounting, send me a message." He reached inside his breast pocket and retrieved his card. When he held it out to her, she didn't immediately accept it. The moment stretched and he waited, assuming she would walk away without it.

"I'm sorry I can't help you," she said as she took the card, her fingers brushing against his in a fleeting touch that left him staring after her.

"LOLA, WATCH THIS!"

Lola turned at hearing her name called from the stage closest to the colonnade. It was well past noon and after she'd finished her interview, she'd decided to go for a walk to escape the chatter and speculation inside the pavilion. The earl's calling card was in her skirt pocket, but if she avoided hearing anything worth repeating, she wouldn't have to decide whether or not to contact him. The shadow of pain visible in his eyes when he'd spoken of his friend still haunted her. She understood the bleak, hopeless feeling of loss and didn't need any reminders.

Now, as she shaded her brow with her hand, she watched her friend Sofia fly across the wooden platform in a series of complicated flips and twists, landing on her feet in an effortless finish.

Lola's interview with Fredrickson this morning had involved the same level of difficulty. Not wanting to say the wrong thing or provoke suspicion, she'd juggled lies with truth in what she hoped was convincing conversation. Things had progressed well enough until he'd casually inquired whether she lived alone or with her family. A stab of regret had sliced through her heart though she'd managed to keep her expression calm. She had nothing to share about her parents and sisters. She'd sacrificed the privilege of knowing their joys and hardships when she'd run away, abandoning her home, leaving everything behind in Ipswich never to be seen again. But she couldn't think about that now. Regret had a way of stealing one's soul.

Having accomplished another tumbling pass, Sofia leapt from the stage and headed in Lola's direction. Together with her two brothers, Sofia comprised The Gallos, an acrobatic act who'd found work at Vauxhall after they'd arrived from Italy five years ago. The sibling trio lived in the same boarding house as Lola.

They occupied the lower, larger rooms, while Lola rented the single room above them. Between working together and staying at the same address, Lola and Sofia had forged a comfortable friendship even though several years separated them in age.

"How was it for you with the questions?" Sofia asked, worry lines creasing her forehead. "It's a terrible thing, no?"

"Yes, it is," Lola said, anxious to change the subject. "You've added another flip to your routine. Your brothers must be pleased."

"*Dio mio.*" Sofia half smiled, rolling her eyes in exaggerated complaint. "They always want me to go faster, fly higher. I keep telling them I'm not a bird."

Lola laughed and relaxed, some of her earlier tension slipping away.

"But you, Lola," Sofia continued. "You move like a little starling on that rope. You are a star at the end of the evening, high above us all."

"Until I misstep," Lola answered, her words meant to remind herself of everything at risk.

"No," Sofia admonished in a rushed tone. "Don't say such a thing. You are brilliant."

"Actually, I meant to go home for a little while instead of taking practice," she said. *Tonight, when she walked the rope would be soon enough.* "But now that the gates will open in a few hours, there's not enough time. Morland and the Runners took up too much of the day."

"Yes, so many questions. They make it sound like we're all in danger." Sofia frowned. "I have my brothers watching over me, but what about you, Lola. Are you frightened?"

"There's nothing to be frightened about." She shook her head to emphasize her answer and reaffirm her confidence. No one knew what she saw and she intended to keep it that way. In another few days, it would all be forgotten and life would continue as usual.

"After the show tonight, we will go home together. Francesco and Alessandro will be with me," Sofia said. "They will protect us."

"I don't think we need to be worried," Lola added. "Besides, Marco watching over me is suffocating enough." Thankfully Marco finished his act and left the grounds earlier than she did. He also lived in the opposite direction. Otherwise, she wondered if he would insist on the same.

"I understand. But what better way to show him you're safe than if we walk home together. Maybe then he will stop hovering. You have the last performance of the night. My brothers and I will wait for you in the pavilion."

Given Sofia's persistence, Lola couldn't disagree. Maybe talking with her friends and laughing all the way home would keep her mind off what had happened as well as the disconcerting confrontation with the earl. She hoped so because nothing else seemed to do the trick.

THEODORE ENTERED WHITE'S FULL-KNOWING HIS return to London would draw notice. Handing over his greatcoat, he made his way toward the back, stopping intermittently for a handshake or word of greeting. Not unlike the gentleman surrounding him, he'd spent several nights a week here before he'd hied off to America. The club provided a place to relax, enjoy the company of his closest friends and hear the latest news, salacious or otherwise. But tonight, he wasn't looking for companionship as much as noise and distraction.

Vauxhall didn't open for another two hours and the more he paced around his town house, the more Wyndham, his man-of-all-things, inquired over his unrest. Wyndham was a loyal servant and irreplaceable valet, already taxed from their recent voyage and now charged with staffing the house on short notice. Wyndham deserved better.

At the moment Theodore's conscience couldn't bear another burden, his emotions frayed thin by Fremont's sudden, unexplained death. He should call on Fremont House soon, though the thought brought with it another layer of despair. He couldn't imagine the heartache Fremont's younger sister experienced. Margaret and Stephan were extremely close and their adventures had often included Theodore. For a time, it was assumed he and Margaret would make a go of it, but once he'd decided to travel to America, he'd rightly encouraged her to seek a future elsewhere. The kind of marriage she deserved. In truth, their affinity was nothing more than kinship developed due to frequency and proximity. Any feelings of affection were strictly familial.

Needing liquor to quiet these thoughts, he signaled for a brandy and settled in a chair near the corner, unsure how much distraction he desired after all. Another hour and he'd have his driver take him over to the south bank. He wasn't exactly sure why he needed to return to Vauxhall. He just knew he must. Was it an attempt to feel closer to Fremont? Or an effort to learn more of what had occurred there? That seemed an impossibility. Nevertheless, he wouldn't waste time trying to reason it out, his emotions still in chaos.

"Essex, you devil! When did you return?" Braden Ulrich, Earl of Huntington, slapped him heartily on the shoulder and slid into the adjacent chair. "You look no worse for your travels. Did you get everything well sorted in America?"

"Huntington." Theodore greeted his friend, the tension in his chest easing by degrees. Perhaps talking to his friends was exactly what he needed this evening. "It's too soon to tell in regard to my venture and as far as our fair city, I've only been home two days now."

He waited, wondering if Fremont's death had already hit the gossip mill. Damn it to hell, coming to White's was a miserable idea.

"Then you've not heard." Huntington's expression lost all conviviality. "Or have you?" He asked tentatively.

"I have, although I don't understand it," Theodore said with grave seriousness before he took another swallow of brandy.

"It does make one wonder, doesn't it? I suppose there's more that needs to come out." Huntington paused as his gaze traveled around the room. Was he taking note who stood within hearing distance or gathering his thoughts? Theodore had no way to know.

"Wonder about what?" Theodore prompted. If his friend knew why Fremont was in Vauxhall last night, if he knew anything connected to the untimely death, it needed to be said.

"Never would I speak unkindly of the dead. You know me better than that, Essex." Huntington exhaled deeply. "But you've been gone for two years. Things have happened. People have changed. You might want to speak to his sister. There's really nothing else to be said."

"Except what you just told me expressed there's quite a bit more to be said," Theodore replied, unable to restrain a note of tempered frustration. "Fremont was a good man. If he found himself in trouble, he would respond appropriately and resolve the conflict. Pestering Margaret when she's only begun mourning her brother is a cruel suggestion."

The longcase clock on the adjacent wall had the good sense to chime six, otherwise Theodore might have continued and said a few unforgiveable things in Fremont's defense. Instead, he stood up, abruptly ending the conversation.

"I've somewhere else to be. Enjoy the rest of your evening, Huntington."

Then he made for the door, quick to retrieve his greatcoat and head out into the night.

Four

The grandstand was packed full with spectators. The weekend usually brought out a bigger crowd and tonight was no exception. Apparently having a murder occur on the grounds less than twenty-four hours earlier did little to discourage sales. Such was the popularity of Vauxhall. Danger was a large part of the allure.

Lola stood on the left platform, her skirt catching a light breeze to dance across the back of her legs, her ribboned sash chasing after it. She looked out across the gardens, beyond the rotunda and picture rooms, in the opposite direction of the pleasure paths.

Simon, the hot air balloon pilot, was completing his last ticketed fare. Seeing the giant balloon float weightlessly through the air always brought a smile to her face, but tonight it failed to charm. In the area adjacent to the balloon's landing circle, she watched as the orchestra pit emptied alongside dinner boxes doing the same. It was nearly time for her to begin. The tightrope was the closing act before the fireworks display.

Biding her time, she shifted toward the grandstand and waved to the visitors, their bright eyes and expectant faces lifted upward as they awaited her daring walk. A familiar tingle of anticipation flowed through her as she glanced to where Morland stood in position at the grandstand gate. His signal, nothing more than a nod of his hat, would tell her when to begin. In the meantime, she would soak in the thrilling experience of living high above the world, out of reach of problems and emotions. Alone, in the shimmering light of multiple lanterns strung between the platforms.

Breath by breath, her world quieted. Simon's balloon was again anchored to the ground. The music that once filled the air with song had ended. At the ready, she sought Morland's signal, but now his back was turned as he spoke to someone lost to the shadows.

With a huff of impatience, she waited. Until at last, she saw him.

The earl had returned. Theodore M. Coventry, third Earl of Essex. That's what his calling card said in two sharp rows of engraved block letters. Even his name was complicated. Nobility always needed *more* than everyone else. Her interest fell away and she moved into position on the platform, focused on the task before her.

The earl's return didn't matter. Nothing mattered except walking the rope. As she waited for Morland's signal, she told herself not to look at Essex, but her brain didn't listen and her eyes followed the earl's tall form as he moved further into view along the walkway. He stopped beneath the platform where she would complete her walk. When he glanced upward their eyes met and that same startling sensation coursed through her. As if he could see inside her. Know her secrets. But that could only be her imagination. *Everyone* stared at her. It was the very purpose of her performance. To be a spectacle. To entertain.

That, she would do. She placed one foot on the rope, her weight causing the slightest waver as she moved gracefully forward, one step after another. The soles of her feet, accustomed to the pressure and texture of the rope, held steady even though her heart thrummed at the knowledge his eyes moved with her. Why had he returned? What could he want? He was a distraction that would lead her to fall if she didn't stop thinking about him.

At the halfway mark, she paused and raised her arms in a graceful arch, the colorful ribbons around her wrists fluttering. Below, the crowd cheered and clapped with excitement. She bent her knees slightly, adjusting the angle of her shoulders to retain her balance. A few more steps and she would be finished and yet the rope suddenly seemed endless. As if she would be forever balanced between one side and the other, undecided where her loyalty belonged.

Dispelling the unsettling thought, she forced herself forward, confident she would not falter. Her skill had been honed through childhood. Unknowingly accomplished, but attained nonetheless. First by balancing on the ornate limestone wall that enclosed the estate's prized rose garden. Then with more daring, on the wrought iron railings surrounding the expansive stables. For her it had been a way to combat boredom. Child's play, nothing more. But now the ability had become her salvation. A delicate and daring act on a tightly strung rope at an unthinkable height. It reminded her of teetering between life's choices, one wrong step could lead to irreparable consequences.

She was nearly at the platform now and brought her eyes to the rope, then to the ground, where the earl intersected her line of vision. Broad shouldered and darkhaired, standing in the one place she needed to focus, he was impossible to ignore.

The impact of his prolonged attention caused her to wobble and the tenuous sway of her body evoked gasps of horror from the crowd though she was quick to compensate. Continuing without error, she reached the wooden platform and curtseyed graciously at the audience's applause. All that risk for one fleeting moment of glory.

Just like the previous night the grandstand emptied quickly. With nothing left to see, the guests departed, anxious to purchase a meat pie or sweet treat before they found a comfortable location to view the fireworks display. Lola lingered, unsure what she would say to the nobleman who waited at the bottom of the ladder. Lord Essex hadn't left like the others. He seemed determined to speak to her again, whether she wished for it to happen or not. She was trapped.

Never a coward, she gathered her cotton wrap around her shoulders, tied it in a tight knot over her heart, and started down the ladder.

"YOU'RE FEARLESS, LOLA." THEODORE WATCHED HER progress as she climbed down the ladder, but then quickly averted his gaze, too aware of her captivating silhouette as she descended. Her costume was nothing more than wisps of gauze and silk which reached mid-calf and left her dainty ankles exposed, the ribbons of her slippers hardly wide enough to cover all her bare, soft skin.

"It is an art as much as a skill, my lord." She turned and offered him a tight smile. "Why are you here?"

"You waste no time on niceties, do you?" He answered, hoping to keep the mood light.

"Is that why you've returned to Vauxhall? For pleasant conversation?" She tugged at the ends of the shawl covering her shoulders. She was either cold or nervous, and it was unusually warm for a mid-May evening.

"No. I've returned to speak to you." He suspected she would appreciate his bluntness. "Would you like to walk while we talk?"

"Surely you must have more important obligations than to waste your time here. What do you need to say?" She worked at the ties at her wrists and removed the colored streamers, rolling them around her fingers and tucking them into the invisible pockets in her skirt.

Clever how she'd switched the focus of their conversation away from herself. For someone who lived in an entirely different arena, she wasn't intimidated by his title, her words as brave as her performance.

"My time is my own."

"Of course, it is," she said with undisguised disdain. She reached up and pulled the pins from her hair, the lengths tumbling down past her ribcage. "I just assumed you'd rather spend it somewhere else."

He didn't answer at first, his attention divided by her actions. A strong pulse of lust worked through him, settling in his groin. He rubbed his fingers together restlessly. He'd gone too long without a woman. That could only be the cause. Although no lady of the ton would ever converse without a chaperone, expose her skin in such tempting fashion, or openly contradict him. Lola's tart words and sweet lips made for a bewitching combination.

"Nothing is more important than finding out what happened to Fremont," he said at last.

"Fremont?"

"My friend," he added, exhaling deeply and leaning his shoulder against one of the wooden poles supporting the tightrope platform. "A man who shouldn't have been killed."

"I understand. Unjust things happen to good people. The world we live in is rarely fair."

The depth of emotion in her words told him she truly did understand, and more. That she'd lived through some kind of tragedy, some undeserved loss. As before he suddenly wished to console or protect her, even though she'd likely reject the kind words he'd offer. She was complicated, this beautiful, talented, interesting woman before him. And more than a little dangerous because of it.

"What will Bow Street do?" She asked, breaking through his thoughts. "About finding the man responsible?"

"Ask questions. Inquire with their usual informants," he said, moving from where he'd leaned on the pole and indicating they should follow the path out of the grandstand area. "I suppose come next week the information will be published in The Quarterly Pursuit."

He didn't hold much hope the newspaper would assist in finding the killer. While it provided details of crimes and informed the public of recent incidents, the facts surrounding the viscount's murder were vague and insufficient.

"I wish I could tell you more about last evening," she said as she moved beside him.

Now there was a cryptic statement. Maybe she knew something. Maybe he was grasping at straws.

"But as I told the Runners, it seemed like every other Friday night here," she continued. "You've troubled yourself coming out and waiting for my performance to end. Perhaps you should speak to Dante. He works in the picture house."

"Dante?" Finally, someone who might have useful information. No one had mentioned the man before.

"Yes, he's an illusionist, and it's said he can communicate with those who have crossed over."

Theodore wasn't sure if her words were sincere or sarcastic, but she didn't give him time to decide.

"Now I'll need to change my clothes before I walk home. If you'll excuse me, my lord."

"I'll escort you home, Lola."

"That isn't necessary."

"Isn't it though? A murder occurred here last night and for all my lofty education," he said this with a note of humor, "I can't imagine a single circumstance where it would be wise for a beautiful woman to be walking alone at night no matter the neighborhood."

He had no idea how the word *beautiful* had worked its way into his comment, but it wasn't a lie.

Her eyes examined him for a long moment, a flicker of some unknown emotion evident there while she debated her decision.

"I will only be a few minutes," she said finally before she turned and went inside the pavilion.

LOLA MADE QUICK WORK OF CHANGING INTO A SIMPLE gown before she slipped back outside, successfully eluding Sofia and her brothers. She felt badly about leaving them waiting and would have approached to explain, but then Marco had appeared and joined their conversation. She didn't want him to accompany her home or offer him a reason to believe she was his responsibility. Their relationship had ended amicably, though at times she wished it hadn't. Perhaps if they'd argued and remained on poor terms, he wouldn't disguise his protective gestures as friendship.

Shaking away these thoughts, she strode toward the earl, a strange fluttery feeling alive in her stomach. He shouldn't make her nervous. She'd spent ample time around noblemen in the past. Beneath his arrogance, wealth and perfectly tied cravat, was a man, skin and bones, like every other. In his case, well-formed skin and bones.

Instead of reassuring her, the realization made the fluttery feeling intensify. He was handsome. She wouldn't deny it. But it mattered little at the moment.

"It's this way." She motioned toward Collyhurst Road since they'd come to the end of the oyster shell path. Another step and they would go beyond Vauxhall grounds. Somehow taking their association into the London streets made it all the more real, all the more complicated.

"Do you walk home alone every evening?" He asked.

"Not always." She avoided a puddle of questionable liquid near the curb. "Sometimes I go home with friends. A few of us live in the same building."

She bit back a knowing smile and wondered if he'd ever spent time in her part of London. She doubted it. Nobs never left

Mayfair unless they needed something. Something they couldn't send someone else to fetch.

They fell into companionable silence, his boot heels marking the way while her slippers brushed softly against the pavement. Yet in the quiet she noticed other, louder things, like the inviting scent of his cologne, bergamot and spice. And the utter strength in his command, the width of his chest and length of his stride. She forced her attention to the immediate surroundings in an act of mercy.

His appearance at Vauxhall this evening was a waste of time. She'd seen nothing more than a long black greatcoat very like the one he wore. For all she knew, he could have committed the murder. Besides, he didn't know what she'd witnessed and she intended for it to stay that way.

At the corner of Collyhurst Road and Kennington Street, she purposely directed him left, taking them on a longer route to the boarding house. Sofia and her brothers would eventually give up on waiting for her and walk home the same way. Lola didn't want to cross paths.

She was so lost in these thoughts that the earl startled her when he spoke, his voice deep and smooth, void of any earlier tension as if he'd relaxed by having distanced himself from the fair grounds.

"How did you come by your skill? I watched you tonight in fascination. Though I clenched my jaw so tightly I know it will pain me come tomorrow." He paused beneath an oil lantern, the sallow light from the lamp pole casting him in partial shadow. "It is an unusual talent."

He'd surprised her. Not just in his concern on her behalf, but by his compliments. "I suppose my daring balancing act will catch up to me someday."

Truer words couldn't be spoken, though it wouldn't be her first fall from grace.

"You know, you rarely answer what I'm asking. Why is that?" He stepped nearer; his face illuminated by the light now.

"I'm not sure, my lord." She looked up and studied him. His eyes were sincere, his expression one of amused curiosity. "Habit, I suppose."

When he didn't reply, she asked a question of her own. No doubt a poor decision. But something about the way he stared at her, the intensity in his gaze and strong cut of his jaw, had her saying and doing things she would probably regret tomorrow. "What is it that you wish to know, my lord?"

"What does it feel like? To take such a dangerous risk and then conquer it repeatedly?" He asked, his voice more serious, as if he truly wished to know. His choice of question was interesting.

"Exhilarating. Incomparable. It's wonderful to be separated from the world, to be above all the struggle and hardship. When I walk the rope, I'm completely in control and that's a freedom I cherish." Her heart squeezed tight. She didn't often confess personal feelings.

"You know, we're not so dissimilar, you and I, when it comes to desiring control and wanting to be free."

She laughed at this. She couldn't help it. Did he really think to compare his life with hers? She did her best to smother any further amusement by resuming their walk. Standing under the lamplight was exposing emotions she'd rather keep in the dark. "You cannot be serious, my lord."

"You needn't be so formal, Lola. I hear my title all day long and we aren't within society. You should call me by my given name."

She laughed again, harder this time. As if he was trying to bamboozle her. "Which one? I don't think I can remember them all."

"No." He stopped walking.

His habit of demanding attention by refusing to move was ironically indicative of how their lives were different. He possessed the luxury of time. She had to keep moving so the past wouldn't catch up with her.

"I would like you to call me Theodore. I insist, so that we're on equal ground. If not, then you must call me Essex. All your *my lording* reminds me of how useless a title is if it can't command a killer to be found or a friend to be returned."

His solemn comments struck a chord within her even though she'd rather his words didn't evoke such emotion.

"Very well," she paused, forcing the last bit. "I will, Theodore."

"Thank you."

They continued, having apparently reached some kind of agreement, though other than his name, she had no idea what it could be.

"Are you originally from London?" He asked as they rounded the corner of the street where she lived.

"No. Ipswich was once my home." She told him the truth because she didn't believe it would ever bear significance. "The boarding house where I have a room is down at the end."

"You have an intriguing view of life, Lola, and I've enjoyed your company." He turned and faced her, sincerity in his eyes. "Thank you for the honor of escorting you home."

"You do like all your pretty words, don't you?" She quipped, uncomfortable with his praise although a smile willed its way to her lips.

He chuckled then, and the sound was rich and decadent, like the hot chocolate her mother used to make in the wintertime. It warmed her from the inside out. And just like that memory, like the last drop in her favorite cup, she didn't want their time to end. But thinking of her mother always reminded her how it *did* have to end.

"My rental is in the next building," she said to break the silence, slightly unnerved by all the conflicted emotions alive within her. She reached into her pocket and took out the ribbon attached to her key. It slipped through her fingers before she could catch it.

The earl bent down and retrieved it without thought. He held it a moment, stared at it, before he looked at her again. When he placed it in her outstretched hand, his fingers wrapped around her palm, his thumb brushing across her skin in a gentle caress. The moment left her breathless.

"Very good then. I'll walk you to the front stairs," he said finally, his words lower, yet somehow more intense than before.

"Lola?" Marco's voice interrupted the night. "Lola, what are you doing?"

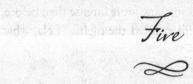

Five

"**M**arco." She rushed to the steps where he waited, unsure how to manage his unexpected appearance and anxious now for the earl to leave.

"Is everything all right?" The earl asked, inserting himself into the conversation and making the situation more complicated.

That was the trap with nobs and gentry, they made life increasingly more difficult.

"Yes," she turned back to reassure him. "You should go. Thank you again for seeing to my safety."

"Think nothing of it."

The earl spoke to her, though his eyes remained on Marco where he stood unmoved on the top step of the building's stoop. She had to diffuse the situation before it escalated. Men and their masculine foolishness would forever cause her frustration.

"I need to talk to you," Marco said, though his attention hadn't wavered either.

She slid her key into the lock and opened the door, waiting for Marco to follow. She knew what the earl would assume, but she was helpless to resolve things otherwise. Any conversation she'd have with Marco had to happen behind closed doors.

They went upstairs and she lit a lantern, not wanting to prolong his visit.

"What is it?" She asked, wondering if he would forget her walking home with the earl in favor of his own problem.

"What did Mr. Deep Pockets want?"

Apparently not.

She sat down at the tiny wooden table that constituted her kitchen and living room though Marco paced to the window and glanced out, probably checking to see if the street was empty now.

"Nothing important." She sighed deeply, tired and wanting to sleep. "He asked about the murder. The man who was killed was his friend. Morland must have mentioned that it occurred during my act and the earl—"

"He's an earl?"

"Yes." Beneath the table, she nudged the leg of the chair opposite her with her foot. "Sit down. Listen to what I'm telling you."

Her words sounded reminiscent of so many conversations within their relationship. Marco was quick to anger and didn't always think things through clearly. She didn't want trouble. Not from him or Morland or the earl. She just wanted to forget about the other night and put it behind her.

Marco sat and rubbed his eyes. He had to be just as exhausted as she.

"The earl asked me if I'd seen anything. That's all. Then he walked me home. He was concerned about my safety."

"But you didn't see anything, so what did you talk about?"

"Nothing out of the ordinary. My walking on the rope." She shook her head. "All this discussion about the murder keeps the event too alive. I want to forget about it. No one is going to be able to identify a man in a black coat. Half of London wears a black coat."

"You saw the man," Marco snapped his head around, his attention renewed. "From up on the platform?"

"A tall man in a black coat." She bit her lower lip, their conversation treading into dangerous territory. But she could trust Marco not to repeat anything. He despised Runners as much as she did.

"You saw his face?"

"No. I didn't say that." Her words were sharp. She wanted him to leave.

"Did you see the murder, Lola? Is that why you're upset? Because you saw what happened?"

"No," she lied, but she wasn't sure he believed her. "I don't want to talk about it anymore. You should leave now."

He stood from the table and checked the window again. It was late and so much had happened. All she wanted was to go to bed.

"Please don't repeat what I've said, Marco. It's useless information and I told Fredrickson the same. I don't want him questioning me further. You know about my past. I can't get involved with the law. If something comes out, I'll have to leave London." She added the last sentence to ensure he kept her trust. They were no longer together, but she was certain he still cared for her. He wouldn't want to see her go.

THEODORE HANDED THE REINS OF HIS HORSE TO THE groom at the mews behind Fremont House. It was an unusually cheerful morning and yet the ample sunlight did little to warm him. Calling on Margaret was the right thing to do, albeit difficult. He'd thought to give her more time to come to terms with her brother's passing, but now he couldn't stay away. Once he'd returned home last night and opened her message, the decision was made.

Margaret's distress had added another layer to the emotional maelstrom already inside him. His return to London and Fremont's sudden death, combined with the intriguing exchanges he'd had with Lola and the complex scene when they'd reached her home, all weighed heavily upon him.

Lola had been laughing, enjoying their conversation, until

she'd heard the other man's voice. That man, *Marco*, had caused an immediate change in her demeanor. All happiness fell away and her eyes lost their sparkle. The other morning, Marco had tried to take Lola's hand in the tent, but she'd pulled it away. Theodore remembered that too.

Still, she'd allowed Marco into her home. It was curious, indeed.

Now, as Theodore approached the back door of Fremont House, he exhaled thoroughly noticing the swags of black drapery over the windows and doorways. Full mourning had begun. Fremont's death would be common knowledge now, not just an overheard rumor or snippet of gossip. His heart ached for Margaret. She was too young to bury her brother. Her parents were also deceased, although she did have a large extended family to assist her. Unfortunately, knowing all this didn't make his visit this morning any easier.

Death was difficult in and of itself, never mind when a loved one was taken without reason, justice or consequence. There were still too many unknowns. He recalled yesterday afternoon at the club when Huntington had alluded to the fact that Fremont's behavior had changed over the two years Theodore had been away, but there was nothing for it. He couldn't question Margaret when she'd only begun to grieve.

He entered through the back door, a frequent visitor to the estate before his travels took him away. The cook's expression brightened upon the sight of him, but then remembering the circumstances, she reclaimed her sadness. He walked through the main hall, knowing the layout as well as his own home, and entered the front drawing room where Margaret waited. She was dressed in black crepe from head to toe, even her dainty hands were covered in black lace gloves. She offered him a weak smile, although her face was tearstained and eyes red and puffy. The silver tea service was already laid out on the sideboard where a maid fussed with the necessary utensils.

"Margaret." He brought her into his arms for a consoling embrace. "I'm so very sorry. I am at a loss for words."

"As am I, Theo." She exhaled a shuddering breath in an attempt to keep her composure, pulling away to move to one of the windows where she looked out. "I struggle to understand everything that has happened. I need answers."

"Right now, Stephen's death is an unexplained tragedy, but that doesn't mean the person responsible won't be brought to justice. I'm in close contact with Bow Street. I have their word I will be notified if any new information is learned."

"Ever since the Runners came to the door, I've been unable to eat or sleep. I can't think straight." She turned, weaving her fingers together as she clasped her hands tight. "This seems like a nightmare I can't wake from. Stephen, killed, in Vauxhall of all places." She sniffled and blinked away fresh tears. "He didn't belong there."

An image of Lola came to mind. Her long dark hair, full lips and graceful body. She was talented and educated, if her vocabulary was any indication. He had the sense she didn't belong there either. But maybe that was the irony of it. Vauxhall's collection of performers belonged nowhere except right where they were.

The maid came forward and poured two cups of tea. When she left, Margaret settled on the couch and he sat in the cane-backed chair opposite her in wait of conversation. He didn't wish to upset her further. No topic seemed a good choice considering the circumstances.

"My brother changed while you were away, Theo." She picked up her teacup and put it down without taking a sip. "At first it was only small things. He would come home late or having had too much to drink. I would inquire casually at the breakfast table the next morning, but he was always quick to assure me he was fine. He'd tell me I worried overmuch."

"That sounds just like him."

"But I don't think I was worrying too much." She picked up her tea again, this time accomplishing a sip. "In retrospect, I feel as though I should have done something. Insisted he stop whatever it was that was making him so unhappy and argumentative. I should have pleaded with him to tell me more. It was unlike him to get foxed and keep irregular hours. Sometimes he never came home at all."

"When you grew concerned, why didn't you write to me?"

"I didn't want to trouble you," she said quickly.

"Was that the only reason?"

"Yes. I don't know. Maybe. You and Stephen left things on such poor terms. He was foolish for quarreling with you the day before you departed for America. It was selfish on his part. I didn't wish to be just as selfish, asking you to end your trip abruptly and return home early."

"I would have done so without a second thought."

"I know." She exhaled a deep breath. "That's exactly why I didn't write to you. I knew you would cut your trip short and come back as soon as possible when it might prove all for naught. Stephen wouldn't listen to me, no matter how many times I tried to discuss my concerns. Colin spoke to him repeatedly on my behalf."

"Colin?"

"Oh, dear. I've been remiss with all that's happened." She took a moment to remove her gloves and raised her left hand in front of her. "I'm engaged to be married. To Colin Everly, Viscount Sidmouth. We thought to hold our wedding sooner than later, but of course, with Stephen's passing, everything will have to wait now," she said the last bit more to herself than to him.

Theodore struggled to place the name, but he couldn't. He was relieved Margaret hadn't been alone through this troubling time and that she'd moved on with her life once he'd left. Hopefully, having to postpone wedding plans until next year wouldn't dampen her spirits further. It could offer her something to look forward to, instead of the reverse.

"Congratulations." It seemed an odd, out of place sentiment

in the dimly lit drawing room. "I'm happy you've found a future with Lord Sidmouth."

"He's a good man. The night the Runners came to the door, I don't know what I would have done if Colin hadn't been by my side." Her voice trembled with solemn emotion, the brief note of joy in her eyes dimmed again.

"Didn't they notify you in the middle of night?" It was past midnight when Bow Street had knocked on his door, though it felt like weeks ago instead of a few days.

"Yes. It was very late."

When she didn't elaborate, he abandoned any more questions. Apparently, Stephen wasn't the only one in the family who'd changed while he'd been away. "Your brother would be comforted to know you had someone with you. Was Stephen pleased by your engagement?"

"Yes." She found a slight smile. "Although he worried about my dowry. I don't know why he ever would. My parents left us financially secure."

Theodore finished his tea and glanced at the waning fire. Margaret's note had indicated she wanted to ask him a favor, yet he couldn't imagine what that would be. Especially now learning of her betrothed. He supposed she might ask for help with the customary house visits as friends and family paid their respects or with the burial. Of course, he would oblige. Otherwise, he was at a loss to what she might need.

"The night Stephen was killed he was supposed to be with me, but for some reason he went to Vauxhall instead. I don't know why. He didn't send me a note. But it must have been important. He wasn't in the habit of breaking our plans."

"No, he wouldn't have done that without good cause," Theodore agreed. "Did he give you any indication that something was amiss? Have you looked through his things?"

"I haven't. Bow Street asked that I do so as soon as possible, but I can't bear going into his rooms." She picked at a loose thread on her skirt. "But you knew him like a brother, perhaps you can assist me."

"Yes, we can start whenever you're ready."

"Thank you." She paused. "But that's not why I asked you to come here today, Theo. I need your help with something else."

"Go on." He waited, unsure about the determined look in her eyes.

"I want to see the place Stephen was killed."

She blurted this out so forcefully it took him a moment to process her request.

"No, you don't." So, this was the favor? She wanted his help defying propriety in every way imaginable. "You're in mourning, Margaret. You can't leave the house or wear anything other than black. I understand how emotional you are at this moment. I'm struggling with my feelings as well, but I can't bring you to Vauxhall Gardens."

"Why not?" She huffed, her eyes now sparked with misplaced anger. "I want to see where my brother drew his last breath. I need to see it. I can't say goodbye to him any other way. When the undertaker delivers his body, he'll be wrapped in wool and be nothing more than a cold corpse—" She choked on a sob but when he rose from the chair to comfort her, she waved him away.

"Margaret, listen to reason. What if someone saw you there?"

"I'll keep my eyes down and wear my cloak, the one with the frilly hood. No one can see me for all the ruffles on the trim. And we can go early. Before it gets crowded. Just straight to the spot so I can see it and stand there and say goodbye to my brother." She struggled with the last words, overcome by emotion, although she managed to get them out.

"You haven't thought this through. Don't you suppose people will recognize you as you stand there and mourn your brother? Instead of being discreet, everyone will take notice. I'm sorry, but I can't take you there." He shook his head slowly. "You're asking me to bring you even more heartache."

"Colin refused, but I thought you would understand." She searched his face, imploring him to agree. "Please don't disappoint me, Theo. Won't you help me make peace with my brother's death? I need to see where he was taken from me."

Said in those terms, he struggled with the words to deny her. Yet he couldn't bring more anguish into her life. If they went about this ill-advised scheme, it needed to be planned carefully.

"There might be a way," he said after several beats of silence. "I've met the manager and can ask if he'll allow us to enter before Vauxhall opens to the public. That way, no one will see you. But we can't stay long, Margaret. I'm not willing to take that chance with your reputation."

"Thank you, Theo." She sank back against the cushions, visibly relieved. "I knew you would help me."

Six

I t was mid-afternoon when Lola headed toward the grandstand to practice in an effort to clear her head. Sleep had come easily last night; exhaustion having won out. But while she rarely remembered her dreams, the images that had tormented her through the night still stayed with her.

In her dream she was walking the rope while Theodore waited on the platform on the other side. He smiled and extended his hand, except when she tried to step forward the rope disappeared. Confused and fearing for her life she'd leapt toward him, but he was too far away and beyond her reach. She fell through the darkness, wildly thrashing at the air around her, while the audience cheered and clapped below. When she'd awoken, her heart thundered in her chest so hard, she'd had to lay quiet for several minutes to calm down.

Now, as she crossed the lawn inside the grandstand, she spied Marco at the top of the platform, crouched low where the line was tied off to the wooden stanchion. Marco played the fiddle and strolled through the grottoes and groves, entertaining people with a lively quick step to accompany his songs. He wasn't a rope walker and had no business atop the platform.

"What are you doing?" She called out before he'd finished descending the ladder. Would nothing return to normal?

"I was checking the knots," he said, coming toward her.

"I always do that before I practice or perform. You know my routine. Besides, you need to stop worrying over me. You're going to give yourself gray hair." She reached up and swept her fingers over the top of his head, the dense curls brushing against her palm. "Now leave. I want to be alone."

He smirked, but he couldn't be surprised by her request. She'd made it often enough when they were together. Practicing her craft demanded complete concentration and she wasn't looking for company or conversation.

He grunted in response, walking backward a few steps before he turned without further complaint, perhaps remembering the way of things. He didn't look back as he made his way across the grass and when he finally left the grandstand, she began warming her muscles with a series of stretches.

She practiced for nearly an hour, perfecting two new arm flourishes within her routine before she decided to stop. The sun had climbed high overhead. It was probably close to noon. She'd find Sofia and together they would eat lunch. Lola hadn't had a chance yet to apologize for not meeting her last night.

She was on her way to the colonnade when she noticed Morland with a man and a woman near the rotunda on the north side of the main entrance. Vauxhall didn't open for hours, so there was no reason for anyone to visit, unless it was connected to what had happened the other night. Keeping to the shadows, she moved closer in want of a better view. A beat later, she recognized Theodore in the company of a young, refined woman. The lady wore a long velvet cloak with the hood drawn up. She hung onto the earl's elbow and his gloved hand rested on her fingers holding them in place. A flicker of disappointment squeezed Lola's heart tight though she had no claims on the earl. It served as a timely reminder any foolish infatuation was better smothered out. Her emotions were a complicated tangle of knots that needed sorting.

She watched as Morland indicated a path leading to the pleasure gardens before he stepped away. Theodore and the lady continued down the walkway. Rejecting every obvious reason for their appearance, Lola followed. Curiosity wouldn't allow her to back away.

"WE'RE STAYING FIFTEEN MINUTES AND NO LONGER. ARE we agreed?" Theodore led Margaret onto the gravel path, keeping them as close to the dense hedgerow as possible. Even though Vauxhall was closed to the public, he wasn't taking any chances. But no one seemed interested in their arrival and while he told himself not to look for a petite beauty with long black hair, he couldn't help himself.

Ever since he'd met Lola last week, she'd lingered in his thoughts. He'd like to blame it on her soft curves, firm muscles, and tempting ripe lips, to label it lust and impulse, but the elusive feeling was something else. *Something more.* The promise of unspoken words. An intangible connection. The look in her eyes. While their worlds might be completely different, for no reason he could explain, he believed they shared an affinity.

"Thank you, Theo." Margaret's reply brought his focus to the present. "I know it may sound odd, but I have no way to say farewell to Stephen. If this is where he had his last moments, I'd like to spend time here and say a prayer."

He nodded, hoping this experience would bring Margaret a modicum of peace. They arrived at the same spot he'd visited two days before. The same day he'd followed Lola after she'd left the tent. Remembering that morning, he looked over his shoulder and was startled to see the empty tightrope platform distinctly outlined against the bright sky. The rotunda and grandstand were too low to the ground to offer a clear vantage point in viewing the inside of the pleasure garden, but that wasn't true of the tightrope platform. Fredrickson had mentioned the guests were watching a performance during the time of the murder. *Lola's act.* The realization she must have seen something more struck him like a hot ember.

He needed to talk to her.

When Margaret finished, he explained his reasoning and deposited her in his carriage where it waited on the corner. He followed the oyster shell path through the gates and aimed toward the grandstand this time, but he didn't walk far. Lola stood just beyond the entrance, almost as if she'd waited for him.

"Why have you returned? Have you nothing better to do with your time?"

Her words were a challenge in that same tart tone that made him want to kiss her as much as contradict her. Desire pulsed through him stronger than ever. For all the sadness and regret at hearing of Fremont's murder, Lola made him feel alive.

"I have a few unanswered questions."

"I told you everything I know. Why don't you bother the Runners instead?" She tossed her hair over her shoulder, the sunlight skimming down the silky lengths as they slid to her back.

"Would you endure one more conversation?"

"No." She sounded angry now. He didn't know why. Her gaze traveled over him slowly from his collar to his boots. "I don't want anyone here seeing me talking to you again. That will only invite trouble."

"I understand," he agreed, giving the surround a cursory glance. "My carriage is parked at the corner of Frazier Street. Can you walk there? We can take a ride. I'll have you back in plenty of time before this evening's show."

He could see the indecision in her expression. Her chin jutted up the slightest.

"I will be there in a few minutes," she said begrudgingly. "How will I know which carriage is yours?"

"My crest is on the door."

"Of course it is." She rolled her eyes, but he noticed the trace of a smile curled her lips.

He walked away, knowing he was drawing her further into his life for more than good reason and selfishly not caring.

HE WAS DRESSED AS AN ORDINARY GENTLEMAN TODAY. Gone was the long greatcoat, expensive waistcoat and intricately folded cravat. For whatever reason, Theodore had worn a white linen shirt and fitted brown trousers. Perhaps to avoid attention, she couldn't know why. But she'd noticed. From the vee of smooth skin at his neck, shadow of dark chest hair beneath his shirt, to the sinful way his muscular thighs moved beneath the fabric of his trousers. She'd definitely noticed.

Yet he was still beyond her reach.

She left without preamble, walking to the corner as she noted the sudden change in weather. Clouds shadowed the sun in increasing shades of gray. Perhaps there would be no show tonight. No reason to hurry back to Vauxhall. She wouldn't mind a night spent at home alone.

Finding his coach without trouble, she knocked lightly on the door. When it opened, she paused. The same woman from the pleasure paths was seated inside, her velvet cloak draped across the entirety of the right bench. Their eyes met but the woman remained quiet.

Theodore sat on the opposite bench, half of which was empty. She had no choice but to sit beside him, otherwise lingering in the street midway inside a nob's carriage would surely come back to haunt her.

The door fell closed. The interior of the carriage was extravagant as would be expected, but it was equally as warm. Theodore sat too closely beside her. He radiated heat, his enticing cologne all the more noticeable for his proximity. But that wasn't the worst of it. The hard press of his thigh against hers was impossible to ignore, the thin layers of her skirt no barrier to his strength. Desire, raw and insistent, unfurled deep within her. She drew a breath, taking in his intoxicating scent and at the same time steeling herself against the sensation it caused. She didn't want to want him.

Together they'd become tangled in a difficult situation, and it would be wise not to make it more complicated.

"What is it you want?" She asked to keep her mind focused on something other than the delicious heat of his thigh.

On the opposite bench, the cloaked lady's eyes widened in surprise. She was very beautiful. No wonder Theodore favored her.

"Lola, this is Lady Margaret, Fremont's sister," Theodore explained. "At Margaret's request, I brought her to see where the incident happened."

Lola noticed his careful choice of words. He must care for the lady deeply. Sincere compassion colored his reply. Lola understood. She was no stranger to pain. "I'm very sorry for your loss. I'm sure your brother did not suffer."

"How do you know?" Margaret asked quickly.

"Did you see something that night?" Theodore asked, his voice quiet, but resolute.

"I would be a fool to look anywhere other than the rope." She glanced between the two of them.

"From the platform then?" He persisted.

"By the time I finished walking the rope, it was already over."

"And how do you know that?" He asked.

"I heard the screams. The evening was busy. The night was like any other until I heard the screams."

Margaret sniffled, but she didn't cry. Lola was impressed with her fortitude. Her eyes fell to where Margaret clasped her hands, the glimmer of a betrothal ring catching the light.

"You are engaged?" She asked, because she couldn't leave that question unanswered.

"I am in mourning," Margaret replied, her eyes going to Theodore. "But next year..."

Margaret didn't finish and Lola turned toward Theodore now. *He was engaged.* It was a puzzle piece that didn't fit because the attraction between herself and Theodore was a force beyond control, a dangerous force, and yet was it possible he had feelings for another?

Anything was possible.

"Margaret and Viscount Sidmouth will delay their plans for the sake of propriety, but no doubt it will be an extraordinarily special day when it arrives," he clarified, somehow understanding what she really wished to know.

Theodore knocked on the roof and the carriage jerked into motion immediately.

"Where are we going?"

"We'll take Margaret home. She shouldn't be out of the house." A rumble of thunder punctuated his sentence.

"Theodore is a dear friend for indulging me," Margaret said after a time. "He has always behaved as an additional brother whether I've liked it or not."

Lola nodded in reply, unsure what to think as Margaret glanced back and forth between her and the earl. Nothing else was said and Lola wondered why Theodore didn't break the unbearable silence. His leg still pressed against hers, firm and insistent, making her body grow hot from the inside out. He had to be aware how their legs rubbed so intimately. Didn't it cause in him the same sensual reaction she experienced? It was nearly unbearable, yet she didn't want to move away.

Eventually, the carriage rolled to a stop before a grand two-story town house with a Portland stone façade. There was a crescent shaped terrace with wrought iron railings that reminded Lola of her childhood bedchambers. She smiled despite herself. Too many times she'd found trouble climbing down from that landing.

"I'll be back in a minute," Theodore said, breaking through her thoughts. "I'm going to walk Margaret to the door."

Lola said goodbye and Margaret quickly stepped down from

the carriage. Thunder sounded, accompanied with a flash of lightning. Poor weather would ruin a show for this evening. Lola didn't mind.

When the rain began, it startled her. Huge, unforgiving drops struck the roof, pummeling the wood in a determined rhythm. She moved the damask curtain aside and peered out the window again, but there was nothing for it. The skies had opened up with a vengeance.

A moment later, Theodore returned, flinging open the carriage door and climbing inside as if he could escape the downpour. He sat on the bench opposite her this time but all that did is offer her a better view of him. His shirt was soaked through, the thin white linen translucent against the muscular outline of his broad shoulders. He half-smiled, seemingly amused by the circumstances, and combed his fingers through his hair, slicking the strands back away from his face though a few droplets clung to the unruly lengths near his collar. She inhaled slowly, his spicy cologne all the more prominent in the damp air. She swallowed, that insistent throb of desire once again making itself known.

He knocked on the roof, the wheels turning before she could recover her bearings.

"You're all wet." She could never confess she was as well.

"I am." His voice was low and intimate. "It happened suddenly."

She knew that feeling too. The pull between them was palpable. Her hands trembled where they rested on the bench. She wasn't one to be overset by emotion. She made decisions and acted on them. She always remained in control. But this, this was something else entirely.

Their eyes met and held. Their breathing matched as their bodies swayed in tandem to the rhythm of the carriage. He leaned forward, his eyes searching her face until his gaze settled on her mouth.

She licked her lips, her tongue darting out and in again, and she heard him exhale heavily.

"Give me your hand."

His gruff command surprised her but she did as she was told, unable to react otherwise.

Seven

He couldn't ignore it any longer. Not after enduring the agony of Lola's thigh pressed against his for the entire ride. He had to touch her, had to feel her skin and taste her mouth. When the tip of her tongue poked out to wet her full, ripe lips, he was so aroused his cock twitched.

"Give me your hand."

Like any respectable gentleman, he only meant to kiss the back of her palm, but when she placed her hand in his, he turned it over and pressed his mouth to the delicate skin on the inside of her wrist, inhaling her sweet musky scent, longing to explore all the other sensual pulse points hidden beneath her clothes.

She slid her fingers into his hair as he lifted his head. Their mouths aligned without hesitation. Her dark lashes lowered. They both moved closer.

He grasped her shoulders, drawing her forward into a deep, sensuous kiss. He'd wanted it to happen from the moment he'd seen her despite the unusual circumstances, and now having denied his desire and finally succumbed to it, she tasted that much more addictive.

She responded immediately, raking her fingers through his

hair, down to his shoulders where she twined her arms around his neck.

"Do you want this, Lola?" He whispered into her ear, his voice low and raspy.

"Yes." Her answer came fast against his jaw. "I do."

He trailed kisses down her slender neck, licking into the heated indentation between her collarbones, relishing her soft flesh, before he returned his mouth to hers. Her embrace tightened. His teeth grazed her lips seeking entry and she opened to him, their tongues rubbing together in a tight rhythm that sent shocks of pleasure to his groin.

In perfect accord their kiss slowed, became less rushed and yet more impactful, neither one of them wanting it to end. He settled his hands across her ribs, his thumbs below her breasts, the temptation to touch almost too much to bear. She mirrored his actions, smoothing her palms over his back, down to his waist, while their kiss continued, the silken warmth of her mouth inviting him in again and again.

When she sucked on his tongue, his breath seized in his chest. She was bold, sensual, *erotic*. His arousal throbbed in a demanding bid for attention. Her world was more carnal, more vibrant, incredibly more *real*. It was madness to want to be part of it.

He moved his hands upward, tracing over the delicious swells of her breasts, raised higher by her arms circling his neck. He wanted to pull down her bodice and taste her creamy flesh, tease her nipples, suckle the rosy tips, but that was better left to nighttime fantasies for now.

He breathed deep, forcing his hands into her hair to keep from acting on impulse. He wrapped his fists in the long silky lengths, having dreamed of it fanned across the pillows of his bed and draped across his body as they came together.

She made a sound in the back of her throat and it pleased him, that intimate noise, that tiny loss of control. Satisfaction thrummed through him, coursing in his veins, sinking deep into his bones. He couldn't think straight for its intensity.

She slid one hand to his waist, along the outside of his thigh and his muscles contracted beneath her touch, but she wasn't finished with her torment. When she placed her palm over his arousal, he couldn't draw his next breath. He broke their kiss, touching his forehead to hers at the same time she caressed his erection. She withdrew right after, the torturous pleasure-pain short-lived.

He pressed a soft kiss to her mouth, not wanting for her to speak just yet. Too many conflicting emotions clouded his mind. Perhaps she experienced the same. She moved back to rest against the bench and several wordless moments passed.

"I hope it rains all night," she said finally, more an unspoken sentiment than anything else.

"And why is that?" He asked, relieved they could resume normal conversation after what had just transpired between them.

"Then there will be no show. No need for me to walk the rope." She looked at him, her eyes clear, that same spark of defiance alive in her expression.

"But you enjoy it, don't you?"

"Yes. I do."

She didn't say more and he rapped on the roof of the carriage. They'd dallied long enough in the circular drive of Fremont House.

"What will you do now that your friend is gone and the killer may never be caught by the authorities?" She asked after the carriage had advanced several blocks.

"I will go on. I will come to accept the injustice, I suppose."

She made a sound that told him she did, in fact, understand.

"What about Lady Margaret?"

Her question surprised him. "She will learn to live with the pain of her loss. She has other family to ease that burden and her upcoming marriage to look forward to." He wasn't sure what Lola was seeking. Reassurance, perhaps?

"We all just go on, don't we?" She said with a wry twist of her lips. "Some of us together, and others alone."

"Lola, I would like us—"

"I miss my family." She stared out the window, the raindrops racing down the glass like a cascade of tears. "I don't think I will ever see them again."

The chance to understand her better overrode what he'd intended to say. His suggestion would keep. "Why don't you return to Ipswich? It isn't very far."

"No, it isn't." She shook her head slowly. "But it may as well be."

He didn't know how to reply to that and instead reached across the width of the carriage and wove his fingers with hers, keeping them connected. At least for the time being.

LOLA WATCHED THE BLUR OF SCENERY THROUGH THE carriage window and blinked back the onset of tears. She wasn't usually maudlin or sentimental about her past, but kissing Theodore so intimately had stirred up all kinds of emotion and the sudden angst threatened to overwhelm her.

Her fingers remained laced with his. Her lips still stung from their passionate embrace. She could easily slip back into his arms and continue what they'd started. But there was the rub, wasn't it? He was an earl. He had no use for a Vauxhall worker other than a little slap and tickle. She knew the way of the aristocracy and the inevitable pain promised at the end of that kind of relationship wasn't worth the risk and heartache.

Drawing a cleansing breath, she beat back this rush of inconvenient truths and conjured the comforting image of her family. Were her parents well and happy? Her sister would be old enough now for a come-out in London. Hopefully Lola's choices hadn't stained her sister's reputation. At the time, there had been no other way to resolve the problem and Lola had taken the matter into her own hands. If her sacrifice saved the family's honor, then so be it. She would make the same decision again in a heartbeat.

The carriage wheels hit a rut in the road and the interior shook from the impact. Theodore tightened his hold on her hand, but he didn't speak. For a man who always had questions, she appreciated him knowing when not to ask them.

Instead, she memorized how he looked in this moment, his shirt still dampened from the rain, his expression a mixture of patience and curiosity. The tightness in her chest eased. He was pleasing to the eye in more ways than she could count.

"Tell me about your family," he said, noticing her attention.

A command, not a question this time. Interesting that the one topic she was most reluctant to discuss was the one he'd chosen. But then, she was to blame. She'd admitted to missing them.

"I have a sister. She is two years younger than me."

"And does she excel at the tightrope?" He asked, a hint of humor in his voice.

"Anna excels at watercolors. She also sings quite prettily."

"Anna," he said thoughtfully. "Lola and Anna. What is your last name?"

Aah, now she had to tread carefully, it would be so easy to misstep.

"York," she answered, acutely aware of how his thumb brushed over her palm in the gentlest of touches. Her entire body responded even though each stroke was featherlight and fleeting.

"Lola York," he said in a charming murmur, disarming her with his handsomeness. "How old are you, Lola York?"

"I don't believe it's polite to ask a woman her age. One would think with your lofty title, you would know the rules of etiquette," she replied in her usual tart tone.

"Indeed." He didn't say more, but instead tugged her forward, their fingers still locked as he settled his mouth over hers.

There was something incredibly intimate about this kiss. The first had been hungry, seeking, wildly assertive, as their lips and tongues tasted and explored in a race to learn each other and satisfy an irrepressible need.

But not this kiss.

This kiss was entirely different. It was unhurried and languid, as subtle as the raindrops that slid down the steamed window glass, yet potent for the spell it cast. This time, they savored and seduced, unconcerned with anything other than the desire to make the moment last, as if time held no significance. Their kiss was exquisitely tender and at the same time fraught with emotion, and in that way, it frightened her with the power it possessed.

Releasing his hold on her, he cradled her face, slanting his mouth at the perfect angle to capture her lips in another long, lingering caress but she pulled away. She opened her eyes noticing his were heavy lidded. Their breathing had become the loudest noise inside the carriage or perhaps it was the pounding of her heart. She couldn't be sure. Her hands trembled and she gripped the edge of the bench so he wouldn't see.

"I should go home now." The quiver of emotion in her voice solidified her decision.

"I'll take you anywhere you want to go."

At least his voice sounded as affected as hers.

"There won't be a show tonight, with all this rain." She kept her eyes on the window, not trusting she wouldn't change her mind.

Theodore knocked on the ceiling and when the driver opened the trap door, the earl gave him Lola's address. With the weather being what it was and their location in Mayfair, it would take some time to reach her part of town, but of one thing she was certain. There'd be no more kissing today.

. . .

It was half seven in the evening, dinner was over and Lola was downstairs visiting Sofia and her brothers. With Vauxhall closed and her emotions recovering from her afternoon with the earl, she needed an effective distraction. Reading a book wouldn't suffice.

"*Dio mio*, my cat loves you more than me," Sofia complained, watching Topolina settle on Lola's lap.

"That's because I feed her scraps when you aren't looking," Lola confessed, stroking the cat's velvety gray fur.

"Don't get used to her affection. Topolina is fickle," Alessandro remarked from the other side of the table. "She is like a ladybird in that respect."

"And what would you know of ladybirds?" Sofia teased.

"Lightskirts are his passion, dear sister," Francesco said from where he leaned against the wall. "He loves women too much to choose just one."

"But not you, Francesco?" Lola asked, accustomed to their lively discussions. "You're ready to settle down?"

Francesco stumbled back; his hand flung over his chest in a dramatic pantomime of his own death. "When I find the right woman, she will own my heart, but until then..." he paused for a rakish chuckle. "I will make good use of my youth and kiss as many women as possible."

The room filled with laughter, although the mention of kissing evoked a slow heat inside Lola. The time spent with Theodore had made her hands tremble and pulse race. When she'd said goodbye and stepped from his carriage, her knees were weak. For a woman who balanced on a rope as her profession, that condition was dangerous indeed.

She reached for her glass of wine and took a hearty sip. "I, for one, am grateful for the poor weather. I needed a night away from Vauxhall."

"Me too," Sofia said. "Although tonight Morland was opening

the Cascade for the first time this season. I was so looking forward to seeing it."

The Cascade was an artificial waterfall located within a three-dimensional landscape at the center of Vauxhall Gardens. The mechanical showpiece used tiny tin sheets on belts to give the appearance of flowing water. Clever use of music and lighting added to the stunning display, making it a sought-after spectacle, especially since it only operated for ten minutes each evening. Otherwise, the Cascade remained hidden behind a decorated curtain waiting to be revealed dramatically for its single nightly presentation.

"It is beautiful," Lola agreed. "But I've had enough excitement lately with what's already happened."

Both on the tightrope platform and inside the earl's carriage.

"*Sì,*" Sofia said, her face lighting up as if she'd just remembered something. "Alessandro, tell Lola what you saw that evening."

Immediately interested, Lola replaced her glass on the table. "What? You saw something?"

"Not at Vauxhall, no. Sofia makes more of it than what it is," he replied, staring at his sister as if he'd wished she'd stayed quiet. "Strange things happen in London all the time. It's nothing."

"We don't know that," Sofia insisted. "Maybe it *is* important, maybe not."

"What?" Lola prompted, impatient with their bickering.

"I'd just left Vauxhall, the exit along Lawn Lane because sometimes I go through the alleyway connected to Langley." Alessandro waved his hands as he explained, his gestures flowing as quickly as his words. "But that night there was a horse there. In the alleyway by itself! A very beautiful stallion! And right in front of me, a man ran into the alley, jumped on the horse's back and went flying out into the streets. *Che roba!* I couldn't believe my eyes. I never saw anything like it. Who leaves such a fine horse unattended? Anyone could have stolen it. I still can't believe it."

Lola sat up so quickly, Topolina leapt from her lap with a yowl. "What did the man look like? Did you see him?"

"No, no." Alessandro scowled, shaking his head as he spoke. "It all took me by surprise. I didn't see anything more than a black horse, so black it blended in with the man's greatcoat. Together they were like a giant shadow melting into the night."

"*Come la morte che viene a trovarci,*" Francesco said solemnly, his expression grave.

"What does that mean?" Lola turned toward Sofia, waiting for her to translate her brother's words.

"Like death coming to visit," Sofia explained. "That's why you should tell the Runners, Alessandro. I wish you would. It could be connected to what happened."

Lola listened, hoping Alessandro would change his mind although she'd already decided she would share the information with Theodore.

"It doesn't matter now," Alessandro said. "I don't want trouble and what happened cannot be changed. We all die sooner or later."

"*Sì, non c'è nessuno che possa saltare così in alta da sfuggire alla morte,*" Francesco lamented.

Lola looked toward Sofia again, but Alessandro translated before his sister could respond.

"There is no one who can jump so high as to escape death."

Eight

Theodore arrived at Fremont House early the next morning. His usual restlessness had plagued him through the night, but he couldn't blame Stephen's death this time. Too often he'd thought of Lola, the sensual promise in her eyes, her eager openmouthed kisses, and the delectable taste of her tongue. He wanted to feel that wicked tongue everywhere on his body. The tempting fantasy made his groin tighten.

Drawing a deep breath, he rapped the brass knocker with more force than necessary and followed the butler into the front drawing room. Just like yesterday, the tea service was in place, and Margaret waited, her attire in accord with proper mourning though she appeared more composed, her eyes no longer red-rimmed. He greeted her, happy to see she'd improved a bit.

"Stephen's body will arrive tomorrow and Colin will stay with me during the house calls." Her tone was calm and matter-of-fact. Speaking of the necessary arrangements couldn't come easily. "I would like very much for you to meet him, Theo. I only wish it was under better circumstances."

"Now that I've returned, I'm certain we will get to know each other." He'd already decided to inquire about Viscount Sidmouth

63

at the club. Perhaps he'd have Wyndham look into the matter as well. His man-of-all-things was quite astute at acquiring information in addition to a variety of *all-things*.

"Thank you again for taking me to Vauxhall yesterday afternoon. It helped ease my mind. I wanted to ask you about the woman you invited into your carriage..." Margaret paused, apparently waiting for him to complete her thought.

"Lola?"

"Yes, Lola." Margaret stirred her tea vigorously. "Do you not care about the scandal you'll cause?"

He walked to the fireplace and leaned against the mantelpiece. "You and I have known each other long enough to forego pretense, Margaret. What is it you'd like to say?"

"I saw how you stared at her when she looked elsewhere and how she did the same to you. And when you both looked at each other, the tension was unmistakable." Margaret glanced to the fire and back again. "I also noticed how long you remained in the drive after I went into the house. Were you having a quarrel?"

Theodore swallowed thoughtfully, unsure what he wanted to share. At the least, he could answer her question truthfully. "No. Not at all."

"I had hoped it was a row." A pinched frown made a fleeting appearance before she continued. "People will talk, Theo."

"I haven't given them anything to talk about." He would not apologize, not to Margaret or to anyone. He wasn't sorry. Nor had he done anything wrong.

"Stephen was involved in something secretive. He didn't confide in me. He dismissed my questions. Now he's gone and I'm left with never knowing what upset him, what drove him to act in a foolhardy manner or why he was at Vauxhall on an evening when we'd already planned to be together. I fear you're doing the very same thing and making imprudent choices. It's maddening."

"Margaret." He strode to where she sat. Her frantic stirring had caused a whirlwind in her tea cup and he gently took it away and placed it on the table. Then he sat beside her on the couch. "Thank you for your concern."

After a long, silent moment, she turned to him. "That's all you're going to say?"

"On that subject, yes." He could hardly explain something to Margaret he hadn't figured out himself. "But I do understand why Stephen's death doesn't make sense. I want to discover his reason for being at Vauxhall as much as you do. That's why I'm glad you've asked me here to go through his things. I hope there's something in his rooms that proves helpful. We can look together."

"You go ahead." She sighed heavily. "I don't have the constitution for it."

"Yes, you do." He stood up, offering her his hand. "I'll be right there beside you. Let's get started."

"What if we find something that changes everything?" she asked, her words barely above a whisper.

"Isn't that our goal?" He waited, relieved when she stood and they began walking toward the hall.

"No, I don't mean in that way," she said as they approached the stairs. "What if Stephen was involved in something that disparages his character or alters the way I remember him? I shouldn't want to learn it then. It's one of the reasons I haven't entered his rooms. I can't bear to discover he was involved in anything unseemly."

"I can't guarantee that won't happen," Theodore said with concern. "But we might discover an important clue revealing what Stephen was involved in. Something that could indicate who wanted to harm him. If there is anything in his rooms that offers Bow Street information to capture his killer, wouldn't you want to find it?"

"Yes," she answered immediately. "I suppose I'm being selfish."

"No, I understand your hesitation. But that makes it no less important."

Their conversation had led them upstairs and to the doorway

of Stephen's rooms. Theodore heard Margaret take a deep breath as they entered and moved through the sitting area into his main chambers.

Everything looked as it should at first glance. Margaret sat at the foot of the bed and waited. He supposed that was the best she could manage.

Stephen's wardrobe consisted of the usual male necessities. Shaving soap, tooth powder, pomade, and cologne water remained untouched beside a small inlaid jewelry chest. Theodore opened it and shifted the contents with one finger. As much as he wanted to discover something to explain Stephen's murder, it still seemed a violation of privacy to be looking through his friend's belongings in such a manner.

"Margaret?" Theodore picked up one of the silver coins he'd uncovered at the bottom of the chest. He brought it to where Margaret sat and placed it in her palm. "This token is stamped with the word *Vauxhall* and the engraving shows a scene. Did Stephen go often?"

"Not that he shared with me." She turned the token over in her hand, looked at it closely and then passed it back to him. "Although his behavior had altered so much, I wouldn't be surprised in the least if he did."

Theodore slid the token into his pocket and returned to sorting through the chest. Aside from one more token with a different engraving, there were two small bronze keys, and a few broken cuff links. He walked to the writing desk next. The expected ink pot, writing paper and blotter lay atop the walnut escritoire, but something about the scene looked a little too arranged and tidy. He made quick work of looking through the drawers, surprised they weren't locked, and still finding nothing useful. He even looked under the blotter which inspired a scoff from Margaret who all the while watched from the foot of the bed.

"Did Stephen keep a journal?"

"I don't believe so, although you can ask Timmons."

"Timmons, yes. I hadn't thought to speak to his valet. That's a very good idea."

"He isn't here right now though. His mother has taken ill and he's gone to be with her in Ipswich. I don't know when he plans to return and quite honestly, with Stephen gone, I'm not sure I have a position for him in the house anymore."

"He went to Ipswich?" Theodore remembered Lola's family lived there. "Whereabouts? Do you know?"

"Not without looking in the household ledger." Margaret stood up and moved to a leather trunk situated beneath one of the oriel windows. "He keeps it in here with all the other budget papers and legal documents men like to read."

"Why didn't he keep these books in his study? Isn't it odd to have them here in his private chambers?"

"I have no idea," Margaret said, untroubled by his questions. "I think Stephen preferred to keep financial matters away from prying eyes. He often met with the estate solicitor here in his sitting room instead of the study or drawing room below."

Theodore didn't know what to make of that unusual habit. Most people didn't invite lawyers or legal men into their private chambers. Turning his attention to the trunk, he found it locked, but remembering the bronze keys in the jewelry chest, he had the trunk opened a moment later. He lifted the lid and then paused a moment to remove his spectacles from his breast pocket.

"What is all of that?" Margaret asked, peering over his shoulder as he sifted through a pile of papers.

"Receipts, I think. Or maybe, vowels."

"Vowels!" Margaret exclaimed. "My brother didn't owe anyone money. He found that dishonorable and would have simply paid his debt instead of risk the embarrassment of someone learning he had overdue obligations."

Theodore's chest tightened the more he sifted through the paperwork. Clearly, Stephen was in debt. Deep debt from what the unpaid receipts, vowels and invoices implied. He tapped the stack of papers into a pile and replaced them in the trunk. Then he picked up the household ledger, an uneasy feeling accompanying the action. He had a strong idea of what he would read within.

The ledger contained page after page of withdrawals from the family account until the sums were completely depleted. Yet it didn't make any sense. Where was all that money going?

"Did Stephen start gambling? Did he wager on horses? Make large purchases or invest in property?" He searched his mind for any reason Fremont would bankrupt the viscountcy. Because from the brief perusal Theodore had at the ledger, that's how it appeared. The accounts were empty and nothing was left.

"No," Margaret said. "And now you have me worried. This is exactly why I didn't want to look at Stephen's things."

"Ignoring facts won't change them," Theodore said, mostly to himself. He thumbed through a few more pages and paused when a wrinkled piece of paper snagged his attention. It wasn't written in Stephen's hand and the message caused a terrible shock to pass through him. He closed the ledger quickly and stood up, relieved to see Margaret no longer watched over his shoulder.

LOLA STOOD OUTSIDE NO. 4 BOW STREET WITH A written note explaining what Alessandro had shared. Even with Sofia's support, she'd had little success in convincing him to report what he'd seen. She understood his hesitation. Interactions with lawmen rarely worked out favorably for immigrants and working-class people, no matter their honesty or cooperation.

Compounding the situation, Lola had no way to contact Theodore and share what she'd learned. Whereas the earl could walk into Vauxhall, or just about anywhere, with authority and privilege, she could hardly do the same with his property, wherever that may be. Somewhere in Mayfair or Westminster, no doubt. That was prime earl territory.

She glanced at the note again. It was hardly a valuable clue. An expensive black horse was as nondescript as a long black greatcoat and likely just as common among the aristocracy. Not that any nobleman or person with common sense would leave an animal of that caliber alone in an alleyway at night. Maybe that was the most telling part. It was a reckless act.

Regardless, Lola couldn't keep the information to herself. What if the Runners had learned other facts that together with this news would lead to finding the killer?

A coach and four rolled down the street, the driver on the box in control of the team of high-stepping dappled grays. She smiled. Her father loved horses. He prided himself on the esteemed reputation of the estate's expansive stable and the superior animals it held. Arabians, Andalusians, Thoroughbreds and Flemish stallions, filled stall after stall. She remembered how fond he was of the grays, but then she pushed the memory aside. Speaking to Theodore about her family yesterday had opened a Pandora's box of memories.

So much so, this morning she'd considered hiring a hack to take her to Bond Street where she could shop for a present for her sister. But sending the package through the post troubled her. What if the markings on the package led her family to discover where she'd run off to? What if one of the solicitors kept their house under watch and somehow obtained the wrapping? Could he trace the post? There were too many unpredictable variables. One foolish mistake would cause an avalanche of trouble.

Instead, she'd hired a hack to take her to Bow Street with the intent of passing Fredrickson or Johns the note outside the office, but perhaps that was a mistake as well. Having it hand-delivered by a messenger boy was a better idea. With no names mentioned in her message and an anonymous delivery, she could breathe easier.

As she worked through the maze of her thoughts, another carriage made its way down the cobbles and this time her breath caught. She recognized the conveyance immediately because it belonged to the earl.

Withdrawing behind the boxwood shrubbery, she watched as the driver aligned the carriage in front of the Bow Street office. When the door opened, Theodore stepped out with a leather portfolio in hand. He was dressed immaculately in fine tailoring that hugged his muscular physique and declared him a dashing gentleman. Although yesterday she'd found him equally desirable in his damp linen shirt.

She gave her head a little shake and watched as he made his way inside without so much as a glance over his shoulder. He wouldn't have come to Bow Street if he didn't have new information to share.

And she did too.

It took her less than a minute to decide what to do next. When the earl's driver jumped down from the box to use a hoof pick on the lead horse, she eased around the back, opened the carriage door and climbed inside.

Nine

Theodore concluded his discussion with Fredrickson and Johns, left the ledger and disturbing message in their possession, and headed for his carriage where it waited near the curb. His notes were tucked into his breast pocket and contained inconsistencies he wanted to review as well as a copy of the words written on the wrinkled paper he'd found at the back of the ledger.

The Runners had assured him they were actively conducting the investigation and he shouldn't worry, but that didn't sit well with him. Not just because the Runners had made little progress. The listing in The Quarterly Pursuit had yet to produce information and Theodore doubted it would. No, more because Fremont was like a brother to him. No matter the circumstances, his friend deserved better than the way he had died.

Indicating for his driver to remain on the box, Theodore opened the carriage door and paused. A smile forced its way out, lightening his mood. He had an unexpected guest. He settled on the bench across from Lola, rapped on the roof, and the carriage lurched forward.

"Good morning," he said, his grin still in place.

Something about Lola made him happy. He couldn't define it any other way. It had been so long since he'd experienced pure happiness, he almost didn't recognize the feeling. The physical attraction, well that was elemental. No living, breathing man could resist Lola's tight body and tempting curves, never mind her delicious heart-shaped mouth. A pulse of lust worked through him as he cleared his throat to help clear his mind.

"Good morning, my lord."

"Lola," he said in a way that made his meaning obvious.

"Good morning, *Theodore*," she answered with a mischievous smirk.

"How is it you're inside my carriage?" He asked. "Not that I have a complaint."

"I saw you arrive while I debated how to go about speaking to Fredrickson. Last night I learned something interesting that could prove helpful in the investigation."

"You promised to contact me and share anything of worth." He hoped he didn't sound arrogant, but he was disappointed she'd thought to go directly to Bow Street before telling him.

"I had no way to find you," she said. "I don't know where you live."

"That can be easily remedied." He knocked on the roof and instructed the driver to his address near Grosvenor Square.

"And why have you come to Bow Street?" she asked, her eyes never leaving his face. "Have you learned something?"

"Yes. Shall we share fact for fact?" he suggested, interested in her information.

"You go first."

He should have expected that response. Removing his gloves, he reached inside his waistcoat and took out the notes he'd written along with his pair of spectacles. When he slid them on, Lola made an appreciative sound from across the bench.

"You wear spectacles?" She asked, a gleam in her eyes. "I like them on you."

A shot of desire cut through him at her compliment. She was forever surprising him.

"Thank you." He cleared his throat again, feeling utterly pleased and foolish for it at the same time. "I went through Fremont's things with Margaret and found a few discordant items I believe are connected to his death." He glanced at Lola, her attention unwavering though she didn't speak. "This is the first."

He retrieved one of the silver tokens from his pocket and handed it to her.

"He had this token?" She asked.

"Two of them, actually. Both different. What can you tell me about them?"

"Each year a new coin is designed and issued to allow unlimited entry into Vauxhall. The tokens are exclusive. Most guests can't afford them or don't plan on visiting often enough to make it worth the guinea. And you found two?"

"Yes," he answered as he replaced the token in his pocket. "I assume there's one for each of the last two years which means, close to the time I left for America, Stephen became involved in something."

"You were in America?" She asked, her eyes going wide. "What was it like? How long were you there?"

"I promise to tell you all about it, but now isn't the time," he said, and then noticing her disappointment, reached across and squeezed her hand, lingering long enough but not so long he'd become distracted. He wanted to soften his words, but in truth his desire to touch her motivated him more. "Now it's your turn."

"I was visiting friends last evening and one of them mentioned having seen something unusual the night of the murder. Alessandro was leaving Vauxhall on his way home and he saw a man in a long black coat enter the alleyway and jump on a stallion that was waiting there unattended."

"And you think it was the murderer?"

"There's no way to know, but the man *was* wearing a long

black greatcoat. Why would anyone leave a horse alone in the dark? It was the alleyway at the end of Langley Lane which is directly behind the pleasure paths if one was to pass through the hedgerow."

"Is that possible? To exit through the hedgerow and reach the street? It looked dense in there and confusing, most especially in the dead of night."

"It wouldn't be easy, but I suppose there are a few areas where the shrubbery isn't especially thick. We can walk the paths and look together if you'd like. Once I learned my way it wasn't confusing at all, and if we find an area that appears trampled or damaged, it could prove someone inside left through the hedgerow and ran to the alleyway where his horse waited."

"That's an idea," he muttered, wondering if Lola had learned her way through the close walks from her own curiosity or the frequency of personal visits there with a man.

"Thank you." She offered him another smile. "Now it's your turn."

"I discovered Fremont was in serious debt. His bank accounts are nearly empty."

"Oh, how terrible. Was Margaret upset?"

"I'm not sure she understood how much her brother drained the finances, but unless there are other monies kept somewhere, the accounts are in low water," he said, frustrated he couldn't connect the strange pieces of information. That note he'd found in the back of the ledger. That, perhaps, was the most worrisome part of it all. "Fremont and I quarreled the morning I left on my trip. He didn't want me to leave London. He'd known about my plans for months, and never said more than a few words. Then, on the morning I was to leave, he visited me and insisted I stay, although he wouldn't give me a reason why he objected. It seemed unlike him to behave so selfishly. Afterward, I wondered if it had anything to do with me encouraging Margaret to look elsewhere for a husband. Otherwise, I don't know what to make of it."

"Was that the last time you spoke to him?"

"Here in London, yes. But we wrote each other often. Things went back to the way they'd always been. He never mentioned our quarrel and neither did I. I was looking forward to meeting him once I'd returned and was settled. Instead, Bow Street knocked on my door." He paused and exhaled heavily. "I can't help thinking he was already worried on that morning I boarded the ship for America and he needed my help and didn't tell me. Nothing makes sense."

Lola reached across and took his hand this time, lacing her fingers with his. "You can't regret what you did not know."

He looked at her lovely face and the genuine concern in her eyes. He wanted to learn more about the beautiful woman before him. He wanted to learn everything. Somehow in the past few days his curiosity had shifted into an unrelenting desire. Perhaps he was unknowingly enchanted from the start. And while they couldn't come from more different worlds, aside from it all, they were woman and man, flesh and blood.

"It's my turn," he said, searching her face but not sure what he searched for.

"I've told you everything."

"Who is Alessandro? You haven't told me that."

"He is an acrobat. Part of the Gallo tumbling act with his brother and sister. Sofia is my closest friend at Vauxhall. They live together in the rooms below me."

She was so forthcoming, he hesitated in asking his next question, knowing it was a ruse to learn something that had nothing to do with Fremont's death.

"And Marco?"

But she was too clever by half and that same playful smile curled her lips. "Marco is also a friend. We once were more than friends, but that ended over a year ago. He's still protective at times and I suppose that's normal, but I don't like his hovering. I am no one's responsibility but my own."

He didn't respond and instead reached for her, pulling her into his arms, her gown dragging across his legs, her body beneath the fabric a cruel temptation.

"Lola." He gathered the lengths of her hair and let the silky strands sift through his fingers. "I don't want to talk anymore. I want to kiss you."

"Then kiss me, Theodore." She reached up to remove his spectacles. Then she straddled his lap, her body pressed to his so close he could feel each syllable brush against his lips. "I want it as much as you do."

IT WAS SHAMEFUL TO ASK FOR A KISS. SCANDALOUS TO be draped across a gentleman's lap. All the etiquette rules and deportment lessons from her youth were wasted and forgotten in the span of a heartbeat. But Lola didn't care.

Something beyond coherent thought had control of her now. *She wanted*. Wanted with an ache inside that could only be satisfied with his kiss and more. She stroked her tongue across his lips, taking his mouth as she gripped his broad shoulders, all that strength and tension alive beneath her fingertips while deep inside her, desire surged, hot and insistent.

He met her challenge. Their tongues twined to rub and slide over and over, her breath coming rough and fast. She tightened her thighs against his, their muscles tensed, as she settled further on his lap. Her skirt had wrapped her waist in disarray, but the hard press of his arousal was evident through the fabric and she reveled in the fact he was just as eager as she.

He held her around the ribs, his fingers splayed as if to lock her in place, while the carriage's motion rocked her back and forth, producing the most delicious sensation between her legs. Need gathered and pulsed deep within her, demanding release. Just a little longer.

It took her a moment to realize the carriage had stopped.

"Christ," he said, sounding very un-earl like.

She moved to the other bench, adjusting her gown and waiting for him to speak. Perhaps he needed another minute.

"Where are we?" She asked, impatient with all her unsatisfied urges and their untimely stop.

"Mayfair. Brook Street. My home," he said in succinct answer.

At least he sounded as affected as she.

She moved the curtain aside and viewed the brick-faced town house with large sash windows and a sophisticated canopy over the door.

"Let's go inside," he said, as if it was of no consequence. As if he brought a Vauxhall performer home every day. She assumed his housekeeper would be shocked.

"Inside?"

"You said you didn't know where I live," he asserted as he knocked on the roof. "I'd like to show you my home."

It was such an unexpected request she almost didn't know how to reply. But considering her body still hummed with pleasure from his kisses and there was the possibility they'd share more kissing once inside, she readily capitulated. "Very well."

The interior of Theodore's home resembled the man she'd come to know. Tasteful decorations and select pieces of furniture filled the rooms, all done in masculine shades of blue, graphite and cranberry. Everything had a place and yet the rooms were warm and welcoming.

A single servant, Wyndham, answered the door and he seemed unbothered by her appearance beside the earl.

"Wyndham, have Cook prepare a tray of refreshments. Once you bring it in, we're not to be disturbed."

Theodore led her into the sitting room. A lively fire burned in the hearth before an overstuffed brocade chair. Elegant works of art graced the wall. A pair of long white tapers burned near the window. Everything about the room was perfect. Very neat and orderly.

Like his life, no doubt.

Unlike hers.

That conclusion extinguished her enthusiasm for further kissing. She was falling into the very same trap she'd warned herself away from. Developing feelings for a man, *for an earl*, when no future existed where they could be together. He was a nobleman, held to the highest standard, a man with dignity and honor.

And just like their worlds, her life was the complete opposite. She'd confessed to a disgraceful crime and then ran from prosecution. In the eyes of society, she was a criminal and criminals didn't usually take tea with kindhearted, devilishly handsome earls. Nor did they kiss them with an open heart.

She could enjoy his attention while it lasted, but she'd be smarter to protect her emotions. Nothing could ever come of their relationship. She needed to remember that most of all.

Wyndham's entry with a large silver tray interrupted her silent musings and she was glad to let them go. Once the servant closed the doors behind him, Theodore strode across the room, gathered her in his arms and kissed her soundly. His fervent attention touched her heart, making her earlier decision that much more difficult. She would never be able to spend time in his company and not become more attached. Already she stood on unsteady ground.

She pulled back the slightest, relishing the warmth and security his embrace provided. Knowing she would miss it. "I need to return to Vauxhall for practice. You wouldn't want me to fall now, would you?"

She'd tried for a teasing tone, but so much truth was disguised in her words they sounded tentative at best.

"I will catch you," he whispered next to her ear and a thrill spiraled through her. "Every time."

Her heart lurched. She couldn't do this. She couldn't hurt his feelings. He already mourned his closest friend. Why had she started something that would only end with pain?

"You think it's that easy?" She pulled from his arms, struggling to protect them both, and refusing to acknowledge the confusion in his eyes.

He took a moment, then another, before he spoke. "I will return to Vauxhall after hours and we can walk the path. Then I will escort you home."

How like him to think he was in control. To dictate what would happen. To expect she would agree without question.

"No," she said quickly, purposely moving farther across the room. "I know my way through the close walks and you've no need to bring me home. That isn't necessary."

"After the danger that has occurred, I disagree."

She'd traded Marco's escort for Theodore's now, although it wasn't the same. That's what made it so dangerous.

"My friends don't take well to nobs. We're very different people from those who live here in Mayfair." She gestured toward one of the velvet-draped windows and moved away, but he came up behind her, gently clasped her shoulders and turned her to face him.

"Lola." Whenever he said her name, his tone, his voice and the emotion there, always reached for her heart. "What's wrong?"

He stood too close. Heat emanated from him. His spicy bergamot cologne filled her lungs. "I need to go." She pulled away before he distracted her with affection and she'd need to distract him with lies. "Don't wait for me after the show."

He stepped back. He didn't stop her when she walked to the door. Nor did he follow her out.

She hurried toward the corner to hail a hackney, cursing herself. She knew better than to make this mistake. Nothing could come of their kisses. Her future would always be uncertain because of what she'd done. Thankfully, Marco was the only person who knew about her past. In her world, truth was often more dangerous than lies.

Ten

Theodore entered White's and nabbed a brandy from a nearby tray. Many of the gentleman in the room wore a black band of mourning around their sleeve resembling his own. He'd visited Fremont House before coming to the club and Margaret was doing as well as could be expected. She was busy with callers offering condolences, so he hadn't approached her, but she had her betrothed at her side and other family members there for support and that eased his mind.

Now he made his way through the hall, down the stairs and into the card room in search of the Earl of Huntington. Huntington enjoyed cards, piquet to be exact, and Theodore hoped to find him at a table. When he'd come to White's last week, Huntington had intimated Fremont's attitude had changed during the last two years. Having discovered evidence to support Huntington's comment, Theodore hoped to convince his friend to elaborate. Too many questions remained unanswered.

"Essex!" Huntington called as Theodore crossed the room. "Come sit in on a hand. I'm fleecing Mowbray. Mayhap you'll bring him some luck."

Theodore approached the table where Huntington sat across

from Alan Gresley, Baron Mowbray. A long while had passed since he'd shared Mowbray's company, but Theodore might never have recognized the man were it not for Huntington's announcement. Mowbray was younger by at least five years, but he appeared older by comparison. His complexion looked ruddy and his hair had gone too long without a cut. Mowbray glanced up, narrowed his eyes at Theodore, and then immediately returned his attention to his cards.

"Mowbray." Theodore greeted the man, although the baron didn't look up again to acknowledge him.

Huntington was also busy examining his cards. Theodore took the empty chair even though he had no intention of playing. He wanted to speak to Huntington alone, but he'd have to wait it out. His friend would never abandon a winning streak.

"How goes it since we last spoke?" Huntington said as he revealed a quint, the high scoring combination of five matched suits causing Mowbray to grumble angrily.

"How many rounds do you have left?" Theodore eyed the table. If the discard pile was any indication, the game was nearly over.

"Two, at best," Huntington said, his voice lowered. "I'm just shy of one hundred."

"Not yet," Mowbray piped up as he displayed his hand of cards. "That's six more points for me."

Theodore leaned closer, his words meant for Huntington only. "How long have you been at this? Mowbray looks a little worse for the wear."

"A few hours," Huntington replied. "This should finish it out."

Huntington revealed a final trick and scored the points he needed. He collected his winnings and stood from the table. "Let's go up to the morning room. Lately Mowbray's a sore loser."

"Then why do you play piquet with him?" Theodore asked as they moved up the stairs.

"He's always after a game and I'm happy to oblige. However, he used to be far better company. It's only the last month or so he's become surly and argumentative. Otherwise, he was always a high-stake player with very deep pockets who enjoyed the game heartily. There were nights we'd gamble into the wee hours. Just not of late." Huntington shrugged, seemingly unbothered by the situation. "So, what did you want to talk about?"

They found two open chairs near the window and Theodore glanced out at the passing traffic, still unsettled by his visit with Lola this morning. She'd left upset and he wasn't sure why. One minute they were sharing sensual kisses and the next she couldn't leave his home fast enough. He took another sip of brandy and put those thoughts away for later examination.

"Last time I was here you mentioned Fremont had changed. How so?" He may as well get right to the point.

"I'm not completely comfortable talking poorly about him now that he's gone, but I believe it's common knowledge in the club that Fremont was having money troubles."

"Yes, I know about that."

"One night, when we'd all had too much liquor, Mowbray confided in me that someone had Fremont in a firm grip," Huntington said quietly.

"What do you mean?"

"Mowbray didn't elaborate, although I understood it to mean extortion of some kind."

"What?" Theodore couldn't have heard his friend correctly.

"Someone demanding money in exchange—"

"Yes, I know what extortion means," Theodore snapped. "Why would anyone bleed Fremont's funds? It's nonsensical. He was friends with everyone and the least confrontational person I know. Every time I think I've solved a problem, another question arises."

Huntington sipped his brandy. "I suppose you could ask Mowbray, although I wouldn't want him to think I've betrayed his confidence and repeated the conversation. I doubt he'll want to play cards with me again after that."

"Is that what's most important here?" Theodore asked, struggling to maintain his patience.

"No, of course not," Huntington replied. "I'd just prefer if you went about your information recognizance in another manner. Maybe you can sit in on a few hands of cards tomorrow evening. I'll bring up the subject of Fremont's passing and we can go from there. That way I don't look like a tongue-wag."

"That's not a terrible idea," Theodore said, hopeful he could lead Mowbray into repeating whatever he knew about Fremont's situation. "All right. I'll meet you here tomorrow evening. How about nine?"

"Yes, that will be all right," Huntington agreed. "But for now, I'm off."

"I'll walk out with you," Theodore answered. "I have somewhere else I need to be."

LOLA LEANED ON THE PLATFORM RAILING AND STARED out beyond the grandstand. It was late afternoon, an hour before the gates opened, and no one was about. It was a good time for her to examine the hedgerows in the close walks.

Scurrying down the ladder, she aimed for the pleasure paths. If she found a place in the shrubbery along Langley Lane that looked damaged, she would share the information with Theodore. She'd told him not to come tonight and walk her home, but part of her wished she hadn't. Kissing him was the only peace her heart experienced since she'd fled Ipswich years ago. Yet kissing him was also the reason she couldn't think clearly.

Impatience and anger simmered inside her. She'd developed feelings for a man who would always be above her reach and had allowed those same feelings to interfere with her concentration. Her mind and heart were at war. So much so, she'd had to stop walking the rope this afternoon for fear she'd make a foolish mistake. She had enough troubles without inviting more.

If her past had taught her anything, it was that the line dividing social class was stronger than the rope that supported her weight each night and even more dangerous. Whenever she lost sight of that divide, danger loomed. It was what caused her to leave home, the same circumstance that changed her family's close relationship with a duke into a confrontation with the law.

Two years ago in Ipswich, her world had upended when the Duke of Leinster accused her father of stealing. The accusation came as a shock since the two men were on good terms for nearly a decade. Her father, a sought-after horse trainer and His Grace, an avid equestrian, were introduced at Tattersall's. They'd become fast friends and eventually His Grace hired Lola's father to run his extensive stables. Lola, her parents and sister, moved into a spacious cottage on estate grounds and in many ways became part of the duke's extended family. His Grace was a reserved, formidable man, but for many years, her family lived a content and comfortable life due to the strong bonds of friendship. A rare and precious friendship considering her father possessed no lofty title.

But everything changed when His Grace accused her father of stealing. Suddenly the distance between their social class overrode more important qualities like uncompromised loyalty, infallible respect, and years of camaraderie. His Grace contacted the authorities and Lola's father was challenged. He had no way to prove his innocence other than his word and since an aristocrat's claim cancels all others, the magistrate didn't investigate the matter. Just like that, Lola's family was displaced from their home, her father taken into custody, and their honor stained.

But Lola couldn't bear the thought of her father suffering for a crime he didn't commit and her mother and sister struggling without him. Her intercession was the only way she could spare the people she loved. One person's sacrifice in exchange for three seemed a very fair trade.

She never questioned her decision, nor did she regret it now. Even if it meant forfeiting her future and keeping Theodore at arm's length. Never indulging in more of his kisses. Never pretending their connection could be more than a temporary, meaningless tumble. Because there was no way their relationship made sense. Not when she was an accused criminal and he, an honorable nobleman. Not when one wrong word or action would destroy those tenuous bonds or worse, expose her past and further humiliate her family.

She breathed deep and entered the close walks, knowing exactly which direction to take. Striding past the place a man had lost his life. Moving farther into the twisting labyrinth of clandestine alcoves until she reached the line of shrubbery that paralleled Langley Lane. She paced along the path slowly, her eyes on the hedges while her mind and heart continued their fierce battle.

If she confided in Theodore and told him about her past, would he respect her decision? Or like most men, would he attempt to remedy the situation? He lived in a different world than Marco. Entitled men possessed power far above the law. But in this case, Theodore's influence would be for naught. The Duke of Leinster was a prideful, arrogant man. Uncompromising and unsympathetic in ways she'd never imagined. His Grace didn't want the truth to come to light. Any interference by Theodore would only exacerbate the situation, and she was not so naïve to believe the problem could be resolved with an apology and conversation. Had that been the case, she would never have had to confess to the crime in the first place.

Blinking hard to clear away these thoughts, she walked on. One of the shrubs near the corner had several broken offshoots. It created a narrow opening, no more than twelve inches wide, but with the flexibility of the branches and the force of someone pushing through, she believed passage could be achieved. The killer had worn a greatcoat for protection. In her thin day gown, she wouldn't attempt to move through, but she had no doubt she'd found the correct spot.

Turning on her heel, she made her way out, her mind debating decisions in the same fashion she followed the maze out of the gardens. She believed Theodore experienced the same pull of desire, the same aching measure of want and need, yet she could never be more to him than an illicit affair. Her mind insisted that to be true while her heart squeezed tight in objection.

When she exited the close walks, Marco was waiting for her.

"Where have you been? I looked for you on the platform. Did you practice today?" He stepped closer.

"I needed time to think." She gestured behind her. "I wanted to walk where it was quiet."

"What were you thinking about?"

"Just my family," she lied, unwilling to share her conflicted emotions concerning the earl. "I miss them."

"Is there no way you can visit them?" His voice was more relaxed now.

"No," she answered adamantly, folding her arms over her chest and standing her ground. She'd had this conversation with Marco in the past and it never served any purpose other than to ignite her temper. "If I go to Ipswich, my parents will urge me to recant my confession. My father will insist he committed the theft, even though I know he would never betray the duke's trust. But my father *will* attempt to save me. He will sacrifice himself in the same way I've chosen to protect him. It's better that I never return. My running away is another layer of guilt added to my confession and the only way to keep my father from prison."

"Are you sure, Lola?"

"Yes." She dropped her arms and straightened her shoulders. "I don't want to talk about it anymore."

Marco glanced toward the pavilion and his expression changed. She followed his line of sight and saw Theodore walking toward them. She breathed deep, soaking in the sight of him. Warning herself to guard her heart.

"Look who's back, acting as if he belongs here," Marco said with a bitter note of sarcasm. "I know why he keeps coming around and it has nothing to do with his dead friend."

"Marco," she said sharply, gravity in her tone. "Don't."

"Good afternoon." Theodore joined them where they stood near the entrance.

"Hello, Lord Essex," Lola said in greeting, but Marco remained silent.

The earl continued regardless of the insult. "I thought to have a look at the hedgerows—"

"Lola doesn't need a keeper," Marco interrupted.

"I would never make that assumption," Theodore said calmly, though there was an edge to his words.

"She doesn't need a protector either," Marco went on, his voice stronger than a moment before. "At least not in you."

"Marco," she warned. "Stop."

Men with their arrogance and bravado. She expected Marco to thump on his chest next.

To his credit, Theodore ignored Marco's taunting. "Lola, if you'll show me the way."

"She doesn't have to obey you," Marco continued; his eyes narrowed as he stared at the earl. "I know Lola better than anyone here at Vauxhall."

"Marco, you need to go." Lola stepped toward him. "This is fine. I'm only showing Lord Essex something that may have to do with the death of his friend. I'll be out of the paths in a few minutes."

Marco gave a sharp nod and turned to leave, but Lola knew their discussion was far from over.

. . .

UNWILLING TO BE DRAWN INTO AN ARGUMENT, Theodore watched Marco walk away. The man was a matter to be settled at a later date. Now Theodore followed Lola into the pleasure paths. They walked in silence, him a few strides behind her. He couldn't complain about the view. Her long hair swished with every step, brushing her lower back and luring his attention to her perfectly rounded bottom, the rest of her just as pleasing to the eye.

He always liked this time of day as the sun was setting and night hadn't yet claimed the sky. When he was a child, he believed all kinds of magical things were possible as dusk fell. Wishes could be made here in the gloaming, the in-between hour, otherworldly and incandescent, as if one was caught between two realities.

"I'm sorry, Theodore."

Her words floated back to him, forcing him to the present. "Does he always behave that way?"

Lola stopped, her silky hair wrapping around her shoulders as she turned abruptly to face him. "I suppose, in light of recent events, he worries on my behalf."

"I mean you no harm."

"I know that, but he doesn't," she said, before she pivoted and continued to follow the gravel path deeper into the close walks.

"You find your way through here well." That knowledge bothered him for several foolish reasons.

"I come in here often," she said, her eyes slow to meet his. "I like to be alone and think," she said at last.

His tension eased and they started to move again. He came up beside her. "What happened this morning? You left angry."

"Why did you bring me to your home?"

"I wanted to talk," he answered plainly.

"Talk about what?"

"Talk about you."

"I'm not such an intriguing subject," she answered with a note of skepticism in her voice.

"You are to me," he said, surprised he needed to explain.

She scoffed and her eyes flashed with some unnamed emotion. "You must be tired of the fancy ladies in the ballroom if you find me intriguing."

"I am and I do," he insisted, unsure of her meaning.

"And you say that as if it's a compliment."

"It is." He'd held back long enough, answering her comments and questions. If she doubted his honesty, he would enlighten her now. "Lola."

She stopped walking and faced him. She waited; his lips pressed tightly together.

"I can't stop thinking about you. It doesn't matter what I'm doing, you're with me. Day or night, you're in my thoughts, and I'll be damned if I allow you to ignore the attraction between us."

She frowned. It wasn't the reaction he'd expected.

"But that's your mistake," she said in that same tart tone that usually amused him. "Like every nob you want something, but you don't consider the consequences or what will be left in the aftermath."

"What are you talking about?"

"What happens, Theodore, after we kiss? After I fall into bed with you? After I fall in—" She stopped before any more words tumbled out.

He reached for her hand and pulled her straight into his arms.

She came willingly.

Eleven

"Tell me you feel nothing and I won't ask you again," Theodore said, his voice thick with emotion. "Just don't lie to me."

Her chin jutted out, but her tempting little mouth stayed quiet. When she pulled back, he released her. Her refusal to answer was answer enough.

"The place I found in the hedges is up here."

She strode to a turn in the path and he followed.

"Here."

She indicated a space in the hedgerow and he examined it closely. With enough force and momentum, someone could pass through and exit on the other side. She'd done a good job. They were deep within the pleasure paths now. During a typical night's entertainment with only moonlight and lantern glow, no one would have noticed.

"You're right." He stepped away from the hedgerow. "Since Bow Street has made little progress, any piece of information is helpful."

"We can have no future." Her blunt change of subject took him by surprise.

90

"I thought you lived in the moment." He moved beside her. "You told me one misstep would bring about the end of your days."

"You have no idea how true that is." Sadness deepened her frown.

"Then tell me."

"No." Her eyes glinted with determination. "Too much truth is more dangerous than walking the rope. I should go now," she said as she started past him.

He reached out and caught her fingers in his. They stood that way a long minute. No sound could be heard aside from a far-off birdcall. With a deliberate pause, he angled his head and gazed into her eyes. When their mouths met, they closed the world out together.

Deepening their kiss, he breathed in the scent of her skin, a fragrance he'd come to know as *Lola*. Fresh, tart, sweet, sensual. His mind spun from it. Wrapping her hair in his fist, he tugged gently, angling her head for better access as he trailed kisses along her jaw, down the graceful arch of her neck to her clavicle where he nipped and tasted, all the while wanting more.

He licked over her pulse and she said his name like a plea, almost an ache. Her body pressed against his, soft to hard, perfectly matched as desire thrummed through him. It was maddening. He needed more of her, all of her.

He reversed their position, turning his back to the hedgerow as he slid his hands over her firm bottom and pulled her closer. She made a low, appreciative sound in the back of her throat. It vibrated through him as their tongues continued their erotic dance.

Her hands, impatient in their exploration, smoothed over his back to his biceps, all the while their kiss created headier bliss into a sense of timelessness.

She passed her palm over the falls of his trousers, the fleeting caress enough to send an arrow of sensation to his groin. Every movement she made was unmistakable and enticing. The heat of her skin tempted just beneath his touch, her dress nothing more than a slip of fabric over a chemise. So, unlike all the layers proper ladies wore like armor around their bodies.

He trailed his fingers along her ribs until he reached the delicate swell at her neckline. She murmured his name, that same breathy restlessness in every syllable. Moving the fabric aside, he lifted her breast, breaking their kiss to lower his head and taste her creamy skin. She arched into him and he stroked his tongue over the hard tight tip causing her to shudder with pleasure.

Her fingers sunk into his hair, holding him to her heart, yet he couldn't continue. He wanted to and so much more, but Lola deserved better than to be ravished on a pleasure path. When they made love, it would be in absolute privacy, wrapped in satin and silk, unhurried and magnificent. Not like the patrons of the close walks, who after a tawdry interlude returned to their regular lives unchanged, easily dismissing what happened only hours before.

Decision made, he carefully withdrew, putting her gown to rights before he wrapped her in his embrace. He rested his chin atop her head and breathed a deep sigh. He didn't know what they had, what they'd created, but whatever it was, there was no denying it had a strong hold on him now.

LOLA KEPT HER EYES CLOSED, RELISHING THE PRECIOUS security of Theodore's embrace. Just one minute longer and then she'd let go. She shouldn't get used to the feeling. Forcing herself to withdraw, she slowly stepped away.

"Don't wait tonight to bring me home. I'm perfectly fine with Sofia and her brothers. We will leave together," Lola said as they moved out of the close walks.

Time shared with Theodore within the pleasure garden was a cherished memory, but that was all it could be. Every time she was with him, she made another mistake and gave in to desire. She needed to end it now before her emotions became more involved. Already it hurt to think of never seeing him again.

"If that is what you want," he said as he watched her closely.

"Do not think yourself clever." He had agreed too easily and she wasn't fooled. "I don't expect to look down the street and see your carriage in the shadows rolling along in silent escort."

He chuckled, low and wonderful. He'd been caught.

"You're too smart for your own good."

"My father used to tell me that," she said with a rueful smile. "Perhaps it is true."

"What time do you finish this evening?" he asked and she wondered if he would still insist on appearing at the end of her act even though she'd told him not to.

"It will be late," she said noncommittedly. "Morland is opening the Cascade for the first time tonight and there will be a bigger crowd than usual. Sofia and I are looking forward to seeing the show. Then all of us, her brothers too, will go home together."

"I see."

They'd reached the pavilion and Lola wondered if Marco watched from afar. Besides, it was almost time to open to the public. Too many performers and workers were moving about the grounds now.

"Best of luck to you in finding out what happened to your friend." She bit her lower lip and glanced away, the finality of her words in direct contrast to the taste of him lingering on her tongue.

"Until next time, Lola," he said before he turned and walked away.

THEODORE ARRIVED AT FREMONT HOUSE BY SEVEN in the evening. Calling hours had ended and he hoped Margaret felt well enough for conversation. Enduring the mourning visits and keeping her emotions under control had to have been exhausting.

He hoped her betrothed was the stand-up sort, able to comfort her and also take control of the situation.

Once inside the drawing room, he helped himself to a brandy. For the entire ride to Fremont House, he'd tried to understand Lola's dismissal. She sought to protect her heart, he supposed, but didn't she realize they were already intertwined. And not just because of Fremont's death. He refused to believe they were drawn together for a few illicit kisses and nothing more.

"Theodore." Margaret came into the drawing room looking more relaxed than when he'd seen her previously. "I'm glad you've returned."

"I know the day must have taken its toll. So many people were here earlier. It's a tribute to how respected and well-liked Stephen was." He placed his brandy on the inlaid rosewood table between them as they settled on opposite chairs. It still felt odd to speak of his friend in the past tense. He couldn't imagine Margaret's difficulty with the same.

"Yes." She sighed. "He will be greatly missed."

"I've conferred with Bow Street but I'm afraid I don't have any more information to share." Sincere frustration laced his words. "Did you hear any gossip or speculation today that could be useful?"

"No, unfortunately." She stood up and walked to the writing desk. "But I did receive a note from Timmons."

She returned to where they sat and handed him a folded piece a paper. Placing it on the table, he reached into his breast pocket and retrieved his spectacles, remembering how Lola had removed them in his carriage and kissed him until he'd forgotten his own name. The untimely but intense memory gave him pause. Belatedly, he slid his spectacles on and opened the valet's note, anxious for meaningful distraction.

"Timmons resigned his position," Margaret shared. "His mother is much improved but he's decided to stay in Ipswich to care for her. I suppose if you want to ask him about Stephen's behavior or whether or not my brother had a journal, you'll have to visit him. He's included his mother's address so I can forward his final wages."

"Yes. I see that here," Theodore said. "It isn't that far of a trip, but I won't be able to go for a few days. I've committed to a game of cards at the club tomorrow night."

"Cards?" Margaret asked as she took the note and placed it on the table. "And that's so important?"

"Actually, yes." He nodded. "Huntington plays piquet regularly and mentioned a comment about Stephen's change in behavior during one of the games. It's my hope that by engaging in a few rounds of cards, I'll be able to discover more."

"I guess any information can be helpful since we know so little."

"Yes, I'm of the same mind," Theodore agreed. "Playing cards with Huntington is a small sacrifice if Lord Mowbray can shed some light on what happened."

"Lord Mowbray? Alan?" Margaret blurted, her voice high and sharp.

When Theodore looked at her, she'd gone pale. What the devil?

"Margaret, what's the matter?" He asked, confused by her sudden, troubled reaction.

"I don't know where to begin. This is so unexpected." She'd calmed, though her pensive frown hadn't changed in the least. "Shortly after you left for America, Lord Mowbray began courting me. I intended, as you suggested, to move on and seek a relationship that could lead to marriage and a family. Stephen was quite disconcerted you'd given me that advice. I think he always hoped you and I...well that matters little now." She huffed a cleansing breath before she continued. "Anyway, Lord Mowbray continued to call and we became a popular couple. His feelings were engaged quickly, while I was unsure whether I truly cared for him or whether he was a convenient suitor. At times I found him lacking in character."

"How so?" Theodore asked.

"He asked indelicate questions that made me uncomfortable, especially when he inquired about my dowry. He was quick to anger whenever I commented on his behavior. At first, I ignored it, but it continued to bother me, so I asked him to cease calling. It ended badly. Alan persisted and it became complicated. He called here at the house and messaged me frequently. He claimed he was heartbroken, but it didn't ring true. I think he was insulted, his self-importance unaccustomed to rejection. Something like that." She wrung her fingers in her lap as she fell quiet.

"Then what happened?" He prompted.

"One day, everything just stopped. He never came by again. I assumed he grew tired of my refusals."

"Margaret, I'm sorry." Theodore fell silent for a moment. "How was it that Stephen allowed this to continue?"

"That was the thing, unfortunately."

"What was the thing?"

"I didn't tell Stephen about the deteriorated relationship. I kept it all from him." She stood up and walked to the fireplace, her back turned as she continued to explain. "I didn't want Stephen to engage Alan in some foolish battle caused by his desire to protect my reputation. They were friendly enough otherwise. I thought I could end the relationship and no one would be the wiser regarding our private problems. Alan and I would part as friends within the public eye."

"This does add another layer to the situation. Stephen would definitely have objected if he'd known Mowbray mistreated you. However, relationships end. If you'd confided in your brother, he might have been able to smooth things over with Mowbray and spared you distress."

"It wasn't that simple."

Margaret turned to face him and Theodore waited for her to

explain further, a sense of foreboding hanging in the air between them.

"Alan and I had become intimate." Margaret looked away again. "I know my brother would have reacted poorly to *that* news."

"Indeed." The one word was all Theodore could manage. He certainly understood the fine line between decorum and desire. Had he less conscience earlier today, he would have laid Lola down on the soft grass of the pleasure gardens and lost himself. "Thank you for confiding in me, Margaret. I realize why hearing Mowbray's name came as a shock, but let's hope my card game tomorrow evening brings resolution to some of the unanswered questions concerning Stephen's murder."

"Yes, that is my wish as well."

VAUXHALL WAS MORE CROWDED THAN LOLA HAD SEEN the entire season and it could only be due to the Cascade presentation that evening. She walked toward the Picture Rooms and Rotunda, closer to the Centre Cross Walk, looking for Sofia so they could enjoy the spectacle together, but the crowd of pleasure seekers milling about the area made it difficult.

When she went up on tiptoe, she could see above those around her and all the way to the display platform. The curtain that concealed the Cascade hung from a screen and was beautifully decorated by artists who changed the landscape painting each year. When show time neared, the curtain would be drawn back dramatically to increase the anticipation.

Lola wanted to move closer, but at the same time hoped to locate Sofia in the crowd. Her friend was similarly petite and that made it all the more difficult. Nevertheless, Lola eased her way through the joyful families and amorous couples to gain a better vantage point. The Cascade only operated once so if she didn't find Sofia for the showing, she would still be able to rejoin her friends inside the pavilion before walking home.

Someone brushed against her from behind and she looked over her shoulder seeing only more spectators filling the area. Everyone was packed in tight now as show time neared. She heard the tinkling of a bell and the curtain slowly drew back evoking awestruck gasps and excited exclamations all around her.

The crowd shifted as eager guests tried to gain a better view, but Lola resisted, refusing to be caught in the momentum. She had a good position for watching the display and didn't want to move before it was over. The show was only ten minutes in length.

Again the crowd surged, an undulation of activity and energy flowing toward the platform, but this time someone pressed against her back. Uncomfortable with the onlooker's nearness, she attempted to pull away but the stranger, *a man*, caught her neck from behind. His fingers slid beneath her hair and held her head forward as he leaned in and spoke into her ear. At the same time, she felt the prick of a sharp weapon pressed into her side.

"Poke your nose where it doesn't belong, Lola, and I'll have to cut it off."

The man shoved her forward and she hit hard against the people in front of her. By the time she spun and recovered, the swell of visitors behind her had absorbed the man as if he'd never existed. The Cascade began that very same moment. The spectators around her stood tightly pressed together, shoulder to shoulder, as they watched the fascinating display of roaring water and soothing music.

Everyone delighted in the enchanting performance.

Everyone except Lola.

Her entire body trembled. Her pulse pounded so loudly in her ears she could hear nothing else.

Twelve

Once the Cascade show had ended and the crowd dispersed, Lola hurried to the pavilion, located Sofia and together they'd walked home with her brothers. Yet Lola had waited until she was upstairs in her room with Sofia before she'd revealed what had happened.

"You need to tell Bow Street," Sofia repeated for the umpteenth time.

"I don't think it will make any difference. I didn't see the man who threatened me. I have nothing to share except his words, and I've learned from the past that words mean little without proof," Lola insisted. "I don't want the Runners to take an interest in me and start prying into my life."

The thought of lawmen pressuring her to answer more questions was distressing enough, but if they somehow connected her to what had happened in Ipswich, her greatest fear of being discovered would be realized. She'd have to run away again and she wasn't ready to leave behind her new life and friends.

Or Theodore.

Nevertheless, the threatening experience had left her shaken. The stranger had called her by name. She supposed being the only rope walker at Vauxhall, the information was available, but that didn't calm her nerves. And she couldn't tell Sofia how frightened she felt because Sofia would try to protect her. She would tell her brothers or worse, tell Marco. Sofia was a good friend and meant well, but none of those possibilities helped Lola.

"Please, Sofia, keep my secret."

"But I worry about you. What if this man is watching you? What if he intends to harm you?"

"He was just trying to scare me," Lola said with false confidence. "And he did. From now on whenever I go out, I will be more careful. And since I have no plans to invite his anger, I think this was a single incident."

"But what if it isn't?" Sofia went on, her voice growing anxious as she waved her hands for emphasis.

"I can take care of myself." She had, for over two years now.

"What about the earl?" Sofia asked with her brows raised. "I think he fancies you. He would want you to be safe. You should tell him. He can protect you."

"No," Lola said firmly. "He would follow me around just like Marco. Besides, what does it matter if he fancies me? We are as different as the sun and the moon." Her heart turned over. She was such a liar. She was drawn to him with the same intensity he'd expressed this afternoon.

"*Dio mio!* The sun needs the moon. They work together to balance the world in light and dark." Sofia tutted her tongue as if Lola was a child who didn't understand. "An earl's attention would make my heartbeat race."

"I think you have that reversed," Lola teased hoping to ease the mood. "If you caught an earl's attention, your brothers would race to chase him away."

"Aah, I suppose that is true," Sofia scoffed. "Anyway, I should return now and see if my overbearing brothers are ready for dinner. Are you feeling better? Do you want me to come back upstairs later?"

"No, I'm fine." Lola returned her friend's smile. "And you're just downstairs if I need you."

"*Sì*. Now lock your door." Sofia paused before she entered the hall. "I will tell Alessandro to check the downstairs door as well."

"Thank you, but I'll be fine," Lola said before she closed the door and turned the latch. Now if only she could convince herself.

WHEN THE SUN ROSE THE NEXT MORNING, LOLA HADN'T changed her mind. She wasn't going to Bow Street, but she would go out. Years ago, as a child in Ipswich, whenever something disappointing happened, her mother took Lola and her sister, Anna, shopping for a new hair ribbon or sweet treat.

Remembering that long ago feeling of her mother's love and concern, Lola left the boarding house and walked a few blocks until she found a hackney for hire. She directed the driver to Bond Street and settled on the seat, taking in the passing scenery as she approached the better part of London. Little by little, the world around her changed.

Men and women in serviceable gray work clothes and stained aprons transformed into gentlemen in distinguished trousers with embroidered waistcoats or ladies dressed in fashionable day gowns of lace-trimmed muslin and imported cotton. Blocks of tightly pressed rental houses and run-down tenements evolved into stately town houses with brick-faced facades, set back from the curb where only decorative pots of lavender marked the entryway. If she needed another reminder of the difference between her world and the earl's, she'd only had to take a ride this morning.

She paid the driver when they reached Bond Street, the hour not long after ten. Window shopping was always enjoyable, but perhaps she'd indulge and purchase something special to ward off the uneasy emotions alive in her heart. She'd developed strong feelings for Theodore. Dare she label it love?

But the situation at Vauxhall last evening and the threatening stranger with his knife at her back provided her a convenient reason to avoid the earl. He'd take one look at her face and know something was wrong because, for no reason she could explain, they'd connected on some strange soul-knowing level. Then he'd ask questions she had no intention of answering and that could only lead to an argument. So, it was for the best to avoid him. Even if she knew she was behaving like a coward.

THEODORE DIRECTED HIS DRIVER TO LOLA'S ADDRESS and climbed into his carriage. The card game this evening was still several hours away and his usual restlessness had taken hold. Even though Lola had insisted he not escort her home last night, he wanted, no, he *needed* to see she was safe. In truth, he needed more. To touch her and breathe her in. Or maybe these were all just excuses to visit her today. He wouldn't lie to himself.

He'd spent most of the morning meeting with his man-of-all-things, assured Wyndham would make all the necessary arrangements for their travel to Ipswich. Theodore hoped speaking to Fremont's valet would prove beneficial. Usually, a gentleman's valet was an invaluable asset, a servant who provided many purposes beyond dressing. Even though Theodore doubted his friend disclosed confidential matters, if Timmons shared knowledge of Fremont's mood or some strange meeting or appointment, the information might shed light on the issue. If Timmons was aware Fremont kept a journal and knew where the book was kept, then that would be worth its weight in gold.

Everything was interconnected and complicated, tangled together like knots in a rope. His thoughts turned to Margaret and the confessions she'd made the day before about having been involved with Lord Mowbray. It certainly added another layer of difficulty to the matter.

The carriage rolled to a stop and shook him to the present. With any luck, Lola would be pleased to see him. As he stepped down, he wondered if that was a fool's wish. He mounted the stairs and knocked on the door to the boarding house. It opened immediately and a young woman stared up at him.

"Lola isn't here," she said with a coy smile. "I'm Sofia Gallo. I live with my brothers in the rooms on the first floor."

"Hello, Miss Gallo. Lola has spoken highly of your friendship," Theodore said. "I am Lord Essex."

"I thought so." Sofia's smile grew wider. "Lola has mentioned you."

A knowing beat passed between them.

"But she isn't here this morning, my lord," Sofia went on, her expression growing pensive and concerned. "I urged her to go to Bow Street, but if I know her as I think I do, she's probably only gone out for a walk."

"Why would she need to go to Bow Street?" he asked, all at once concerned. "Is something wrong?"

"*Dio mio!*" Sofia huffed and hesitated. "I've said too much. Lola will be angry with me." She stepped out onto the stoop and closed the door so they could speak privately.

"I believe you've said exactly what you'd intended to say," he assured her. "Now please be a good friend to her and tell me why you're worried."

"It is better, I think." Sofia hooked her finger in a loose curl near her cheek and tucked it behind her ear. "Lola is always so strong, but in this she needs protection."

"What happened?" He asked, trying hard to keep a leash on his patience.

"Last night, when Lola watched the Cascade, it was a mob," Sofia explained. "So many people. It was ridiculous. She was alone in the crowd and a man moved up behind her." Her words came out quickly now, her hands gesturing in circles in front of her as if to hurry them even faster. "He held her neck so she couldn't see him or pull away and he pressed a weapon to her back as he told her to mind her business. He said he would hurt her if it happened again."

Theodore's chest pounded, his heart in an anxious, angry rhythm. "Is Lola all right? Did she share anything else?"

"Lola is strong. She never shows weakness, but I know she is shaken," Sofia said. "She didn't see the man so she thinks it is a waste of time to talk to the Runners. That's all I know."

"She doesn't want to inform Bow Street?"

"No." Sofia scowled, her own frustration evident. "Lola keeps secrets she doesn't share with anyone. Not even me. She fears the Runners will pry into her personal life."

"Did she tell you anything else about this stranger?" he asked.

"Not very much. She couldn't see him, but Lola said he wasn't much taller than she. His mouth aligned with her ear when he held her neck."

"Anything else?" Theodore's temper ticked up another notch. A man of smaller stature was hardly an effective clue.

"He smelled of cigar smoke and cologne," Sofia added, a confused grimace on her face. "I know that sounds strange, but that's all she remembered. It happened very fast."

"He was a gentleman," Theodore said, thinking out loud. "Thank you, Miss Gallo. I'm glad you were here to talk to Lola."

"She is my friend. I don't want anything to happen to her and please call me Sofia," she answered, a slight smile making a reappearance. "At least whenever my brothers are not about."

LOLA STROLLED ALONG THE BOND STREET BAZAAR, the spacious shopping area one of her favorite spots in all of London. It was a good decision to come here. She felt better just by being outside and away from the confines of her neighborhood. It brought back memories from her past. Good memories. Things she'd kept tucked away, reluctant to revive for fear of the pain they'd cause, but she'd been wrong to ignore them.

She paused before a magnificent window display in front of Harding Howell & Company, one of the city's finest department stores. The grand scene in the showcase was one of a lavishly decorated drawing room filled with all the wonderful treasures available within the store. It portrayed a life of uncomplicated luxury from the Ormolu clock on the mantel to the decadent Turkish rug gracing the floor. It immediately reminded her of Theodore and the tasteful interior of his home. Like one of the Vauxhall illusions, it tempted her to believe she could fit into such a life.

The next window was tailored more to the lady shopper. An elegant chaise upholstered in crimson velvet sat at the center of the display. Various feminine fripperies were draped throughout the interior, silky robes, frilly hats, hand-stitched leather gloves and delicate imported French underthings. The latter also reminded her of Theodore. The fire in his eyes right before he kissed her was a thing to behold. What would he look like were he to undress her and find a silky bit of lace beneath her skirt? The idea brought a mischievous smile to her lips and when she saw her reflection in the window a bubble of laughter escaped.

Moving on, she walked closer to the entrance of the extravagant shop, but then stopped, frozen in place by what she saw across the street. Her sister was being handed up into a carriage. Lola gasped. But it couldn't be Anna. Pushing through the cluster of people near the curb, Lola tried to gain a closer look, but it proved a waste of time. The door to the carriage shut and the driver slapped the reins, the equipage fast to move into the flow of traffic and on down the street.

Doubting her eyes, she told herself that while the woman may have looked like Anna, it had to be a mistake. Maybe she'd imagined it, too caught up in reminiscence from the past. Nevertheless, the familiar pain of longing and regret overrode her previous enjoyment. The awful emotions were an ever-present shadow, always at the ready to remind of her choices in the past.

Thirteen

Wanting to expend some of his tension, Theodore rode his horse to White's instead of taking his carriage. After handing off the reins to a stableboy in the mews, he followed the slates leading to the entrance of the club. It was nearly nine o'clock. Time for his game of cards with Huntington and Mowbray.

Time for Lola to walk the rope at Vauxhall.

He'd tried unsuccessfully to find her this afternoon. In a city of over one million people, attempting to locate one petite, fiery-eyed beauty when he had no idea where she'd gone, was an impossible task. Finding Fremont's killer seemed easier. Theodore hoped tonight's appointment would provide useful information. Otherwise, he'd rather be at Vauxhall.

These feelings were telling. He cared deeply for Lola and could no longer push the truth away and dismiss it with excuses of lust. But he had no idea if she felt the same. She was maddening. One minute she was pressed up against him, her lips and tongue driving him crazy with desire, and the next she was insisting he keep his distance.

Although hearing she'd been threatened and still might be in danger cleared his thinking. He would share his feelings this evening.

Regardless of this plan, nothing could transpire until after the card game. And he needed to be focused, attuned to every detail at the club. Fremont's death had uncovered so many unexpected twists and turns thus far, Theodore didn't want to miss a telling clue.

He entered the club, nodding to acquaintances as he strode toward the card room, noticing the familiar scent of cigar smoke and men's cologne water. Was the stranger who'd threatened Lola right here in the club with him? He clenched his fists in frustration. The few facts he had—

dark hair, dark horse, medium build—were hardly useful.

"Huntington. Mowbray." He approached the two men across the room. When he reached them, Huntington stood up for a hearty handshake, but the baron stayed seated, only sparing a nod in greeting.

"I told Mowbray you'd be joining us this evening," Huntington said as they settled around the table. "It's always invigorating to add new blood to the game."

"Thank you for the invitation," Theodore said. He was anxious to get to the core of the issue but he knew he'd have to act the carefree gambler and instill a sense of harmless companionship before Mowbray would start talking. The gentleman looked as surly and reticent as when Theodore had seen him days ago.

"Essex is recently home from America." Huntington picked up the deck of cards and began to deal. "Good you returned in one piece. I hear men over there are savage and uncivilized while women have far too many freedoms. It's an odd combination."

"I think you listen to too much gossip," Theodore answered, pleased his friend had unknowingly initiated a pathway into the conversation Theodore most wanted to have tonight. "Americans are unique. That's true. But I found their confidence and outspokenness to be refreshing. I've never had difficulty accepting differences." Lola came to mind and he stifled a smile before he continued. "It was a good trip and I accomplished several interesting investment ventures, although returning home to the news of Fremont's death was a shock I never anticipated."

Mowbray rearranged his cards and took a long sip of brandy, but he didn't readily add to the conversation.

"Yes. Wretched news," Huntington said as he discarded and drew three new cards. "The two of you were good friends, weren't you?"

"For many years, yes," Theodore continued. "It will be a balm to my grief when more is learned about what happened."

He went quiet, hoping Mowbray would comment or at least concur, but the baron hardly moved. He stared at his cards, only placing them down on the table to push a lock of hair from his forehead and drink more brandy.

"It's a devil of a mystery," Huntington said after revealing his points and marking everyone's score for the round. "Don't you agree, Mowbray?"

Mowbray raised his head, shook another dark lock from his forehead and commented for the first time since they'd begun playing. His expression was unreadable. "English gentlemen, for all their fine breeding and education, can be just as savage as those American men of whom you speak. I wouldn't be surprised if Fremont was tangled up in something complicated and desperate, a conflict that ultimately brought about his demise."

The chilling comment held the table silent for several awkward minutes. Fremont was a likable fellow as evidenced by the huge turnout for his viewing. Complicated and desperate weren't words Theodore would ever associate with his friend. Quite the opposite. Fremont was always after a bit of simple, good-natured fun. Nothing more.

"That sounds rather grim," Huntington said at last.

"I suppose." Mowbray shuffled the deck and began to deal.

"I'd heard someone had Fremont tightly in their grasp. Perhaps the situation went awry and his death was a result."

Theodore eyed Mowbray steadily. What did the baron know? He spoke as if he had factual information instead of repeated rumor.

"I can't imagine why anyone would cause trouble for Fremont. But I suppose if someone was in a bad way and had money troubles, the situation could lead to desperate actions," Theodore replied. "It's my hope that in due time the truth will be told."

Mowbray finished his brandy but didn't say more. Huntington eyed Theodore, his brows raised expectantly. Eventually, the conversation progressed to politics and horses. Not another word was said in regard to the murder.

Two hours later, Mowbray collected his coins and left the club. Theodore and Huntington walked to the mews as they discussed the evening.

"I'd hardly call that successful," Huntington said. "Mowbray's behavior was odd. His remarks hint at knowledge but he didn't clarify anything beyond his own opinion."

"Yes, that was disappointing, although I can't dismiss his words so easily," Theodore said as they reached the mews. "Let me know if he says anything of interest during one of your future games. It could be he wasn't as comfortable with me sitting in or he may have a comment about that very circumstance the next time you play."

"I will." Huntington accepted his gray from the stable hand and gestured toward the back exit. "There he goes now."

Theodore watched Mowbray melt into the night, his black greatcoat flapping against his stallion's ebony hide as he rode away.

LOLA SAID GOOD NIGHT TO SOFIA AND HER BROTHERS before she went upstairs to her room. Her performance this evening went smoothly. She'd walked the rope with perfection, her mind clear and sense of balance in place. The stranger's threat still caused her worry, but she wouldn't allow it to steal her composure. All she could do was continue to be careful whenever she was alone. Her contrary emotions regarding Theodore were already overwhelming.

She changed into a loose blouse and calf-length skirt before she moved to the window and looked out at the night sky. What was Theodore doing right now? She assumed he kept a full social schedule of the Season's ongoing events as most titled gentlemen preferred to do. Right now, he was probably waltzing across a glittering ballroom with a beautiful debutante in his arms. Afterward he'd escort her home in his sophisticated carriage. Would she allow him a kiss when her maid wasn't looking? Foolish woman, who wouldn't want his kiss?

The sound of approaching horse hooves drew her attention from the stars to the street and with it came an involuntary shiver. All Sofia's warnings made Lola suspicious of shadows. But when a lone horseman came into view, her heart sped up for a different reason. An unbidden smile curled her mouth.

Theodore looked incredibly handsome atop his mount. He stopped when he reached her building and glanced up at the second floor, his smile matching hers when he spied her at the window.

She hurried downstairs and unlocked the door, anxious to avoid Sofia's brothers in case they'd noticed Theodore's arrival. He tied off his horse at the side of the house and Lola scowled. If Theodore stayed awhile, it would be a miracle if the animal was still there.

He paused on the pavement before the front stoop.

"I wanted to see that you are well."

His voice was a low rumble that resonated within her.

"Why wouldn't I be?" she asked, taking him in, his handsome profile limned in the glow of moonlight, his eyes holding her captive.

"I was here this morning. Sofia and I spoke about the incident last night. Will you tell me what happened?"

Her smile fell away. Sofia hadn't mentioned talking to Theodore. "Yes, but you should come upstairs. I can't talk to you here like this."

He followed her inside and when they reached her room, she purposedly walked to the other side of the space, wanting distance so she could think clearly.

She watched as he removed his gloves and took in the modest interior. A small table and two wooden chairs. A single bed. A narrow chest of drawers. Her life wasn't at all like the fancy window displays in the shop on Bond Street. He placed his gloves on the table. The act struck her as intimate and domestic.

"Are you all right?" He closed the space between them in a handful of strides.

So much for keeping her distance.

"Yes," she said without pause. "I was frightened and I guess that was the whole purpose of his threat."

"Sofia said this man approached you from behind and held your neck." He collected her hair and moved it over her shoulder, his fingertips inspecting the skin at her nape with the gentlest of touches. "And that he shoved you into the crowd afterward. Were you hurt?"

"No." She breathed deep, not wanting him to sense how the incident still upset her. "He pressed something to my side. A knife, I suppose. But I am fine."

He watched her closely, searching for truth in her eyes, or maybe searching for lies. "Where?"

She huffed again, feeling flustered by his nearness and intense show of concern. "Here."

She lifted the hem of her blouse just far enough to reveal the patch of skin in question. She watched his expression change. A muscle ticked in the side of his jaw and his dark brows drew together.

"It's just a small bruise," she said to mollify him. "And it doesn't matter anyway because there's no way for me to know who did this. I didn't see him."

"Is there anything else you noticed about him?"

"When he spoke into my ear, he seemed similar to my size, so he wasn't very tall." She fluttered her lashes. "Not tall and broad like you."

The compliment might have amused him. His mouth quirked the slightest.

"And he smelled of cigar smoke and some cedar scented cologne water. Nothing at all like yours. Yours is quite inviting," she said the latter sentence softly, hoping to diffuse his tense expression further.

"I'm not so easily distracted, Lola." He cradled her face in his palms. "Until this matter with Fremont's murder is resolved, you need protection."

It would be easy to agree. To go up on her toes and fall under the spell of his kiss. But something stopped her.

"I can take care of myself," she assured him. "I've been on my own for over two years."

He smoothed his thumb over her cheek before he took his hands away. She immediately felt the loss of his touch.

"Why? Did your family force you to leave?"

"No." She almost laughed for knowing the truth of it. "Nothing like that."

"Then why not return to Ipswich? Leave Vauxhall for a few weeks and spend time with your family. I'm sure they would be happy to see you and it will also keep you safe. As much as I'd like to be your protector day and night, we both know that's impossible. I have other responsibilities that prevent me from—"

"You don't have to say it." Her voice came out in a harsh whisper, her emotions all over the place now from the sincerity of his concern and mention of her family.

"Say what?" he asked in an incredulous tone.

"That you shouldn't keep company with me. That you can't be seen in public with me." She straightened her shoulders, preparing herself for his reply.

"Lola, you're wrong," he stated plainly. "That's not what I meant. If Bow Street was doing a better job of finding who attacked Fremont, I wouldn't be so invested. When I spoke to them this afternoon, they hadn't any new information. Even after I explained what had happened to you last night—"

"What?" Her temper flared. "*I* didn't go to Bow Street because *I* didn't want them to know. You had no right to tell them. That was my decision and mine alone." She paced to the other side of the room, frustrated the situation had spun further out of control, but also knowing she was being unreasonable and starting an argument he didn't deserve. She just couldn't stop herself. Arguing seemed safer than losing her heart.

"I've no right?" He took a moment as if carefully considering what he would say next. When he spoke, his voice possessed a solemnness she'd never heard before. "If you are in danger, Lola, I will not stand aside. Someone, probably the man who murdered my friend, returned to Vauxhall and accosted you. Bow Street had to be notified. But even if you'd dismiss your own safety so callously, any evidence that will help the investigation gives me the right to inform them."

"I'm sorry." She couldn't tell him why she was reluctant to speak with the Runners. The threat of discovery frightened her more than the threat to her personal safety. "But that still doesn't mean you'd be comfortable being seen with me. I'm not some sheltered debutante. I know too well how the world works and earls don't take Vauxhall performers anywhere they can be seen together."

"This one will," he said, closing the distance between them for a second time, his voice losing all its previous indignation. "I would be proud to have you on my arm no matter what the occasion, whether it's the Prince Regent's annual jubilee or the firework display at Vauxhall. How could you not realize that?"

"My experience taught me a nobleman's word is not always to be trusted."

"That is true of all people, not just noblemen, and I've only been honest with you," he answered, a dubious gleam in his eyes.

"I know. I just wouldn't want to stain your honor," she insisted, knowing it was her fear of believing him that motivated her argument now. "In your world, reputation is life-blood."

"I don't give a damn about anyone's opinion except the people I care about and I care about you." He crossed the room and clasped her elbow, turning her gently. "Whenever you're ready, I'll take you out for the evening. All you have to do is tell me the date. Does that please you?"

She gave a little nod, not trusting herself to speak. He tipped up her chin. His eyes searched hers and his gaze became heated. Her pulse spiked in response.

She was a fool. Balanced between the past and future, between her choices and freedom, obligation and pleasure.

Pleasure.

She'd already given up so much.

She wanted this one pleasure.

Fourteen

Lola went up on her toes and touched her mouth to his. It was the spark that set the inferno ablaze.

She wanted him.

The knowledge burned through him.

He wanted her more.

Grasping her hips, he brought her against his length, her body enfolded to his. She gasped, a soft startled sound, before she offered her tempting lips to be taken. He immediately obliged. Their kiss was deep and consuming. The heat of her body through her gauzy blouse enticed him to hurry though he didn't want to rush. Everywhere he touched held the promise of pleasure. Her perfectly round breasts, firm bottom, and shapely legs. Her hair, long and silky, as it trailed over the back of his hands. The sensual rub of her tongue seeking his attention in an eager game of chase.

He pulled away, only a fraction, their breathing rough and fast. "You fascinate me, Lola. I've wanted you since the moment I saw you."

"And we have this moment," she said, silencing him from further confession with an openmouthed kiss.

He stepped back, unsure where he led them but unwilling to

break contact. They found their way to the single mattress and toppled down together. She lay beneath him, the bed hardly wide enough to share.

When we make love, it will be in absolute privacy, wrapped in satin and silk, unhurried and magnificent.

They had privacy and little else, though he knew this night would be a night to remember always.

He turned onto his side giving Lola the best of the mattress, her long dark hair strewn across the pillow beneath her head, her eyes closed. She shivered even though the room was warm. He bent and kissed her mouth hungrily, moving to her throat next, feeling the tremor of her gasp against his mouth as he explored the enticing curve of her neck.

Her hip pressed tight against his groin, the flimsy fabric of her skirt barely a barrier to her heat. Her body shifted with impatience and invitation. Need hummed through him. He reached down and smoothed his hand along her leg, tracing the graceful curve of her ankle, firm muscle of her calf, and delicate pulse behind her knee. She shivered as his fingertips lingered at the edge of her skirt.

"Theodore," she said, half whisper, half sigh. "Make it stop."

"Make what stop, Lola?" He traced a lazy, swirling design on her skin.

"Me wanting you," she rasped, her hips shifting on the mattress beneath his touch.

"Does this help?" He moved his hand higher, his palm flat on the creamy flesh of her inner thigh, so hot and smooth, he could feel her every tremble.

"No," she answered, her tone indecisive, as if she wanted what she couldn't have and pleaded with him to solve the problem.

He had every intention of giving her what she wanted.

Her blouse was pulled tight across her chest now, her pert breasts visible through the fabric. Lowering his head, he took one of the sensitive buds in his mouth, sucking gently through the cloth and then licking harder. She whimpered his name and her legs parted, her hip rubbing against his erection in the same wicked rhythm as his tongue on her breast.

He moved his hand higher beneath her skirt, all the way to the opening in her pantalets, the silky fabric damp against his palm. A piercing shot of lust raced through him, making him harder still. The air between them was heated, their bodies pressed tight in the single bed. Her scent, fresh and musky, fired his desire white hot.

He touched her again, his fingertip sliding into her delicate folds where she was incredibly soft and wet. He stroked, teasing at first, but then more insistent, finding the tight nub at her core and causing her to tremble with need.

At last, he delved a finger inside her and she murmured a sound of relief, her body welcoming him. She was hot and ready, her breath coming fast as her hips pressed into the mattress. He lifted his head, wanting to watch her lovely face as he withdrew his finger and entered again, tormenting and teasing, over and over again. She arched toward him, greedy for more, and he slipped another finger inside, her body quivering in need, demanding he please her. Slick with want, her muscles contracted around his fingers. She reached up and grasped his shirt, pulling his mouth to hers as she writhed beneath his touch, finding release, her contented gasp a sensual sound he'd never forget.

LOLA LAY NESTLED AGAINST THEODORE WHILE SHE tried to reclaim herself. There were no words for the sensation she'd just experienced. Nothing seemed adequate. She'd come apart and couldn't be put back together in the same way ever again.

She'd wanted pleasure, but with that came so much more. She tilted her head and looked into his handsome face. He gazed at her with an emotion in his eyes she couldn't label. She understood why. She also felt overwhelmed.

After a moment, he leaned down and kissed her forehead, the

gesture too tender. She breathed deep, shielding herself from the callings of her heart.

"Now I want to touch you," she said, her tone intentionally firm in an attempt to recover control. How dare he make her feel things she didn't want to feel? She would exact her revenge. "All of you."

With a charming smile, he rose from the bed and removed his waistcoat, placing it on the back of one the chairs at the table.

"You look so handsome in your spectacles," she said. "You should wear them."

He obeyed, slipping them on before he walked toward her in his shirt and trousers. She was already standing, setting her clothes to rights.

"Sit here," she said next.

"What?" His expression showed his confusion.

"Sit on the end of the mattress," she explained, mischief in her voice. "It's my turn now."

"And here I thought you'd just had your turn," he murmured, low and teasing.

"Aah, so much like a man, to think that receiving is more pleasurable than giving."

He didn't argue, his expression intense as he sat down.

She heard him inhale and exhale deeply. Was he preparing himself? A devilish grin danced about her lips.

She settled in front of him, kneeling with her legs folded beneath her skirt.

"You're very flexible," he said.

"I am," she agreed as she leaned between his knees and ran her hands up the front of his shirt. "You'd be surprised the positions I can get myself into."

He made a sound in his throat, something between a grunt and a groan.

She brought her mouth closer to his while her fingertip traced his jaw, the bristle of new whiskers pleasing to the touch. Then she carefully untied his cravat, drawing the long white strip of linen from around his neck in one deliberate movement.

"I suppose this has a variety of uses," she said playfully as she abandoned it to the floor.

His shirt gaped open to reveal a vee of hair-dusted skin. She pushed her fingers through his chest hair, enjoying the texture, and then continued her exploration with the contours of his pectoral muscles, lower to the ridges of his abdomen, every muscle tensed and smooth to her touch. Her midriff rubbed against the falls of his trousers and his arousal twitched in reaction to the pressure. He eased back slightly, more relaxed now, and she withdrew a little.

"I like touching you too," she said as her fingers worked the buttons of his trousers, pushing aside the wool and linen. She glanced up at his face. His eyes were heavy-lidded as he watched her, but his jaw held tight.

"Lola," he said, his voice nothing more than a smoky rasp.

"Do you want me to stop?" she asked, struggling to keep her expression passive.

"No," he answered immediately.

He turned his head and his spectacles slid down his nose. She abandoned the buttons on his trousers and reached up to push his spectacles back into place.

"Now, where was I?" she asked innocently as she leaned in for a long kiss. When his spectacles were steamed, she placed them aside. "Oh, yes, now I remember."

She slipped her hand below the fabric of his trousers, setting her palm against the length of his erection. He grunted and his body jerked forward. He reached for her shoulders but she gently returned his hands to his side. This time, she made the rules.

She held his arousal for a moment, his flesh hot and hard within her caress, then she stroked him firmly, up the length of his thick cock and down again, all the while watching his reaction. His eyes were closed now and a lock of hair had fallen forward across his brow. Her heart turned over in her chest and she forced her eyes away, afraid to look too long. She already felt too much.

The room was silent. The air was still, heavy with the scent of their intimacy and the magnitude of their emotions. She dared another glance at his handsome face. His eyes were still closed, but he'd relaxed now and surrendered to the wicked sensations of her attention.

She stroked down the length of his arousal one more time before she leaned in and closed her mouth around the tip. His breathing seized and his entire body went rigid.

"Lola."

The word sounded like a growl and she saw him grip the edge of the bedframe.

She stifled a smile and brushed her tongue against the sensitive ridge, but her wicked revenge ended there. He tangled his hand in her hair and drew her up, his mouth silencing her objection as he kissed her hard.

Reaching between them, she wrapped her fingers around his length and resumed the pain-pleasure, working him as their kiss continued. He was so hard and slick in her hand, she only managed one more stroke before he broke away with a harsh grunt, spending himself against his bare abdomen.

Lola sat back on her heels. The disheveled earl in front of her looked nothing like the haughty nobleman who'd caught her on the close walks all those weeks ago.

She stood up and retrieved a wet cloth and towel for him. While he collected himself and put his clothing to rights, she went into the kitchen, reveling in what had passed between them. It couldn't be anything more than indulgent pleasure. She knew that in her head, but her heart was proving more difficult to convince.

Shaking away that problem for now, she went to the cabinet and took out a bottle of wine. She poured two glasses and they sat on the side of the bed, drinking their claret and exchanging knowing glances in silence.

"I SHOULD LEAVE." THEODORE SET DOWN HIS EMPTY glass and stood. "It's late and I don't want to steal your sleep."

She followed, setting her glass beside his. "You're right. No good can come from walking the rope while tired."

"You don't need any added danger in your act." He reached for her, drawing her into his arms and lacing his fingers with hers. "I visited you this evening to confirm you were safe, but that doesn't mean I won't continue to worry about you. I know you're intelligent and cautious, Lola, but please, until everything connected to Fremont's death is resolved, don't take any unnecessary chances."

"I won't," she said, her words sincere.

"I don't want anything to happen to you," he continued. "Especially since I need to travel for a few days. I dislike the thought of being away from you."

She pulled back so she could look at his face. Her lips were kiss swollen and her hair slightly mussed. She looked well-loved and beautiful.

"You're going away?" Her delicate brows drew together though her eyes were wide in question.

"I have some unfinished business to resolve, but I won't be gone long." He hesitated saying anything further.

He didn't want Lola involved more than she was already or having knowledge that could lead others to question her. He trusted her not to break his confidence, but he'd rather no one knew of his trip to speak to Fremont's valet until after he'd returned. Even Bow Street hadn't thought to pursue Timmons. It was a credit to Margaret's suggestion and his own desire to see Fremont's murder solved, that Theodore was making the trip.

He'd also considered the fact Lola's family lived in Ipswich. Whenever he'd spoken of her parents, Lola's demeanor had changed completely. She'd become angry and defensive. Without a doubt there was more he needed to learn about her past. He hoped she would confide in him when she was ready.

That said, he didn't want to cause an argument and upset her at this time of night when they'd just shared such intimacy. Their time spent together was too special. He knew if they quarreled and he left for Ipswich soon after, he'd be distracted by their disagreement and that would interfere when he finally spoke with Timmons.

He pulled her back into his embrace, breathing her in and settling her cheek against his chest. In truth, he could barely think straight now. His body still simmered from her every delicious touch and he didn't want anything, not Fremont's murder, Lola's past, or circumstances beyond their control, to interfere.

Fifteen

The next morning, Lola followed the oyster shell walkway into Vauxhall Gardens. She wore a smile for no particular reason. Or perhaps she did have one; the secret she shared with Theodore and no one else. *A good secret.* Unlike all the others she kept. This secret made her hopeful. Even knowing they could only have a physical relationship, her body hummed from his kisses last night. His kisses, and so much more.

Looking ahead toward the promenade, she quickly averted her path, veering off behind the pavilion to keep out of sight. The Bow Street Runners had returned and were standing in conversation with Morland near one of the supper boxes. She didn't know if they'd come because Theodore informed them about the incident last night or if the Runners had other questions to ask, but in either situation she didn't wish to be seen.

She hurried toward the Gothic Ruins, an elaborate garden full of towering statuary and sleek columns recreating ancient monuments from England, Italy, and beyond. The archways and follies there provided the perfect place to hide for a while, especially since the surroundings were so pretty. In that way, the Gothic Ruins were the complete opposite of the Pleasure Paths. The mood was airy and light compared to the intended privacy of the close walks. Here, roses in every color filled rotund plaster urns, intermittently spaced between ironwork benches where variegated colored lamps painted with transparent designs hung overhead on ornate hooks.

Shortly after she'd entered, she heard a violin's sentimental serenade. Marco sat perched on the wide marble platform of the Baroque fountain at the center of the tiled square. He lowered his bow when he noticed her approach.

"Are you hiding too?" she asked in lieu of a greeting.

"Not at all." He put down his violin and placed his bow in the leather bag at his feet. "I was practicing a new song. Why are you hiding?"

"Morland is talking to the Runners again," she said, wondering if Sofia had told anyone else about what had happened during the presentation of the Cascade, but Marco looked unbothered.

"I don't know who's worse to have nosing around here. Your nob or those Runners."

"Lord Essex is only trying to find out what happened to his friend," she said and settled on the edge of the fountain beside him, tracing her fingertips across the surface of the water to cause a series of ripples.

"How quickly you rush to his defense," Marco said. "You're taken with him."

"Why would you say that?" she asked, watching him closely.

"I can see it in your eyes, in everything about you," he said, his voice lower.

She shifted uncomfortably, not sure how to respond.

"He's only using you, Lola."

"That's not true," she replied, shaking her head in disagreement.

"It's what nobs do. You know that. They use people like us and then when they become bored, they discard us just as easily. Their only loyalty is to themselves."

"Not this time."

"You trust him more than me?"

"That's not what I'm saying." Lola knew Marco had his own reasons for resenting members of the aristocracy, but she wouldn't allow him to speak poorly of Theodore. "The earl isn't like that."

He laughed, although the sound held no humor. "Since when do you believe otherwise? Look what happened with your father. Years of loyal friendship meant nothing to the duke when it threatened his purse and pride."

She couldn't argue his point because it was true, but she had to say something to convince Marco this situation was unique. "You don't know Lord Essex. He's different. He wouldn't lie to me."

"Would you know it if he did? You live outside his world. You only know what he tells you."

She swallowed her immediate objection, disliking Marco's accusations because, again, he was probably right. She had no way to know what Theodore did when he wasn't with her. It was a matter of trust. But that fact mocked her. She hadn't trusted the earl enough to be honest with him since the start.

"Maybe he has no need to lie," Marco continued even though she'd remained quiet.

"Why would you say that?" She looked at him, her frustration making her tone sharp.

"If you simply give him what he's after—" Marco didn't finish his sentence, the implication clear.

She pushed off the edge of the fountain and stood. She'd heard enough. "How I spend my time is no longer your concern."

"I know. You tell me often enough. But as your friend, it's difficult to stand by and watch you make poor choices."

"Then don't watch," she said, turning her back and walking away.

She knew Marco meant well, even if his words were partially fueled by jealousy, but she still didn't want to argue about it. She'd already decided whatever she shared with Theodore could only be physical because the reasons were immutable.

They came from different worlds with different rules.

She was running from prosecution.

Hell, York wasn't even her real last name.

There was so much she couldn't tell him and yet when they were together, when they kissed, the connection they shared made her believe nothing truer ever existed.

She kept going, taking the longest possible route back to the grandstand, and then she climbed the ladder to her platform, took off her slippers, and walked the rope in an attempt to restore her balance.

THEODORE SAT ACROSS FROM WYNDHAM INSIDE THE carriage. His valet had a portfolio of paperwork spread on the seat beside him, but Theodore was in no mood for discussions regarding investments or household budgets.

It was a peculiar anomaly that one hour spent in someone's company could impact him in such a way he could think of little else. And while he was always plagued by restlessness, last evening after he'd ridden home from Lola's building, he'd prowled around his house like one of the panthers held captive in the Tower of London's menagerie. He hadn't wanted to leave her. And after he had, he'd only wanted to return.

Now, he'd just departed his town house to travel to Ipswich and the desire to see Lola was stronger than ever. He had no sensible way to explain it. He rapped on the carriage roof and his driver opened the trap door.

"One stop before we continue, Jenkins," he said, ignoring Wyndham's inquisitive stare. "Take me to Vauxhall Gardens."

"My lord?" Wyndham asked as soon as the carriage moved on.

"I need to fetch something important before we continue."

One of Lola's kisses. But he wasn't about to share that with his man-of-all-things.

Wyndham returned to the papers strewn across the bench and Theodore watched their progress through the square window. He was behaving the lovesick fool. He didn't care. He answered to no one and had neither demanding father nor doting mother to lecture him on the decorum of the earldom. He could do whatever the bloody hell he wanted.

Hopefully, Lola would be easy to locate. He assumed she would be practicing.

When he arrived, he headed directly for the grandstand, but it wasn't Lola on the platform as he approached. It was Marco. From what he could tell, Marco was securing the ropes where they stretched from one wooden stanchion to the other. That couldn't be his responsibility. Besides, Lola wasn't anywhere to be seen.

"She's not here," Marco called as he descended the ladder and stalked across the grass to where Theodore stood.

"Why are you here?" Theodore asked, wary of the man's actions.

"I work here," Marco said plainly. "I belong here."

The latter was said with obvious contempt.

"Why were you on Lola's platform?" Theodore asked, watching Marco carefully.

"We argued earlier. I wanted to make it right." He gestured to the rope above their heads. "Then I thought to check the knots. To make sure everything is as it should be for her performance tonight."

"Lola always checks the ropes."

"So now you know her better than me?" Marco said. "I told you the other day. Lola doesn't need a keeper. Especially not some titled gentleman who believes he's better than everyone else."

"Lola can make her own decisions," Theodore said, keeping his temper in check. Arguing with Marco would prove a waste of time.

"That's true as long as she's not being lied to," Marco scoffed. "She'll never be able to trust you because eventually she'll realize you're the same as the nob who made her leave her family and Ipswich. You don't care about anybody but yourself. That's why you're here now, right? You want something else."

"Marco!"

Sofia's voice cut across the lawn and both men turned to see her approach.

"Hello, Miss Gallo."

Marco jerked his head around, apparently surprised Theodore knew Sofia by name.

"Lord Essex." Sofia smiled slightly before she spoke to Marco. "*Dio mio!* What are you doing? Lola will be upset."

Marco stared at Theodore for a long moment before he turned to Sofia. "Somebody around here has to start telling the truth." Then he walked away.

"I'm sorry, my lord," Sofia apologized hurriedly. "Marco has too much emotion for his own good. He forgets, sometimes, that Lola is her own woman."

"Then it's good he has you as a friend to remind him," Theodore said, scanning the area for any sign of Lola. "Where is Lola? I wanted to talk to her for a moment."

"I haven't seen her." Sofia shrugged. "I wish I could be more helpful."

Theodore thanked the young acrobat and walked back to his carriage, unsettled for a number of reasons. He didn't like not knowing where Lola was and if she was safe. She'd promised to be careful, but he wasn't sure if her definition of the word was in kind to his own. Then there was the matter of Marco and finding him on the tightrope platform. Was he really checking the ropes? Theodore couldn't be sure. Additionally, Marco's outburst concerning Lola's past was as confusing as it was troubling. He'd made it sound as if a nobleman had forced Lola to leave Ipswich and abandon her family. How could that be true?

His driver wasn't going to like it, but another detour was necessary. Theodore would stop at Bow Street to tell Fredrickson and Johns where to notify him in Ipswich if anything new came to light. At times it seemed as if he was going in circles, but with any luck the trip to speak to Fremont's valet would prove beneficial. Hopefully, Timmons would offer some much-needed clarity.

LOLA WAVED TO THE GATHERED SPECTATORS SEATED IN the grandstand as she prepared to step onto the rope. It was nine o'clock. Time for her performance and then she could go home. All day her emotions had shilly-shallied between contentedness and frustration. Her time spent with Theodore warmed her from the inside out and yet her argument with Marco and his inability to behave reasonably dampened her joy. Deep down, where she buried her greatest fears, she wondered if Marco had the right of it. But now was not the time to weigh doubt against hope.

Instead, she drew a deep breath and cleared her mind. Focused on the end of the rope where it was knotted tightly to the wooden stanchion on the other side of the platform, she placed her right foot and then her left.

A sound of hushed awe rose up from the crowd below. Some spectators perceived the risk and danger, while others doubted her ability to stay balanced. She proved them all wrong every time. At mid-rope she paused and arched her arms in a graceful display of poetic expression, not unlike a ballerina's elegant dance. A rush of applause filled the air around her, carrying her all the way to the end of the rope. Her smile burst through as she once again waved to the crowd.

With the show over, the grandstands cleared quickly, but as Lola gathered her slippers and shawl, she noticed Fredrickson and Johns lingering near the bottom of the ladder. There would be no escaping their questions now. Huffing a breath of annoyance, she moved down the ladder and faced the Runners.

"You wish to speak to me?" she asked, aware it was the obvious assumption.

"Just a few minutes of your time, Miss York," Fredrickson said, his tone even and expression calm. "I've learned there was a threat made to your person the other night."

"During the presentation of the Cascade." She looked from one investigator to the other. "Yes. A man came up behind me."

"And was that the extent of the interaction?" Johns asked, his pencil and pad in hand.

"No," Lola continued. "He held my neck and told me to mind my own business. He had some kind of weapon. He pressed it to my side."

"And why didn't you bring this to our attention?" Fredrickson asked, his stare more serious than moments before.

"I didn't want the person, this stranger, to think he was in further danger of discovery. I feared he would return and hurt me because I'd notified Bow Street."

It wasn't the truth, at least not completely. The thought did cross her mind that the stranger could target her again, but the true motivation for avoiding the Runners had to do with her family's past. She wasn't about to share any of that information.

"We're trying to solve Lord Fremont's murder. Even the smallest detail is important," Johns commented.

"I understand your hesitation," Fredrickson said, although Lola wondered if he was sincere. "Can you give me a description of the man who accosted you?"

"No," Lola said quickly. "I mean, I wish I could. But he approached me from behind and pushed me away after he threatened me. I never saw him. It was too crowded. All I know is that he wasn't very tall because when he spoke in my ear he just leaned forward."

"Thank you," Johns said, making a note on his pad. "In the future, if you see this man or have any other troubling interactions, you must notify us."

"I didn't see him, so I can't recognize him," Lola repeated, her agitation growing. "I never expected Lord Essex to go to you with the information."

"In an investigation, most especially when we're trying to expose someone who took the life of a nobleman, all information should be shared," Johns said.

"It's important we know as much as possible, otherwise the opposite of your intention could result," Fredrickson elaborated. "If Lord Essex hadn't informed us of what had occurred, we wouldn't be aware of the stranger's return to Vauxhall. That fact leads us to other clues we can investigate. Furthermore, it pinpoints you as a target. You should take extra care with your safety. We have it in mind to post a few Runners here in everyday clothing each night."

"Well, then I'll be sure to offer Lord Essex my gratitude for his concern over my wellbeing," she said, trying to extricate herself from the conversation now that it seemed complete.

"That will have to wait until he returns from Ipswich," Johns said with a casual chuckle.

"Ipswich?" she asked, her pulse taking a leap. "What do you mean?"

"The earl advised us he would be away from London for a few days. He wanted us to be informed of his whereabouts in case there was a development in this situation," Fredrickson explained further.

"That's a fine example of what you need to do as well," John added. "If anything else occurs that could be connected to this matter, you should report it to Bow Street straightaway."

Lola nodded woodenly, her ears ringing with panic. Last night, Theodore had mentioned his travel. He'd called it unfinished business and she hadn't given it another thought, her body still tingling from their intimacies. But it couldn't be a coincidence. That seemed impossible now.

Ipswich was a quaint village, with charming coastline views

and about two dozen wool farmers. There were a few larger estates, like the Duke of Leinster's country seat, but the majority of the townspeople were simple and hardworking. She doubted Theodore had a pressing business meeting there. So, was he conducting an investigation of his own? An investigation into her past? Even the smallest question asked to the wrong person could cause her whole world to come crashing down.

She swallowed an onslaught of emotion and watched as the lawmen walked away. Instead of relief, her nerves were strung tight. Her heart ached in her chest. Marco was right. Theodore had lied. Or worse, he'd set out to discover what she'd worked so hard to keep hidden. She busied her trembling fingers with the knot in her shawl and walked toward the pavilion, consumed with worry. She didn't want to run away again, but now it seemed she might not have a choice.

Sixteen

Theodore relaxed against the plush banquette in his carriage and watched as the landscape transformed from city bustle to pastoral countryside. Wyndham was deep into house accounts on the opposite bench and Theodore welcomed the quiet. Hopefully the roads would remain clear.

He hadn't visited Ipswich in over fifteen years, yet he remembered the occasion fondly. He'd attended an autumnal house party with his parents at the Duke of Leinster's country seat. Theodore was only a lad at the time, caught in the awkward age of thirteen when he was too young to pursue the ladies and too old to play tag or other childish games. He recalled walking down to the expansive stables in search of an interesting way to pass the time since he thoroughly enjoyed horses and had heard his father speak of the duke's prized Arabians.

But even though Theodore reached the livery yard that afternoon, he never saw the horses, too distracted by a sprite of a girl who balanced atop the wrought iron fence posts that wrapped around the perimeter of the spacious horse enclosure.

The fencing stood several feet off the ground and the posts were narrow in width. At first glance he thought the girl foolish, certain she'd slip and break her neck while he'd have to suffer the memory of witnessing the tragedy of her fall. Yet the girl balanced easily, her surefooted steps a sight to behold.

Eventually, an older man with gray hair at his temples came out of the stable and chastised her. The man's admonishment sent her running, her dark braids whipping in the wind as she fled. Theodore didn't see her again for the rest of the party. Yet years later, sometimes for no reason he could explain, he thought of that daring girl and wondered what had become of her.

Shaking himself free from the long-ago memory, he glanced at the sun as it slid toward the horizon. The forty-five mile trip to Ipswich was too far to accomplish in one day and he'd rather stop at a comfortable coaching inn before the hour grew later. He wouldn't mind a hot meal and the horses needed rest. Besides, unlike Wyndham who seemed perfectly content to sit inside the stifling carriage interior for countless hours, Theodore needed to stretch his legs and take some fresh air. He rapped on the ceiling and instructed Jenkins to bring them to The Blue Lantern, the finest coaching inn along their route. Then he eased his head back against the banquette, closed his eyes, and summoned an image of Lola.

On Sunday Vauxhall was closed and Lola needed a distraction to keep her from pacing around her room in a one-sided debate concerning Theodore's motives. To this end, she was relieved when Sofia knocked on her door and suggested they visit Gunter's Tea Shop after lunch and indulge in a flavored ice.

Gunter's was located on the east side of Berkley Square in Mayfair and one of the few places a proper lady could go without a chaperone or societal censure. Neither Lola or Sofia was born into the gentry, so that fact didn't signify, but it did ensure the eatery would be crowded and that assuaged Sofia's brothers who were concerned about their safety. As was the popular custom, orders for the sweet confection were taken by the staff and hand-delivered in little glass cups outside in the square where the customers waited. This too assured Sofia's brothers of the unlikelihood anything worrisome would occur.

However, none of these details mattered to Sofia who hid an underlying motive for choosing the location. Sofia had an eye for fashion and dreamed of designing stylish gowns made of imported silk and tatted French lace worn by fashionable, affluent ladies. Gunter's was somewhere she could observe the latest dress silhouettes, admire the current shape of sleeves and necklines, and ogle bits of trim on embellished skirt hems without ever entering a stuffy drawing room or fancy ballroom. Afterward, Sofia would go home and draw what she'd seen in a sketch book kept under her bed. Lola knew that, for Sofia, the afternoon outing was an act of reconnaissance, but Lola merely looked forward to a cup of flavored ice and an escape from her rented room.

"I am undecided between the lavender or maple flavor," Sofia said, her fingertip tapping lightly on her upper lip as if she deliberated an important problem. "Although last time Alessandro had the pineapple mousse and it was absolutely divine."

"I'm tempted by the bergamot," Lola said, knowing she'd chosen it because it reminded her of Theodore's cologne. If only he didn't smell so good. *And make her feel so good.*

They gave their order to the server and settled at a small table in the square where they sat in the waning rays of the afternoon sun. Lola watched Sofia's gaze flit from one lovely lady to another, her sharp mind cataloguing every pelisse, reticule and bonnet.

"Thank you for suggesting we come here. I needed a diversion today," Lola said with a wry twist of her lips.

"It's okay," Sofia said as she brought her attention to their conversation. "I know what it feels like to be frightened."

"I'm not frightened," Lola answered quickly. "At least, not overmuch. I don't think there will be another incident like what happened in front of the Cascade."

"Oh, I'm not talking about that." Sofia laughed softly. "I meant about you and Lord Essex. Emotion can be terrifying."

Lola only listened, unsure how to respond.

"But that's what makes it so precious, no?" Sofia continued. "When you finally find that one person who understands you without words. Someone who knows exactly what you need even when you have no idea. A man who can look at you a certain way and make your chest squeeze so tight, it's like he's reaching in and touching your heart."

A tear slipped down Sofia's cheek and she quickly wiped it away.

"Who was he?" Lola asked, taken aback by Sofia's sorrowful admission.

"It doesn't matter." Sofia sighed deeply. "I'm here in London and I must be happy now. But I wanted to tell you that I know how it feels to have a secret and live everyday wondering if that secret will be revealed. I understand."

"Here we are, ladies."

The server arrived with their ices, but neither Lola or Sofia picked up the spoon to eat.

"Will you ever see him again?" Lola asked, unsettled by the thought Sofia carried such sadness.

"I don't know. I hope so. My heart won't believe otherwise. But he may no longer feel the same. There's no way for me to know," Sofia said with a tremor in her voice.

"Have you written to him?" Lola couldn't help but ask.

"Only once. But that was months ago." Sofia lifted her spoon and toyed with the top of her maple ice. "I told him not to answer me. I can't receive his letters without causing a problem with my brothers. Besides if I did write to him again, I'm afraid of what he might say. That maybe he'd gone on with life after I'd left Italy. Except now, I wish I knew. Then my heart wouldn't ache so much. I think most of my pain is caused by the unknowing. It's all very confusing."

"Sofia." Lola reached across the table and clasped her friend's hand, offering her a warm, comforting squeeze. "I'm so sorry. I had no idea."

"How could you?" Sofia answered, her expression more composed now. "I never told you. Although, I'm certain everyone at Vauxhall has secrets they keep hidden. Many of us are misfits, but we're also talented performers in more ways than one."

"I have an idea," Lola said, allowing a spoonful of sweet citrus to melt on her tongue before she continued. "If you ever write to him again, you should tell him to send his return letter to my address. After I pick up my post, I'll deliver his letter to you when we're alone. You won't have to worry about your brothers finding out."

"You would do that for me?"

"Of course,," Lola said, pleased Sofia's face had brightened.

"Thank you." Sofia nodded. "If I ever decide to write to him again, I'll do that."

A couple walked by their table. A demure young woman in a pale pink day gown held fast to the elbow of her dashing gentleman escort. Lola watched them cross the square and when she turned back to Sofia, her friend had a knowing smile on her face.

"You care about Lord Essex," Sofia said in a hushed whisper. "Very much, I think."

"Yes, I do," Lola answered. "I thought I could control how much I allowed myself to feel. But now, I'm not sure."

"Does he feel the same way about you?"

"I think so," Lola said, a frown turning her lips. "But nothing can come of it, so I'm a fool."

"Don't say that, Lola. You're anything but a fool and besides, love doesn't pay attention to the rules," Sofia insisted with a sigh of frustration.

"But the rest of the world does," Lola replied. "I would never bring disgrace to Lord Essex's doorstep."

She swallowed another spoonful of ice, her thoughts returning to whether or not at this very moment Theodore was in Ipswich asking questions about her. Would it be possible for him to discover her family and the scandal that occurred with the Duke of Leinster? She'd adopted a different last name when she'd arrived in London, but that didn't mean the truth wasn't there right under the surface waiting to be exposed. Theodore was intelligent. It wouldn't be hard for him to put the pieces together if he learned a few curious facts. The way he pursued the cause of Lord Fremont's death was an example of his clever mind and determination.

"Happiness is almost as elusive as love," Sofia said to break the silence. "Don't make any decisions until you're absolutely sure of what you want. Sometimes I wonder if things might have turned out better for me if I'd chosen differently."

Lola looked at Sofia across the table, feeling very much in kind. "Sadly, that's another thing we have in common."

THEODORE ARRIVED IN IPSWICH THE NEXT MORNING with every intention of visiting Timmons straightaway. The second day of travel had gone smoothly and he'd broken his fast at the only lodging house in town where he'd secured a room for himself, as well as his valet and driver. The lodging house was a large two-story building with at least a dozen rooms and a cozy sitting area in addition to the modest dining room where meals were served. The keeper of the establishment, an older man with only a small patch of gray hair left on his head, boasted to Theodore upon his arrival that the lodging house was the oldest building in all of Ipswich. Additionally, he shared how he'd worked most of his sixty years in the lodging business, the inn having been passed down through his family for generations.

Honored to have an earl taking a room, the vociferous innkeeper was eager to assure Theodore the accommodations included the most modern conveniences and that any special requests would be met with the utmost expediency. Because of the innkeeper's lengthy descriptions, Theodore didn't extricate himself from the conversation and travel by horse to Timmons' mother's home until almost eleven o'clock.

The address was easy to locate and when he knocked on the door of the quaint countryside cottage, Theodore was pleased when Timmons answered the door. Having written to the valet beforehand, Timmons knew of the reason behind Theodore's visit and they fell into conversation quite readily.

"It was a pleasure and an honor to serve Lord Fremont," Timmons began once they were seated in ladder-backed chairs near the fireplace. "He embraced life in every way. It saddens me to learn he met such a tragic end and I deeply regret not being able to pay my respects to Lady Margaret more formally. My mother is getting on in years and while her health has taken a turn for the better, I don't feel comfortable leaving her alone for very long."

"I'm certain Lady Margaret understands," Theodore said. "I'm also at a loss for what happened to Fremont and hope by talking to you today I can learn something that will help in finding out what happened."

"Yes, I'm happy to assist any way that I can."

"Did Fremont's mood change during the last few weeks you served him? Do you know of any meetings or confrontations that may have occurred?" Theodore asked.

"Lord Fremont was always the jolly sort. Even when things went wrong, he'd find a way to brighten the mood." Timmons paused and rubbed his chin thoughtfully. "I recall the week before his death, he was distracted and unusually tense. I know that because he snapped at me a few times during morning dressing and he didn't often do that."

"Did he mention anything out of the ordinary or tell you why he was upset?"

"No, but I assumed he was angry over another argument with

Viscount Sidmouth. Lord Fremont didn't see eye to eye with the viscount and with Margaret excited about the wedding and badgering his lordship about plans, Viscount Sidmouth was often caught in the middle of it."

"In what way, Timmons?" Theodore asked, anxious to gain a better understanding. "Lady Margaret implied that her brother was happy with the match."

"I can't speak to that, my lord, but Lady Margaret was anxious to move ahead with wedding plans and Lord Fremont wanted his sister to wait. Viscount Sidmouth appealed to him several times on Lady Margaret's behalf and it always ended in a row."

"Why would that be?" Theodore murmured under his breath.

"I cannot say for sure, but I suspect it was due to a financial issue," Timmons replied, though he sounded uncomfortable with the admission.

"And why do you think that?" Theodore asked, shaking his head at the twists and turns of the conversation.

"Lady Margaret desired a grand event and Viscount Sidmouth expected a sizable dowry," Timmons explained, his face pinching with displeasure. "I'm sorry to say..."

"Out with it, Timmons." Theodore's patience was worn thin.

"Yes. Right." Timmons took a deep breath. "I overhead Lord Fremont meeting with his solicitor in his bedchamber one afternoon. I was in the dressing room polishing his Hessians and I suppose his lordship forgot I was there. Anyway, I tried not to listen, but I was otherwise trapped and once the meeting was underway, I couldn't show myself without both of them knowing I'd already heard part of their conversation."

"It's all right, Timmons," Theodore reassured the valet. "Fremont would never have thought ill of you."

"Yes. Thank you for saying so, my lord." Timmons straightened in his chair. "But what I heard exchanged between the two men is the troubling part, I'm afraid."

Theodore waited, the tip of his boot tapping a fast beat on the wooden floorboards.

"Lord Fremont was selling off his belongings. Personal items and family heirlooms. He referred to a ruby cravat pin and pair of silver candlesticks while talking to his solicitor. Later that day when I checked, the cravat pin was gone from his jewel box and the candlesticks were no longer atop the chiffonier in the hall. I began to walk through the house and take notice of every detail and that's when I realized other items were gone too. A trio of oil paintings from the guest bedroom, a prized collection of rare coins kept on display, and an imported porcelain vase from the mantel in the sitting room. Little by little, items were disappearing."

"I can see why you grew concerned and you were correct in your assumption," Theodore said. "I've learned Fremont was indeed troubled by monetary issues. Thank you for sharing what you'd experienced."

"I wish I knew more and could be of more help."

"You may still be," Theodore continued. "Do you know if Fremont kept a journal? It's my hope that, if he did, he may have written a detailed accounting of what was happening and therefore help Bow Street and myself piece all these scraps of information together."

"Oh yes." Timmons smiled for the first time during their meeting. "Lord Fremont was always one for writing. He kept a leather-bound journal and wrote in it daily. There were times when he'd fall asleep over it and I'd have to wake him gently, the ink pot still in hand."

"That is excellent, Timmons." A jolt of adrenaline shot through Theodore and he stood up, anxious to hear more. "Where did Fremont keep his journal? I've already been through his bedchambers and haven't seen anything like it."

"Oh, that is troubling," Timmons said, his expression falling back into despair. "I'm afraid I don't have the answer to that question."

"Of course, I understand. A journal is a highly personal item."

Theodore paced a few steps before he turned back to Timmons. "Thank you. You've brought a greater understanding to this situation. If by chance you remember anything else, please send me a message."

"I will do that, my lord." Timmons stood and they made their way toward the door.

"I hope your mother continues to improve and you enjoy your retirement here in Ipswich," Theodore said before he departed, the valet's information as troubling as it was helpful.

Theodore rode his horse to the lodging house, anxious to send Margaret a message and travel back to London. He'd neglected his initial intention to ask at the club about Viscount Sidmouth and he wondered now how much Margaret was keeping from him considering every conversation he'd had with her revealed new facts.

Pertinent facts.

Yet she wasn't the only one to blame. He'd become distracted by Lola. Lost in her kisses when he should have been seeking answers to questions. Nevertheless, he couldn't regret the time spent with her or how anxious he was to see her again. Even though he'd left London, she'd stayed with him.

He was still in the middle of this thought when he entered the lodging house and nearly collided with the loquacious innkeeper.

"You mentioned you've lived in Ipswich your whole life, didn't you?" Theodore asked, sparing a minute to pursue another subject altogether.

"Yes. Since I was a lad." The innkeeper nodded proudly. "That's too many years to count."

"I have a friend who grew up here. Her name is Miss York. By chance do you know her family?"

"Miss York," the innkeeper repeated, his entire pate furrowed in thought. "No, I'm afraid I don't recall the name. How curious. I pride myself on being the town historian. It's not often that I don't recognize one of the families who has lived here."

"Never mind. I didn't mean to trouble you." Theodore was too eager to write and send his note to Margaret to be caught in another long conversation with the man. "I'll ask Lola about it the next time we speak."

"Did you say her name is Lola York?" The innkeeper asked, his expression curious. "I don't know anyone with the surname York, but I do know of a beautiful young woman named Lola. Long dark hair and eyes that dare you to blink. Such a shame what occurred. So much sadness. I'm sure her family would be greatly relieved to hear from her again if events turned in that direction."

Theodore waited, but this time the innkeeper fell silent.

"What happened?" He'd expected the man to forge ahead with a long, detailed narrative.

"Are you acquainted with His Grace, the Duke of Leinster?"

"Our paths cross from time to time," Theodore replied, although it was an exaggeration of the truth. He didn't know His Grace directly, but if the innkeeper thought him a friend of the duke's, perhaps the man would get on with the telling.

Instead, the innkeeper looked troubled. "His Grace owns the property on the hill. It's his country seat. A few years ago, a problem occurred there. That's really all I can share."

"That's all? That's nothing," Theodore said, his frustration coming through in his words.

"I cannot speak poorly of a peer. It would compromise my personal integrity. Especially when you and he are acquainted and likely to meet again in the future. You should ask him yourself as you consider him a friend," the innkeeper said before he excused himself and walked away.

Theodore closed his eyes, summoning his last reserve of patience. He strode to his room and wrote *two* messages. One for Margaret and one for Lola. He dispatched them at the front desk of the lodging house and then ordered Wyndham to prepare for their departure. He was tired of mistruths, complications, and secrecy. It was time to demand answers.

Seventeen

Lola was leaving for Vauxhall when a messenger arrived. At first, she was unsure if she wanted to read what the letter contained, having convinced herself Theodore had exhumed every ugly truth buried in her past while he was in Ipswich. But eventually, in an act of preservation so she could walk the rope with peace of mind and know exactly where she stood with him, she opened the note. Relief rushed through her when she found an endearing message instead of harsh accusations written inside.

Lola,

I've missed you and will come by this evening at eleven o'clock. Leave a candle in the window if you will see me. I hope to see the light.

Theodore

His words weren't troubling. The opposite, in fact. But she was too unnerved by his trip to Ipswich to convince herself any good would come of it.

She managed to ignore these insecurities while she performed and later talked to friends, though as soon as she returned home with Sofia and her brothers, Lola went upstairs to bathe and change her clothes. She put the candle in the window early.

When Theodore finally arrived at eleven o'clock, her conflicted emotions had a stronger hold. She tiptoed downstairs and greeted him with a slight smile. Then they moved up to her room in silence.

He followed her inside and pulled her into his arms before they exchanged a word, their kiss all the communication needed for the time being. His mouth slanted over hers again and again, his kisses anxious and yet enduring, and she met each caress equally as if they both wished to reaffirm their desire.

"I thought of you all the way home," he murmured as he nuzzled kisses down her neck. He banded his arm around her waist to tighten his hold, her breasts crushed against his broad chest, warm and secure, making it far too easy to dismiss her concerns and questions. When he broke away, he buried his face in her hair and breathed her in before he moved his lips against her ear, his words nothing more than a rasp. "I couldn't wait to see you."

Her heart tripped over itself, a feeling of being cherished in a way she'd never experienced causing the leap in her pulse. Still, she couldn't ignore what she desperately needed to ask, hoping he'd answer honestly.

"Where were you?" Her cheek was pressed to his chest now and she could hear the steady rhythm of his heart. Each breath brought with it the familiar scent of his cologne.

"I traveled to Ipswich to meet with Fremont's valet in hope he could offer insight in regard to what happened. He's retired now and lives there with his mother."

Spoken in his low tenor, every syllable reverberated through her as she listened to his explanation with an odd combination of relief and happiness.

"Is that all the business you sought?"

He set her back from his embrace gently, though he didn't let go, his eyes taking her in, lingering on her mouth as if he was contemplating another kiss. "Yes. It's the reason I went, although Ipswich is charming. You must have enjoyed growing up in such idyllic surroundings."

Was he playing a game or did he speak sincerely? Uneasiness with her own deceit impaired her judgment.

And her desire to be honest with him and bare her soul.

In more ways than one.

The need to confide in him tempted her. To unburden herself and share the choices she'd made and consequences she'd endured. Yet those same choices would ultimately keep them apart.

"It's a lovely town," she said as she dropped her gaze and touched a fingertip to the buttons of his waistcoat. He must have removed his greatcoat and gloves after tying off his horse.

"Have you no wish to visit again?"

His question was innocent enough, though she took a deep breath before she answered. "No. An unfortunate incident occurred there and I'm in no hurry to return."

He must have sensed her inner conflict and tugged her forward, back into his arms and the maelstrom of emotions his kisses caused inside her. Yet, when he bowed his head to take her mouth he paused, his expression possessive and fierce. "Did someone force their attentions on you?"

The question was asked with such lethal calm, emotion welled in her throat.

Was that what he thought? He looked as if he would hunt down anyone she named and usher them to their death. She swallowed before she answered.

"No. Nothing like that," she said and placed her palm on his jaw, easing away the tightness with a stroke of her thumb. "Kiss me now, Theodore. I don't want to talk anymore."

He did as he was told, kissing her thoroughly, drawing her tongue into the silken warmth of his mouth. All the while he walked them backward until they'd reached her narrow bed. Without losing contact, he leaned down and snatched the coverlet, blanket and pillow before they moved in front of the fire. There he pulled back far enough to spread the thick blanket atop the wool rug creating a comfortable cushion. She toed off her slippers, her bare feet peeping out from the hem of her day gown.

"I want to see all of you." He tugged at the ribbon near her collarbones, the bodice of her dress loosening as he spread the neckline wide, easing it over one shoulder than another until it slithered to the floor to leave her in a silky sheer chemise, pantalets, and nothing else.

"And I want the same," she replied, as she smoothed her hands up his chest, mimicking his actions by untying his cravat and casting it to the floor.

She removed his waistcoat before she slipped her hands under the hem of his shirt, his skin hot and smooth to the touch, his muscles hard and tensed. A swirl of sensual heat pooled in her stomach. Lower, where she grew damp with longing. She collected the fabric as she raised his shirt but then he took control, his arms crossed overhead in an undeniably masculine pose as he pulled his shirt off and abandoned it beside his cravat. She licked her lips, wanting to touch and taste him everywhere, and at the same time remain motionless because he looked magnificent in nothing but trousers.

"It's your turn, Lola," he said, tracing the curve of her neck with exquisite tenderness, leaving a trail of sensation in his wake.

She waited and watched, the flicker of emotion in his eyes something to savor. Another wave of pleasure bloomed inside her, the deliciousness of anticipation almost too much to bear. She slipped her chemise off one shoulder, then the other, allowing the fabric to float down to the floor in a whisper. She stood before him in nothing but pantalets with the dancing flames of the fire behind her and the ends of her hair teasing her lower back. She let him have a good, long look, and then she smiled slowly.

. . .

THEODORE INHALED A STILTED BREATH, THEN ANOTHER. He'd somehow forgotten to breathe. Before him, silhouetted by the flickering glow of firelight, Lola waited. Her body was something to behold, all firm muscle, sleek lines and enticing curves. Her pert breasts were deliciously round, the rosy tips of her areolas pinched tight. He exhaled slowly in an attempt to temper the surge of primal lust battering his rib cage like a wild animal trying to escape its cage.

Forcing his eyes to hers, he caught the gleam of invitation and realized the minx toyed with him. Two could play at that game. He closed the distance between them, threading his fingers through her hair and settling his other hand on her hip, her skin satiny soft. He leaned in as if to kiss her, her lids falling closed, but he moved past her ripe, heart-shaped mouth, and instead smoothed his palm up along her narrow waist until he held her breast. She gasped as he lowered his mouth and took the dusky tip between his lips, drawing on it to stroke wickedly with his tongue.

She squirmed within his grasp, her huff of breath becoming more of a sensual sigh. Then she circled his neck with her arms and speared her fingers into his hair as if to hold him still. He would have none of it.

He splayed his hand across her back, down to cup her firm bottom, before he lowered her to the coverlet, all the while his teeth and tongue teased her breasts. She shivered within his hold and he gazed at her, her skin aglow from the firelight and utterly beautiful. She still wore her pantalets and desire pumped through him again, this time stronger, his erection already hard and anxious.

"Come here," she said and lifted a hand to reach for him.

He eluded her grasp as he sank to his knees. He wanted to savor her and would not hurry. Circling her ankles with his fingers, he ran his palms up her calves, all smooth skin and shapely muscle, across the sensitive curve at the back of her knees, and higher until he reached her pantalets, sliding them off before he eased her legs apart. Her eyes fell closed as she waited for his touch. He settled on the rug, his exhale on her inner thighs causing her lids to flutter open again.

"I want you to touch me," she said, a note of aching want in her voice.

"I will," he murmured. "Be patient."

She wriggled on the coverlet, apparently unsettled by his reply, and he watched her muscles contract, her battle with desire as strained as his.

He traced the creases of her thighs with a featherlight touch, then the indentation of her navel, his mouth a breath away from her sex, the musky sweet scent of her longing causing his pulse to pound hard and fast, each of his exhales making her shiver. A lovely prickling of sensation dotted her skin.

"Theodore," she said on a breathy plea.

"Yes, Lola."

"I want you to touch me now."

"I am touching you," he teased wickedly as he drew a delicate line across her inner thigh with his fingertip. "Don't you feel it?"

"Yes." She shifted, raising her bottom slightly and resettling on the soft coverlet. "Yes, I feel it everywhere."

He shifted too. Moving forward, he wrapped his arm across her flat stomach, anchoring her, while his other hand played along her hip.

"Be still," he commanded right before he licked into her sex, finding her slick and hot and ready for him. She moaned with pleasure, her hips rising up to press against his arm. She tasted as delicious as he'd imagined, her soft warm skin drenched with want as he delved deeper, each sweep between her folds causing her to tremble with sensation. He flicked his tongue over the sweet little bud at her core, holding her tight as she endured his exquisite torment, her breathing ragged now.

He lay on his stomach, surrounded by her incredible softness, and yet his own body was rigid. His cock throbbed and demanded release. One more taste and she cried out, her hands clenching the coverlet, her fingers wrapped as tight as her climax. He pulled back to watch, her beauty and strength combined, his own breathing as fast and harsh as hers. He nuzzled her thigh, and she shifted away from him with a weak objection. He kissed her there, pressing his lips to her warmth as he smiled against her skin.

LOLA TRIED TO FOCUS. SHE CLOSED HER EYES. OPENED them again. Nothing was effective. Her heart pounded, her body simmered with sensitivity, and when she reached for Theodore, her fingers only reached his hair so she took hold and tugged. He moved above her, his wool trousers brushing across the top of her legs in yet another onslaught of sensation.

"You're still wearing your clothes," she said more as an observation than a complaint, her voice a little husky.

"That's true," he agreed, dipping down to kiss her, taking his time.

Perhaps he needed a minute for his own pulse to resume a normal beat, but she couldn't allow that to happen. Not after the extraordinary pleasure he'd given her. She wanted him to feel equally as satisfied.

She wriggled from beneath his weight and he moved to lay on his back, the smooth skin of his shoulders turning golden from the flames. She found the buttons of his falls, making quick work of releasing them. His abdomen's muscles flexed as her knuckles skimmed his flesh. Then she passed her hands over him, learning the shape and contours of his body, the hard muscles and deep ridges of his chest, until at last she traced the dark line of hair downward, below the waistband of his trousers. He inhaled sharply when she pushed the fabric aside and took his thick erection in hand.

She closed her fingers around him, his satiny smooth arousal hot and hard against her palm. He inhaled sharply as she passed her fingers down his length, stroking him slowly at first, but then with more intention. His eyes were closed and he'd thrown one arm over his head. The flames cast shadows against his profile, his muscles outlined in burnished gold. How glorious he looked in the firelight.

She glanced down his length, his body taut with pleasure and anticipation.

"Don't stop," he hissed, drawing her attention back to his face.

She curled closer to his side, the tips of her breasts teasing his chest, her hand still stroking him as she leaned in and kissed him with more emotion than she'd ever confessed, until her heart threatened to betray her completely. Breaking away, she whispered kisses along his jaw, closing her eyes in kind to his so she wouldn't say something she shouldn't.

"Lola," he uttered, just that one word, before he placed his hand over hers and found his release.

LATER AFTER THEY'D PUT THEMSELVES TO RIGHTS, THEY remained near the waning fire, the hour well past midnight. Theodore supported his weight on his elbow, his body aligned with hers, a shelter from the chilly room even though she'd wrapped herself in the blanket.

"You are beautiful in all ways," he said, skimming his hand over her shoulder, down her arm and across her flat stomach hidden beneath the covers.

His kind words made her chest tighten because they weren't true. She'd avoided the truth. Concealed her past. If he knew all her troubles, he would leave her. It would be for the best, though the idea of that happening pierced her heart like an arrow.

"Have you been careful?" he asked while she worked her way through the maze of her tangled thoughts.

"You were only gone a handful of days," she answered and nestled closer to his chest.

"That doesn't matter." He tucked her closer still. "I don't want anything to happen to you."

She reached up and touched his lips, moving her hand to cradle his cheek. Their eyes matched.

"You care about me," she whispered so softly he almost didn't hear her.

"Of course, I care." He turned his mouth into her palm and placed a kiss there. "I care more than you know. More than even I'd realized."

Only the fire hissed and crackled for a long moment, their shared emotion palpable.

"Theodore," she turned on her side so she could look at him directly. "There's something I should tell you, something important you need to know."

"No." He inhaled deeply, his jaw held tight. "Not now. Not tonight. This time, I'm the one who doesn't want to talk anymore."

She stared into his eyes, seeing so much more than affection, and nodded her agreement. Leaning in to meet his kiss, they both fell back into bliss.

Eighteen

The next morning Theodore planned to visit Margaret, but first he summoned his man-of-all-things. He needed Wyndham to look into the matter of Viscount Sidmouth's history. Wyndham was excellent at ferreting out information better society would rather keep hidden, and he did this purely by his association with the servants who worked within the Upper Ten's households.

Theodore still intended to ask specific questions at White's concerning the viscount, but that would have to wait. Finding Fremont's journal was the persistent thought occupying his mind.

Well, that, and the lingering pleasures of his late-night visit with Lola. The sun looked brighter in the sky just by having spent time with her last evening. Now, as he walked to his carriage, he couldn't keep his smile contained. He'd wanted to tell her so many things and she seemed to want to do the same. Except he'd seen a flicker of sadness in her eyes and he silenced her with a kiss instead. Perhaps it was better they didn't share words with the same freedom as their affections.

Even if he'd developed feelings for her.

Because he'd developed feelings for her.

Nevertheless, he wasn't one to take personal relationships lightly and he suspected she was the same. Which was why he hadn't wanted to hear whatever she'd wanted to say last night.

Conflicted by logic and emotion, he pushed aside these muddled thoughts for later consideration and approached his carriage, directing his driver to take him to Fremont House. He arrived shortly after and was pleased when Margaret met him in the drawing room as it was earlier than usual calling hours.

"How are you holding up?" He asked as soon as he entered.

The constant flow of visitors and prolonged confinement due to mourning would be exhausting for anyone, but more pointedly someone like Margaret who thrived on social activity and conversation.

"As well as can be expected, I suppose." She wrinkled her nose as she sat in the nearest armchair. "I've reduced visiting to one hour in the afternoon as the flow of people paying their respects has dwindled. The burial is planned for next week." She knitted her fingers together in her lap. "Now that the shock of all this has subsided, I've come to realize how much I will miss my brother."

"I understand," Theodore said from where he stood near the window. And he did, having lost both his parents at a young age. "It will get easier. Time passes whether we like it or not."

"That's true, although I don't know what I would have done if you hadn't returned from America when you did. You've helped me a great deal," she said, smoothing her skirt in an act of habit. "At least, I have my wedding to look forward to next year."

"Yes," Theodore said, thankful for the seamless entry into the conversation he most wanted to share. "I haven't had the pleasure of getting to know Viscount Sidmouth as of yet, but I hope we can remedy that soon. Did he and your brother spend much time together? Did you all get on well?"

"Those are peculiar questions, don't you think?" she asked, popping up from her chair and pacing to the hearth. "I told you once before my brother approved of the match."

"Yes, you did." Theodore strode closer, hoping Margaret would trust him enough to be completely honest. "But when I spoke to Timmons, he mentioned your brother and betrothed had had repeated arguments. I was surprised to learn this since you never said anything to that effect."

"Why would that matter?" Margaret drew her shoulders back, uncomfortable to be caught in a difficult conversation. "Stephen worried too much over money issues. I asked Colin to speak to him about our wedding plans and my dowry. They quarreled. That's all there was to it. I never mentioned it to you because it has nothing to do with what happened to my brother."

"I'm struggling to understand why you concealed this when any information could be helpful in locating Stephen's killer," Theodore replied.

"Are you suggesting Colin was connected to Stephen's death?" Margaret asked, her tone indignant.

"Of course not," Theodore scoffed. "But gaining a better understanding of your brother's experiences will help us learn what he was thinking. It could lead to discovering what happened. I'm surprised I'd have to explain this to you, Margaret."

She didn't speak for a moment and Theodore wondered if she would ask him to leave.

"I didn't want you to think poorly of Colin," Margaret said with a reluctant frown. "Now that Stephen is gone and you've returned, it will be the three of us spending time together often. At least that is my hope, that we will be each other's family. I couldn't allow you to form a low opinion of my soon-to-be husband."

"You still should have told me," Theodore said, struggling to keep a hold on his patience.

"So, they disagreed about the wedding plans. I don't see why it bears mentioning. It casts Colin in a poor light when he was only acting on my behalf," Margaret persisted.

Theodore wouldn't point out how selfishly she'd behaved.

Again. But he could give her what she so desperately wanted. Time spent in each other's company.

"I'd like to meet Viscount Sidmouth and get to know him better. Why don't we arrange a quiet get together here at Fremont House? I know socializing is forbidden while you're in mourning but we could consider this more of a family meeting."

"Yes." Margaret immediately brightened. "I'd like that very much."

"Excellent," Theodore said. "I would enjoy it as well."

They'd seemed to have reached a truce of sorts, although he still had other questions for Margaret and so he continued to smooth over the rough edges.

"Stephen would have wanted you to have the wedding of your dreams, but being concerned about the finances, it might have caused him to react out of character when speaking with Lord Sidmouth."

"Perhaps that's true, although I still wonder what Stephen was doing at Vauxhall. If he was sincerely worried over our financial security, why would he waste money in a pleasure garden? The people there are beneath us." Her tone echoed every ounce of disapproval in her words.

"I wouldn't be so quick to judge the guests who frequent Vauxhall. All levels of the aristocracy have enjoyed the entertainment offered there, including many of your acquaintances, no doubt. I understand the Prince Regent has visited on more than one occasion."

"Oh, I wasn't commenting on our friends." She crimped a smile, her expression merely tolerant. "I was referring to the performers. Considering their choice of employment and lifestyle, it is obvious they lack morals and personal integrity." She reclaimed her seat, completely comfortable airing her haughty prejudice.

"I would think after meeting Miss York the other afternoon, you'd formed a better opinion." He measured his words carefully, not wishing to engage in a conversation of this nature and at the same time unable to allow Margaret's comment to stand.

"I suspected you would reply in that way," she said, with a flit of her eyes upward. "If you're going to cause a scandal, I do hope you'll keep it confined to Vauxhall. You're an earl, Theodore. Better society would enjoy nothing more than to besmirch you."

"And doesn't that last sentence speak volumes," he snapped.

"Oh, don't become irritable. I'm stating the facts. If you take up with *Miss York* you'll damage your reputation and shame your heritage. There's nothing for it."

"I find your concern for my reputation a tad hypocritical considering what you've shared concerning your relationships with Lord Mowbray and Viscount Sidmouth," Theodore said starkly, the remark made in retaliation, albeit true.

"Theodore!" Margaret's brows drew together, her expression a mixture of shock and disapproval. "I can't believe you just said that."

"It needed to be said. Your comments were petty and you're behaving in a manner beneath you. I advise you to keep your opinion regarding Miss York and her fellow performers at Vauxhall to yourself going forward." He curled his fingers into fists at his sides and then reopened them, determined to continue in a calmer tone. "Now more importantly, if your brother was at Vauxhall, he must have had a reason, something that superseded anything else that evening."

"I don't know what you mean," Margaret replied sourly.

"He had plans with you that same night and yet he ignored them."

"The reason why still remains unanswered." She paused, her voice losing its bluster. "The longer this goes on, the more I feel I hardly knew my brother at all."

"It's my hope we can locate his journal and then many of these questions, if not all of them, will be answered."

"His journal? I'd forgotten you were inquiring with Timmons about that." Margaret perked up. "What did he say?"

"He didn't know the location of the book, unfortunately, but Timmons did confirm Stephen wrote in a journal often. I know we searched through his belongings and his bedchambers, but we must have overlooked it. Timmons didn't know where Stephen kept the book, but he did share that it has a brown leather cover with a black binding cord securing a lock."

"I don't recall seeing anything like that." Margaret frowned. "Although I wasn't often in Stephen's rooms."

"Right," Theodore said, pushing on. "Timmons also mentioned items from the house being sold. Paintings and other valuables disappearing on a steady basis."

"I asked Stephen about that once and he mentioned wanting to rid the house of its old décor, so whenever I noticed a crystal vase or some other antique had disappeared, I assumed Stephen wanted them gone and he would purchase new collectibles when he was ready." Margaret's expression grew pinched with worry. "In day-to-day life, these situations all sound mundane, but now, in light of what happened, I feel foolish for not realizing something was terribly wrong."

"No good will come of blaming yourself," Theodore said, hoping to ease her distress. He walked over to where she stood by the window. "Would you mind if I went up to Stephen's bedchambers to search for the journal again? I'd also like to have a look in his study if its not in his rooms."

"Yes, that's fine." Margaret sighed. "I'm sorry, Theodore, about my comments earlier, in regard to the Vauxhall performers. I didn't mean to upset you. My emotions are all over the place."

"I understand and appreciate your apology," he said, not wanting for there to be anger between them. "But that doesn't change what I said or how you should regard Miss York in the future."

Content to have the last word on the subject, he left the room and went upstairs to begin his search.

"TELL ME EVERYTHING," SOFIA DEMANDED WITH A SLY smile. "And don't leave out a single detail."

Lola smiled in return, their table located in a shady corner of the square in front of Gunter's Tea Shop. They'd returned for the second time this week, this visit coming at Lola's suggestion. Her skin still hummed from the feel of Theodore's body next to hers, the thrill of his kisses and the precious intimacy they'd shared. Maybe an ice would cool her from the inside out.

"I didn't know what to expect by his visit actually. I worried he might be disappointed with me after traveling to Ipswich," Lola said as she spooned up a mouthful of lavender ice.

"Why would he be disappointed?" Sofia asked, her attention on the cup of saffron mousse in front of her. "Ipswich was where you grew up. What else is there to find out?"

"Ipswich is also the place I fled to come to London." Lola placed her spoon atop her napkin, prepared to supply all the details Sofia requested, even if they pertained to a completely different subject. She trusted her friend without question. "Two years ago, my father was wrongly accused of a crime. No one believed his claim of innocence and his words went unheard by the magistrate who automatically accepted the nob's insistence my father stole from him." Lola paused, sighing heavily as she closed her eyes tight and opened them again. It would be a relief to talk about the secret she carried around inside, but that didn't make it less difficult. "I couldn't allow my father to go to prison. It would have destroyed him and broken my mother and sister. It was horrible enough to be displaced from our home and realize a decade long friendship meant very little when it involved a matter of money. I couldn't stand by and watch my father be punished for something he didn't do. He had no choice in the matter, but I did, and I made a decision that changed everything."

Sofia looked at her with wide eyes, her dessert forgotten. "*Dio mio*. What did you do?"

"I confessed to the crime," Lola said matter-of-factly. "I knew enough about the situation to create a credible story. My father was released from custody and I was to be taken before the magistrate the following day, but that night I fled Ipswich. It didn't fix the problem completely, but at least my family stayed together."

"But they're not," Sofia protested. "You're here in London, apart from them. Don't you miss them?"

"Yes, very much." Lola picked up her spoon and stabbed her ice with more force than necessary. "But there was no other way for me to help."

"That's as terrible as it is amazing," Sofia replied.

"Why do you say that?" Lola asked, unsure how anything about her story seemed amazing.

"You're far braver than me," Sofia said with awe in her voice. "I mean, I knew that already from watching you walk the rope, but to sacrifice yourself to save your father..." Sofia's eyes widened again. "That's truly amazing."

"I don't think of it that way."

"You left everything behind? And you haven't seen your family since?" Sofia prodded; her tone incredulous.

"That's right. Although the other day, when I was window shopping along Bond Street, I had this moment where I thought I saw my sister," Lola replied, her own voice taking on a note of wonder.

"Could it have been her?"

"I suppose. She's old enough now to be courted, but I hardly think she'd be in a position to enter polite society. Not with my family being displaced and carrying the shame of my confession of a crime. I just hope in time a different scandal makes all of this seem like old history and my sister will have the chance to find a respectable husband." Lola exhaled heavily.

"What about *your* future?" Sofia said, taking up her spoon again.

"You mean I can't just go on walking the rope forever?" Lola teased. "You said I'm talented. Just imagine how good I'll be twenty years from now."

"Lola," Sofia said, disbelief in her tone.

"I know." Lola tried to laugh, the effort not completely successful. "I suppose that's part of the sacrifice I accepted when I stepped forward and took responsibility for my decisions. I knew I had to do something and balancing embarrassment for their child against imprisonment for my father made the choice obvious to me."

"Please know I'll never repeat a word of this." Sofia laid her open palm on her heart. "Your secret is safe with me."

"Thank you," Lola said, swallowing a well of emotion. "Marco knows, but sometimes I wish I'd never told him."

"Don't worry about him. He's too hotheaded for his own good, but deep down I know he cares about you," Sofia said, shaking her head sympathetically.

"Exactly, that might be the bigger problem." Lola nibbled at her lower lip before she picked up her spoon and went back to her ice. "Honestly, I like the bergamot better."

"Of course, you do and from what you told me earlier, I know why," Sofia said with a wink. "When will you see Lord Essex again?"

"I don't know, but I hope its sooner rather than later." She paused, regretting her choice of words.

Hope.

Hope was such an unreliable emotion.

"You know, whenever you're expecting a late-night visit if you need my help, you only have to ask. I can effectively keep my brothers busy so they don't notice the earl's arrival," Sofia said, licking the last of her dessert from the spoon.

"Thank you," Lola answered. "You're a wonderful friend."

"I'm happy to help you." Sofia grinned. "And some day, when I send my letter, I know you'll return the favor."

Lola reached across the table and laced her fingers with Sofia's. "You can be certain I will."

Nineteen

T heodore entered White's in need of a brandy. His search of Fremont's bedchambers and study had yielded nothing except more questions. A journal was a personal item usually kept in one's private rooms and yet there was no locked leather book with black cording found anywhere in Fremont House.

He considered stopping at Bow Street and inquiring with the Runners in regard to their progress in the investigation, but at the last minute he'd decided to come to the club instead. Maybe he could garner some snippet of speculation or piece of information that would prove useful. The message on the note he'd found in the back of Fremont's household ledger haunted him still.

Sum to be paid on the last Friday of every month and delivered on the eastmost path of the Pleasure Garden within Vauxhall.

Without more detail, the words were too vague to prove Fremont was a victim of extortion, although it seemed the sensible assumption. However, it was difficult to decipher if the scrawled sentence was written in Stephen's hand or someone else's and that complicated the matter. Was he the recipient of this demand or had he made a note to himself? And how did he end up fatally stabbed if he'd adhered to the delivery instructions?

Too many questions badgered him and he rubbed his temple, wishing he was kissing Lola instead of standing in the entry hall of his club. He wondered for the umpteenth time what she was doing, wanting to learn everything about her; how she spent her time when she wasn't practicing or performing, her interests and experiences, what fragrance she preferred and flavor of trifle was her favorite. He could no longer deny his feelings, and he'd developed more than a few of them.

He'd barely completed this thought when he spied Huntington across the room. Theodore hadn't heard from his friend since they'd played cards with Baron Mowbray and therefore assumed there was no news to share, but circumstances changed rather quickly of late. With a wag of his chin, he indicated they should meet at a private corner of the room.

"Good to see you, Huntington." Theodore greeted him with a handshake.

"Likewise," Huntington said. "Have you any news on Fremont's death?"

"There are few clues to follow, unfortunately." He scowled as he shared the words aloud. "It's all bloody frustrating."

"And Bow Street?" Huntington asked. "Have they uncovered anything useful?"

"Nothing of which I've been informed." He signaled to a footman for a brandy. "How goes things with you?"

"The usual," Huntington said, though he donned a sly grin. "Although I may not be spending as many evenings within these walls in the upcoming weeks. I've met someone who has me accepting invitations to dinner parties and luncheons just for the chance to spend time in her company."

Theodore's brows went up in question. Much like himself, Huntington rarely expressed interest in society's schedule other than an occasional obligatory event but then again, Theodore had been away for two years. While his friend was once a sworn bachelor and regular at White's making use of the brandy and gambling as his primary vocation, it didn't mean Huntington hadn't changed his outlook toward the future.

The idea gave Theodore pause. He wasn't looking for any kind of personal relationship when he'd returned to England and yet here he was at his club wishing he was with Lola instead.

"Who is she?" he asked Huntington, tucking away thoughts of Lola for his late-night fantasies.

"I'd rather not say until I'm sure my story will have a happy ending." Huntington's grin grew wider. "Besides, it's good sport to keep you in suspense."

Theodore chuckled, accustomed to his friend's clever sense of humor. "What about Mowbray? If there's news to share about the baron, I'd prefer you told me now."

"Actually," Huntington looked over his left and right shoulder respectively before he continued, "the Baron has had a significant change in luck."

"Is that so?" Theodore replied. "The evening we spent playing cards, he hadn't had a very good run. Mowbray already appeared on a downward slide and I credited his disagreeable temperament to that cause. Nevertheless, if he continued to gamble so recklessly, I wouldn't be surprised to hear he's brought about his own ruin."

"He's become an all-around miserable fellow." Huntington nodded knowingly. "He hasn't visited the cardroom in several days and I've heard he challenged some poor chap to fisticuffs over an accusation of cheating."

"Nothing good can come of that."

"Indeed. He deserves whatever he gets." Huntington's expression grew devilish. "He's too foolish to stop gambling when he's got pockets to let."

"Purse-pinched?"

"Worse, entirely out of gingerbread," Huntington said as they both accepted a glass of brandy from the footman's tray. "Damned low water and on the rocks."

"Completely cleaned out," Theodore added to their battle of words. "Not a sixpence to scratch with or feather to fly."

"Rolled-up and run off his legs," Huntington went on, enjoying their parry of jests. "In other words, his windmill has dwindled to a nutshell."

"You win," Theodore said in reference to their banter. He sipped his brandy before he continued in a more serious tone. "It does make me wonder what Mowbray was thinking, squandering his money in such a manner. It's like he couldn't control himself from causing his own financial ruin."

It was a good thing Margaret had ended that relationship, especially now, considering Mowbray's decline.

"I can't speak to his thinking. We only played cards and didn't socialize beyond the club." Huntington fell silent, although he pepped up a beat later. "If I'm successful in wooing the lovely lady in my sights, why don't you find someone who will tolerate you for a few hours and we'll make it a grand afternoon together?"

"Interesting choice of words," Theodore said with a smirk.

"No, I'm serious. We can plan an outing. A picnic or drive in the country," Huntington elaborated.

"This may surprise you, but I already know who I would ask to accompany me," Theodore shared.

"Is that so?" Huntington looked impressed. "By all means, tell me more about this mystery lady. You've certainly worked quickly considering you've just returned home."

"Our association was unexpected," Theodore began, a sense of satisfaction and pleasure settling inside him. "And she's remarkable."

The description he'd just given Huntington was inadequate in myriad ways. Lola was far more than remarkable. Anyone who met her would easily notice her beauty, intelligence and graceful nature, but she was also generous, caring and to his delight, seductive. If he paused to deliberate further, his list would become endless. She exceeded all the necessary qualities demanded of elegant ladies of ton who did little more than flit around a ballroom without a thought in their head or hold tea parties to disguise their gossip.

He was all at once struck with the image of Lola amid a candlelit ballroom, an exquisite off the shoulder gown tracing her delicate curves, her long silky hair done up in an elaborate style, while her eyes twinkled and her luscious mouth tempted him to defy etiquette and kiss her right there in front of everyone. He'd be proud to have her on his arm and anyone who had something unkind to say about it could go straight to the devil.

Suddenly, he wanted nothing more than to see her. He glanced at the longcase clock in the opposite corner, annoyed to note the time was only half eight.

"Well, well, well," Huntington drawled after a long sip of brandy. "If I haven't just seen the show."

"That being?" Theodore asked, even though his smile hadn't disappeared.

"Your face, your eyes..." Huntington gestured in a circle with his hand. "For a moment there, Essex, you appeared the star-crossed lover."

"Star-crossed? Not at all." He chuckled while he objected. "That particular story has a terrible ending. My version is quite the opposite." He finished his drink and set the glass on the bookshelf near his shoulder. He couldn't show up at Vauxhall again and stand below the tightrope gawking at Lola.

But he certainly wanted to.

Maybe a brisk walk would help burn off his never-ending restlessness. He struggled to wipe the smile from his face.

"I'm off." He chanced a look at Huntington who continued to stare at him in amusement. "Stay in touch, especially if you manage to speak to the elusive lady you've mentioned. We can plan our outing if somehow *you* meet with success."

Having had the last laugh, he made for the door, anxious to take in the night air.

LOLA MANEUVERED THROUGH THE LIVELY CROWD, fighting the flow of visitors who were headed in the opposite direction. She still had time before her performance and wanted to visit the kitchens and get something to eat. She hadn't taken the time earlier and now her stomach complained noisily. She noticed Marco near the columns along the Picture Room promenade. He played his fiddle to the delight of a small circle of people who gaily clapped along. Sofia probably had the right of it. While at times Marco overreacted, Lola wanted to believe he had her best interests at heart.

Continuing on toward the supper boxes, she skirted a group of young men who'd already over-imbibed. The liquor had loosened their tongues and she ignored their lewd comments and bids for attention as she passed, scurrying to a more indirect path to the kitchens in hopes she wouldn't meet with further nonsense. Clearly, she'd underestimated the number of guests packed into this part of the grounds. The only way she'd have enough time to eat and return to the grandstand for her performance would be if she truly hurried, but making her way proved just as difficult on this path as the other.

Dedicated to the most exclusive supper boxes, this clearing had a direct view of the pavilion and was situated in an ideal location near the orchestra pit. All around her wealth and extravagance glittered in the form of the well-heeled elite in their valuable jewelry and dashing attire. In a moment of self-consciousness, she glanced down at her gauzy skirt and plain muslin shawl. Did Theodore compare her appearance to the refined ladies of the ton?

A sudden, sinking pressure consumed her chest. She didn't belong in Theodore's world anymore than he belonged in her life now. He'd offered to take her out, prove to her that it wouldn't matter, but she doubted it would be so easy. There was a time when she might have blended seamlessly into High Society, but now everything had changed. She'd already sacrificed so much, the realization she should end things with Theodore before she developed stronger feelings for him seemed the smartest path forward, even if her heart squeezed tight at the thought of never seeing him again.

A portly man with two tankards of ale clasped in his hand bumped into her shoulder causing her to startle. Pushing past the man, she skimmed the supper boxes in an effort to reach the kitchens without further delay, but a familiar outburst of male laughter struck her so suddenly it was as if someone had pulled her close and slapped her cheek. The blood in her veins turned cold.

Across the lawn in one of the more elaborate boxes, the Duke of Leinster stood with his drink in hand. He didn't face her, though she could see his profile clearly. While it wasn't farfetched to see a nobleman in one of the luxurious supper boxes, his appearance was so unexpected after she'd only just reflected on her past, she couldn't stop staring in his direction.

"Lola!"

She jerked her head to the right, relieved to see Marco force his way through the crowd.

"Lola, what's wrong?" He came up beside her. "You look like you've seen a ghost."

"Walk with me." She grasped his arm, both pushing and pulling him away from the supper boxes.

"What is it?" He followed her into the kitchens, concern etched across his face.

"I saw someone from Ipswich. It was the duke." She stopped inside an alcove that served as a pass-through for workers and closed her eyes in an attempt to catch her breath. She needed to clear her mind and settle her nerves. "I don't know why it upset me so much. I guess it was a shock, especially with everything that has happened lately."

"Did he see you?" Marco asked, leaning against the wall, his brows lowered in question.

"No." She took another deep breath, feeling more like herself.

"Then you have nothing to worry about."

"But I do," she said, sadness filling her words. "What if these are all signs my time here is ending. That my luck's run out and soon, I'll have to run too."

"You don't believe that, do you?" Marco took her hand in his and squeezed it, wrapping his other hand on top. "You're just rattled from seeing the duke here at Vauxhall, where you feel safe because that part of your life is over. It ended badly, but you're never going back to that world. You have no use for dishonest prigs and their nasty condescension, and there's nothing there for you anymore. I want you to forget about the duke and all the problems he caused. Everything will be okay."

She listened to Marco, reminding herself his words were meant to console and, at the same time, trying to convince herself his advice didn't conceal an underlying motive. When Marco spoke of nobs he included Theodore in his statement and yet that was the one choice she wasn't ready to make.

Or was she?

Twenty

L ola wasn't surprised to see Theodore's carriage waiting near the corner when she approached the boarding house later that evening. She stared at his elegant equipage, unsure if she should feel excitement or disappointment. They couldn't continue their relationship. Too much was at stake.

Sofia and her brothers were busy talking a few strides ahead of her, but as they climbed the front steps Lola managed to subtly indicate her intent to her friend. Once Sofia and her brothers were indoors, Lola discreetly turned around and hurried toward the carriage.

The door cracked open before she reached for the latch and she climbed inside, the warmth an immediate balm to the chilly night air. The interior carried the decadent scent of Theodore's cologne, enticing her to sit on the cushioned velvet bench and sink into pleasure instead of initiate the discussion she'd mentally rehearsed all evening. He smiled when she settled across from him, his handsome features highlighted by the lantern's golden glow.

Allowing their relationship to progress as far as it had was fool-ish. She knew better than to betray her own heart, but now she had no other choice. Nothing good would come of the situation they'd created.

"I hope you don't mind that I waited for you," he said, his eyes reflecting a glint from the candle's flame, his expression full of affection. "I only came by to say good night. I know you must want to go to sleep."

Her heart pounded in her chest.

What she wanted had nothing to do with sleep.

When she didn't immediately respond, he continued.

"I won't keep you."

A truer sentence was never spoken. He couldn't possibly keep her. Not once the truth was told.

Doubt clouded his eyes as the quiet stretched.

"No." She forced out a smile, unwilling to allow him to think she wasn't pleased to see him, because she was, and therein lay the problem. "I'm glad you're here."

He exhaled thoroughly. Was he worried what she might say? That was ridiculous. He was an earl. A powerful man with the world in his pocket. She told herself she was nothing more to him than an interesting diversion, but she couldn't believe her own lie.

"How was Vauxhall tonight? Was it crowded?"

His questions forced her to get on with things.

"Theodore," she began hesitantly as she considered what needed to be said. "I think I know how you feel…"

Half of his delicious mouth curled upward and he took her hand, threading their fingers together, making each of her words more difficult to produce. His thumb stroked over her skin, smoothing away the betraying tremble, luring her away from her decision.

"Shall I tell you how I feel or show you, Lola?"

He reached up and touched her cheek. His fingertips lingered at her jaw, tracing gently over her lips to cause her to shiver.

"I didn't come here tonight to do anything other than say good night. I needed to at least see you," he said, his voice low and husky. "But I'd like to spend time with you tomorrow evening. I can send my carriage. All you need do is leave the boarding house and climb in. I have something special planned. Will you join me?"

"I'm not sure," she answered quickly, her previous decisions silenced by the riot of conflicting emotions alive within her. "I've nothing to wear."

This time he smiled fully. "We won't be going out. At least not tomorrow evening, although my friend Huntington is planning a future outing and has invited us along. Tomorrow night, I'd like us to spend time together at my home, so we can get to know each other better away from Vauxhall and the prying eyes of your neighbors."

He made it sound so normal, so easy, yet she knew it was a mistake. To follow this path further would only lead to heartache and pain. Her wits were stronger than her heart. That's how she'd had the strength to leave Ipswich. But even knowing that didn't ease the ache holding her captive.

Perhaps he sensed her hesitation. He tugged her closer, his fingers still woven with hers.

"What's wrong?" he asked, his brows lowered in genuine concern. "Did something happen tonight that upset you?"

"There was such a huge crowd I couldn't see straight," she said, hedging his question.

"Not a desirable situation for a tightrope walker," he murmured, bringing his mouth in line with hers. "Close your eyes."

The words brushed against her lips and she did as she was told, seeking the comfort he offered. His hands grasped her hips and lifted her, settling her across his lap, encircled in his embrace. She wrapped her arms around his neck, no longer wanting to think about difficult decisions and heartache.

His mouth captured hers with exquisite tenderness, coaxing her to relax against his strength, soothing her with each caress of his tongue. He made no demands, only taking what she was willing to give and, in that moment, she wanted to give him everything.

When they broke apart, he gazed into her eyes, his expression incredibly sincere. "I can help you if you let me."

"Help me with what?" she asked, purposely ignoring all the rehearsed words she'd planned earlier.

"Whatever is troubling you," he answered softly. "Your friend mentioned there was an issue in your past."

"Sofia said that?"

"No." His jaw tightened. "Another of your friends."

"Marco," she said with finality. "He talks too much."

"Who told me doesn't matter as much as what was said," Theodore murmured against her brow, placing a kiss at her temple.

"There's nothing you can do." She pulled back far enough to stare into his eyes. "You have to let it be."

"If that's what you wish." He pulled her close again, resting his chin atop her head. "Tell me you'll visit with me tomorrow."

She listened to his breathing, cherishing his warmth, her arms wrapped around his neck, her heart held in his hands.

"I will," she said at last. "Send your carriage at eleven o'clock."

LOLA WAS JUMPY AS A RABBIT THE FOLLOWING DAY. Weakened by emotion, she'd committed to meeting with Theodore, but now with distance and clarity she worried over her decision. Self-preservation wasn't her only motive. She meant to protect his future as much as her own. It didn't matter her heart would break in the process.

Restless and agitated, she looked through the trunk where she kept her clothing and decided to return to the Bond Street Bazaar and buy a new shawl. She remembered the beautiful display in the window of Harding Howell & Company on the same day she'd thought she'd seen her sister.

Memories of Anna's melodic laughter and warm disposition

flooded her. She missed her family, her sister most of all. Weeks ago, when Lola had gone to Bond Street to purchase Anna a present, she'd never accomplished the task. But she could remedy that today and she'd invite Sofia to accompany her. Feeling better for having a purpose to her morning, she dressed quickly and went downstairs. Not thirty minutes later, the two ladies were inside a hackney on their way to the shopping district.

"I don't remember the last time I bought something new to wear," Lola said. She tugged on the knot of her well-worn shawl. "I won't miss this old thing at all."

"You should purchase an entirely new outfit. Something for your visit with Lord Essex this evening," Sofia said with a gleam in her eyes. "The timing couldn't be better."

Lola had confided in Sofia about her late-night assignation while they rode toward Bond Street, wanting her friend to be aware she'd be out. "I don't know. Why would I deliberately purchase something new if I'm going to tell him we can't see each other anymore?"

Saying the words aloud caused a sharp pang in her chest.

"*Dio mio*," Sofia groaned. "I thought I'd convinced you otherwise. You should enjoy your time with him and not worry about the future. No one can predict what will happen tomorrow."

"Do you really believe that?" Lola asked. "I'm fairly certain I know what will happen if I continue to spend time with the earl." She swallowed, pushing back on emotion, aware it was too late. It had already happened.

She loved him.

"Both of our futures changed unexpectedly," Sofia continued in a more serious tone. "All my plans were destroyed by my brothers' decisions and they never took my feelings into consideration. I was forced to leave my heart and country behind in Italy. I'm not going to live that way anymore."

"You're right." Lola reached around Sofia's shoulders and

hugged her close. "But if I buy a new outfit, then you must buy one too."

"Oh, you don't have to work hard to convince me." Sofia's expression brightened. "Besides, whether you decide to continue to see the earl or walk away from him, you should look good doing it and I'm just the person to help you. Everyone believes the prettiest fashions come from France, but they're wrong. Italy is far superior in creating style."

They laughed, feeling better for their conversation and excited for their outing. When the hackney stopped, they quickly paid the driver and headed toward the shops.

THEODORE STOOD IN THE ENTRY HALL OF HIS TOWN house as he finished his conversation with Wyndham. He'd given his man-of-all-things a lengthy list of preparations and also instructed him to release the staff for the night. Once everything was in order, Theodore wished for privacy on the premises.

"Is there anything else, my lord?" Wyndham asked, poised for further directions.

"That will be all here in the house," Theodore said as he pulled on his gloves. "Have one of the stable boys prepare a stall in the mews. I intend to purchase a horse today."

"Very good," Wyndham replied with a nod.

"And one last thing." Theodore paused, a step from the doorway. "Did you learn anything in regard to your inquiries concerning Lord Sidmouth?"

"Not as of yet, my lord, although I believe I will know more by the morrow." Wyndham's usual professional composure eased. "I, too, have plans for this evening."

Theodore eyed Wyndham knowingly and left, following the slates to where a footman waited holding the reins of his horse.

Tattersall's was located on Hyde Park Corner and it was a pleasant ride through the park to reach the bloodstock auction.

Having an appreciation of horses from an early age served as an advantage considering the significance of the purchase he intended to make today. He trusted no one except himself to make the selection.

Theodore anticipated the popular market house would be crowded and wasn't surprised by how many elaborate coaches and phaetons packed the courtyard. He maneuvered his steed straight into the covered alleys and further into the stables without pause. Dismounting, he handed off the reins and proceeded to where the horses were housed before bidding began.

Many of the noblemen who favored Tattersall's collected horseflesh for show and prestige, but Theodore appreciated the animals on another level entirely. He hoped Lola liked to ride. He had a feeling she did, her spirit daring and carefree. If not, he'd enjoy teaching her if she was interested in learning. He could picture her riding alongside him in the field behind Essex house, her long hair whipping free and laughter in the air, as they raced the wind together.

With that in mind, he focused on the mares, walking along the stalls until he happened upon an elegant chestnut Arabian that embodied the image he'd conjured. The young horse immediately trotted to the gate and he rubbed her nose with affection. She appeared healthy and fit. The notice attached to the outside of the stall detailed her superior lineage.

Noting the lot number, he made his way toward the auction house, having to pass through the lounge first. Inside was even more crowded than outside and he recognized several familiar faces. As he strode past one of the subscription rooms, he glanced inside, surprised to see the Duke of Leinster in conversation at a table with three other peers.

Theodore immediately recalled the innkeeper's advice that he speak directly with His Grace concerning the incident that may have involved Lola. Much like Fremont's murder, there were still too many pieces missing to make sense of the situation. Without knowing more, Theodore couldn't approach the duke and eloquently bring up the subject especially if the problem presented a hardship of some kind. Regardless of coincidence and opportunity, he preferred that Lola trust him enough to reveal whatever troubled her. Hopefully tonight was another step toward earning that trust.

Comfortable with his decision, he left the lounge and entered the courtyard where gentlemen were gathered around the stone cupola at the center in a desire to be closer to the auctioneer and activity. With another ten minutes until the bidding began, he leaned against one of the stone columns to wait. His body was tense with anticipation, but it wasn't caused by the auction. The realization he would have Lola all to himself for hours this evening simmered in his blood.

The sound of a gavel marked the start of the auction and things progressed vigorously from that point on. The courtyard grew more crowded as the most select animals were left until the final round and everyone from broker to farmer enjoyed watching the rigorous competition to win the last bid.

"Lot 317," the auctioneer called loudly. "Arabian breed, mare, fifteen hands high, four years old. Chestnut with marked withers. Let the bidding begin."

The horse he'd chosen was presented and the mare looked even more lovely in the daylight as when he'd viewed her in the stables. Raising his hand, Theodore signaled the clerk, while several other men around him did the same. Winning wouldn't come easily, but he had no intention of losing.

After a series of bids had raised the mare's price considerably, the field of interested bidders thinned. Eight men became five, dwindled to three, and then only two. Theodore raised his hand to signal an increase in his bid to one thousand pounds. A wave of speculation and comment rippled through the crowd. Men now stood in clusters around the courtyard, removed from the cupola to discuss the vicious bidding war in the same way they would retell the story at their dinner table later that evening.

Theodore had no idea which gentleman continued to outbid him, as the man was represented by a Tattersall's worker, who again raised the price with a wave of his hand. Pushing from the column where he'd leaned, Theodore walked closer to the auctioneer. He had no intention of losing because his gesture went unseen.

"Who is outbidding me?" The angry query echoed across the courtyard and the crowd hushed immediately.

Theodore turned to see the Duke of Leinster enter the area. He passed by the Tattersall's agent who'd apparently represented his bids and continued until he stopped five strides from Theodore.

"Theodore Coventry, Earl of Essex." Theodore bowed his head in greeting. "I mean no disrespect, Your Grace."

"Then you will forfeit the bid."

"I didn't say that," Theodore replied.

"This mare isn't worth such an egregious amount. Are you driving up the price on purpose?" His Grace asked.

"Not at all," Theodore replied. "I have every intention of winning this auction."

No one in the crowd made a sound. The auctioneer waited while the Duke of Leinster glared at Theodore for what seemed an endless minute. Theodore suspected His Grace would spare his own reputation considering the large audience who watched with rapt attention.

"One thousand two hundred pounds," the Duke of Leinster announced loudly.

"One thousand five hundred pounds," Theodore countered right after.

"I shall remember you, Essex," the duke said cryptically, before he nodded at the auctioneer, turned his back and walked away.

Twenty-One

Only a few minutes had passed since Lola last checked the time. Her pulse fluttered, anxious with longing and anticipation, until finally at exactly eleven o'clock Theodore's carriage arrived. Locking her door and pocketing the key, she made her way downstairs and into the night. Just like the day before, the door to the carriage opened before she reached for it and she climbed in without hesitation.

"Good evening, Lola," Theodore said, his voice low and rich. He was dressed impeccably in waistcoat, shirt, and trousers. His cravat was tied loosely leaving a shadowy vee of skin visible at his neck.

"Hello, Theodore," she said, her voice calmer than her heartbeat. She settled on the cushioned bench and the carriage began to move.

"You're breathtaking." He reached for her hand and brought it to his lips, pressing her skin to his mouth before he released her, the warm kiss full of sensual promise, the moment far too short.

"Thank you," she said coyly, omitting how she and Sofia had painstakingly considered her gown and underthings.

Silence enveloped them as he took her in from top to bottom.

His eyes followed the curve of her shoulder, lingering at the open neckline of her dress where the rose-colored silk was shirred tight to hug her curves. His gaze traveled lower to the line of her skirt, down to where she'd gently pulled the fabric aside and pointed the toe of her new slippers.

"Silk stockings," he said, his words husky with desire. "Is that a white dove flying across your ankle?"

She slid her leg out further, just enough to expose her lower calf and the fine embroidery decorating her imported stockings. "Sofia says I balance like a little bird on the tightrope. She helped me choose these stockings among...other things."

The last two words whispered out and hung in the air, increasing the delightful tension that radiated between them. His gaze had returned to hers and a delicious heat began in her belly quick to remind of all the pleasures to be had this evening.

He cleared his throat before he spoke again. "I have a surprise for you as well."

"Is that so?" she asked, grateful for the change of topic.

She'd left her hair down, knowing how much he enjoyed threading his fingers through the lengths and now she brushed a stray strand from her cheek to keep herself from reaching for him. He looked incredibly handsome in the lantern's glow, his dark hair catching a gloss from the candlelight, his strong features made sharp by the shadows.

"I'll show you as soon as we reach Essex House," he said, a slight smile accompanying his explanation. "I hope you like it."

"I'm sure I will," she replied, caught in the intimate magic of their flirtatious conversation.

"Tell me what you do when you're not defying gravity," he said, his eyes just as intense as always. "I want to learn everything about you."

Her breath caught, surprised by his candid admission.

"Everything?" she asked. A beat of panic accompanied the

word, but she dismissed it, unwilling to sacrifice the enthralling mood between them for a reminder of worry.

"As much as you'll tell me," he replied. "Do you like the theater? Reading poetry? Riding?"

His genuine interest helped her relax and a soft laugh escaped. "Yes, to all those things. Especially the latter. I haven't ridden since I left home, but I do miss it. There's glorious countryside in Ipswich, perfect for riding, and my childhood home was located near an extensive stable. My mother complained that my father spent more time there than with us in the house. She was only teasing him, but she may have been correct. He has a great love of horses, and I suppose he and I have that in common."

A sad note crept into her voice and she quickly brightened, but it was too late. He'd listened and watched, not missing the subtle change in tone.

"You miss your family," he said, reaching for her hand again, holding it a moment in his own.

"Yes, I do," she answered before she rushed on. "What is it you enjoy when you're not being an earl?"

He laughed, a chuckle from deep in his chest, and the sound heated her blood like expensive brandy.

She was lost.

Terribly lost in love.

"I'm always an earl," he began, a roguish smile transforming his features. "But, when no one is watching, I break as many rules as possible."

The carriage hit a rut in the road, catching her by surprise, and he reached across to grasp her shoulders and brace her gently. The motion brought them nearly nose to nose. She breathed him in, his alluring cologne tempting her, his mouth less than a whisper away.

The need to close that hair's breadth of space thrummed in her veins, to touch her lips to his and taste him. Her longing soon became an ache begging to be fulfilled, yet with a deep breath he resettled on his side of the carriage, the suspended moment gone. She wasn't the only one affected, though. He purposely glanced out the window and she saw him swallow twice, his throat moving beneath his loosened cravat.

The carriage rolled to a stop with blessed timing, the air within fraught with sensual tension.

"Allow me to escort you," he said, recovering his usual charm.

She took his hand as they exited and he unhooked the lantern on the outside of the carriage to carry with them. Nodding to his driver, he led her along the fine gravel walkway toward the mews, not the house. Feeling confused, she slanted a look in his direction in time to catch his devilish grin.

THEODORE DREW ANOTHER DEEP BREATH, TAKING IN the night air in an effort to cool his ardor. The need to touch Lola pounded in his veins, his body in tune to her every movement. Tonight, she looked enchanting, her appearance made all the more beguiling by the light scent of her perfume, a mixture of captivating jasmine and delicate musk. How the little minx had managed to become more desirable escaped him.

When she'd spoken of her family, he'd heard the sadness in her voice, though she'd worked to conceal it. He wanted to soothe away her despair, but she needed to trust him first, not just with her secrets, but with her heart.

As they approached the mews, he stifled a grin of satisfaction, anticipating her pleasure at seeing the chestnut Arabian. She'd mentioned her love of riding. He'd chosen well.

Wyndham had followed his instructions to the letter and the mews were well-lighted and quiet. Theodore hooked the lantern on the wall near the entrance and walked with Lola to the stall where his prized stallion was housed, keeping to the cobbles so her new slippers wouldn't become ruined.

"This is Mercury," he said as he smoothed his hand down the horse's forelock. "I'm certain he would like to meet you."

She reached up and ran her palm over the horse's muzzle. "Hello, Mercury. You're a fine fellow, aren't you?"

The stallion nickered in answer.

"Smart too," Theodore said.

"He's an Arabian, isn't he?"

"Yes." He'd had a feeling she'd appreciate horses, but he was even more impressed with her keen eye. "I admire the breed's even temperament and superior stamina."

"They're strikingly beautiful animals. My father taught me about all kinds of horses, but Arabians have always captivated me. They embody compact strength and yet move with elegance and grace."

"Just as you do," he said, gazing at her lovely profile.

She looked up into his eyes and he again fought the desire to kiss her. Now was the perfect time for her gift.

"Let's walk to the next stall," he suggested. "I have another Arabian to show you."

Lola's face lit up as soon as she saw the chestnut mare. The horse seemed equally pleased with her attention, moving to the gate and prancing prettily as if putting on a show.

"She's beautiful," Lola said, appreciation in her voice. "What's her name?"

"She doesn't have one," he said, matter-of-factly.

"Why not?" Lola exclaimed, clearly aggrieved on the horse's behalf.

"You haven't given her one yet," he replied, smiling through the words.

"What? I don't understand." She canted her head, her expression confused.

"She's for you. A gift," he said, drawing her back against his chest as they admired the animal together. "I thought you might like to go riding with me sometime, and if you do, I want you to have a horse that exemplifies your strength, beauty and grace. With that in mind, I visited Tattersall's yesterday and arranged for her to be brought here."

She twisted, turning in his embrace so she faced him. "You bought me a horse?"

Her question was a mixture of inquiry and awe.

"Yes," he answered as he gazed into her eyes. "I chose her for you."

"I don't know what to say." Her surprise was evident. She hesitated, but eventually her smile broke through.

"Do you like her?" he asked.

They moved closer to the stall and the horse approached once again.

"Yes, very much," Lola said, reaching up to stroke the Arabian affectionately.

"Then there isn't anything else to say. I'm happy you're pleased."

"It's not that simple," she insisted.

"It is if you'll allow it to be," he answered.

"Theodore, this is a very thoughtful gesture and she's a magnificent horse, but I can't accept your gift," she said sincerely.

"Yes, you can, because I chose her just for *you*. No one else." He rested his hands on her shoulders and felt a shiver pass through her. "Let's go up to the house. It's cold and I've kept you here too long."

"Thank you so much. I'm stunned by your generosity." She wrapped her hand around his elbow, holding tight as they began their walk out of the mews. "I don't know what else to say."

"Say good-bye to your horse," he said with humor in his voice.

She stopped, looking at him first before she glanced over her shoulder. "I'll see you soon, Venus."

"Venus?" he asked, staring down at her as they continued to make their way toward the house. "You've already decided on her name? Are you sure?"

"I am." She smiled up at him. "She'll be running alongside Mercury, won't she?"

"Yes." He placed his hand atop hers and squeezed her fingers. "I certainly hope so."

LOLA ATTEMPTED TO CALM HER EMOTIONS AS THEY entered Theodore's town house through the back door and moved down the hall. A giddy, unfamiliar feeling swirled inside her, but she couldn't allow it to take hold.

He bought her a horse?

He bought her a horse.

She was surprised by the extravagant gift and at the same time utterly delighted. Nevertheless, she'd promised herself tonight was an anomaly. Clearly, he was thinking beyond this evening even when she'd forbidden herself from doing the same.

"Would you like something to warm you?" he asked once they'd entered the drawing room. "There's port, sherry and brandy."

"Port will be fine," she said as she took in the room.

A lively fire danced in the hearth. Before it, two brocade chairs flanked a satinwood table where a tray with biscuits and cheese waited along with a bottle of wine and two crystal glasses. On the mantel, a Chinoiserie vase overflowed with a large bouquet of roses in every color imaginable. She walked closer to the fireplace and removed her shawl, draping it over the arm of one of the chairs. "Everything looks lovely. You must have a wonderful staff."

"*You* look lovely." He came forward with two glasses of wine. "I wanted the house to be quiet for our time together, so I arranged for my staff to be released for the evening."

She smiled softly, touched by his thoughtfulness although she couldn't ignore how neatly his life was *arranged* compared to hers. "It's all a little overwhelming."

"That wasn't my intent. I want you to feel comfortable here." He handed her a glass, raising his slightly as he spoke. "To us."

She lifted her glass in kind. "To this evening."

"One of many," he added before they both took a sip of wine.

"I'd rather we didn't plan too far ahead," she said, striving to keep her tone light. "It would probably be for the best."

"Best for whom?" he asked with a disarming smile. "Not for me."

"Yes, for you," she insisted, though her voice held little conviction. "You just don't realize it yet."

"Why would you say that?" He took her glass and set it down on the table next to his before he drew her into his arms.

She relished the warmth offered by his embrace even as she voiced the truth. "We are from two worlds that never shall mix."

"You don't believe that or you wouldn't be here," he countered. "Besides, who's to define where one world begins or ends, or how the two blend together?"

"We should talk about something else," she said, looking up into his handsome face and mentally calling herself a fool a thousand times over. "I don't want to ruin our evening."

"You're here in my arms," he said in an intimate murmur. "It's impossible for this evening to be anything besides perfection."

He didn't allow her a rebuttal, leaning in to capture her mouth in a long, lingering kiss that made her breathless and that suited her fine since his declaration left her speechless.

Twenty-Two

T heodore deepened their kiss and tightened his embrace, wanting Lola to understand what he offered. It was more than a gesture of affection. More than a piece of his heart. Much more. Tonight, he offered a bond. A promise. The precious possibility that they could experience the world together, side by side.

He couldn't identify the exact moment he'd fallen in love. Perhaps it was an ongoing process that had begun the first time he'd laid eyes on her, that very first day when she'd challenged him with her tart words, or later, when he'd tasted her sweet, sensual kisses. But there was no denying it now. He couldn't envision a future without her in it.

He wasn't certain if she felt the same, but he knew she desired him with the same intense longing as his own. That was evident in more than her kisses.

When she pressed closer to his chest, he slid his hand upward, splaying his fingers against her back to caress the soft skin where her neckline dipped lower in invitation. He trailed his other hand down over the curve of her firm bottom. She trembled and he broke away to nuzzle kisses along her cheek, bury his face in her hair, and breathe in her scent as a desperate act to temper his ardor.

"I adore you, Lola," he said, his voice raspy. "At times it feels as though I'll go mad from wanting to see you and touch you."

"I feel that same madness." Her words whispered against his jaw as her hands came up between them and rested on his chest. "When we're apart I spend all day wondering when I will see you again, and then, when we're together, the time always goes too fast."

He kissed her temple, his lips gentle though her words aroused him further. Need and want thrummed with insistence in his veins. To know she experienced the same attraction made him wish he could carry her into his bedchambers and keep her there forever.

He groaned, the image causing desire to pulse heavily in his groin. He took her lips in another deep, openmouthed kiss and when they came apart, their breathing ragged, his every muscle was strained to the breaking point.

"Shall we go upstairs?" he asked, his voice hoarse as he gazed into her eyes, her skin flushed a fetching shade of pink.

She blinked, her long lashes lowering before she raised her eyes to his, a coy smile curling her kiss-swollen lips. "Yes, nothing would please me more."

He reached for her hand, lacing their fingers as they walked toward the hall. Without a word they moved up the staircase and further, their footsteps muted by the carpet runner, until they reached the double doors of his bedchamber.

He glanced at her. His heart beat hard in kind to the rest of him. Yet he had to be sure. Had to know, she was sure. She sensed what he asked as soon as their eyes met.

"Yes, Theodore."

He turned the latch, their fingers tight as he tugged her inside his rooms and closed the doors behind them.

· · ·

Lola drew a deep breath, overwhelmed by the scene before her. Theodore released her, crossing the room to tend the fire while she stepped through the dimly lit sitting room and into his bedchamber. The enormous room beckoned her closer, warm and inviting with its mahogany furniture and sophisticated décor, yet there was no ignoring the massive four-poster bed at its center. The counterpane and pillows seemed to overflow while the flickering shadows from the flames in the firebox danced along the pale bedlinens.

Theodore stood near the hearth. Having finished his task, he turned and watched her now, his eyes causing her to shiver with anticipation and at the same time, her skin heated with desire, her body sensitive and restless. The way he stared at her took her breath away.

She went to him, though she didn't wrap her arms around him to meet his embrace. Instead, she loosened the knot of his cravat, dropping it to the floorboards before she set to work on the buttons of his waistcoat, discarding the garment soon after.

He grasped her hands, pausing her fevered pace. His eyes gleamed with an inscrutable emotion. Her heart squeezed tight as if he'd captured the delicate organ and held it in his hands instead of holding her fingers. In one fluid motion, he carefully reversed her position.

"We have all night, Lola," he said as he smoothed her hair over her shoulders. "There's no reason to rush when we've both waited and wanted this for so long."

He kissed a path to the curve of her shoulder, murmuring words of endearment against her skin while, one by one, his nimble fingers released the row of ivory buttons at the back of her gown. When the silk parted, she heard his sharp inhale and bit back her grin. Her chemise was imported French lace and nothing more than a sheer pattern of gossamer flowers against her skin. She was pleased he liked it.

"Aren't you full of delicious surprises?" he said with a throaty hum of approval. He stroked the shallow curve of her spine and buried his mouth at her nape before he brought his hand around to cup her breast, his hot kisses on her skin causing her nipples to pebble beneath the lace. Unable to stand still, she turned and lowered her gown, one sleeve then the other, until it floated to the floorboards in a puddle at her feet.

"You're still dressed," she said, touching her fingertips to the top of her chemise, watching his eyes follow her every move.

He walked to the bed, sat and removed his boots before he stood and discarded his shirt and trousers. His body was magnificent, powerful strength and composed elegance, broad shoulders, and sculpted legs of lean muscle. That same curl of desire wound through her, causing her to press her thighs together in an effort to quiet the demanding pulse at her core.

Wanting to be closer, she moved to where he sat on the edge of the mattress and he pulled her forward between his knees, the heated friction of his thighs through her silk stockings evoking a sensual shiver. He held her waist and she placed her hands on his bare shoulders. His muscles tensed beneath her touch though his eyes held a wicked gleam. With a fingertip, he traced the swirling lace design pulled taut across her breasts before he slowly lowered the straps of her chemise. It fell to her hips and he swept it to the floor with her pantalets, leaving her in just stockings and slippers. She swallowed, the wait excruciating and, at the same time, her body hummed with anticipation.

Watching her, he smoothed one hand upward, over her ribs to her breast and then across to the tip, tight and sensitive, while his other hand held her waist in a firm grip. She gasped, alive with pleasure as she clenched her thighs tighter, the need there ever more insistent.

His eyes never left hers as he caressed and teased her, and when he finally took her breast into his mouth, her legs threatened to betray her. His tongue rubbed over her skin like hot velvet, each stroke tormenting pleasure. She grasped him tighter, her fingertips pressed into his muscles in an attempt to stay upright while he wrapped an arm around her lower back to lock her in place.

"You're so beautiful, Lola," he rasped, his hands skimming over her waist, around to her bottom and down the length of her thighs, his every touch leaving her more aroused. When he ran his fingertips along the edge of her stockings, she trembled from his sensual caress, her body taut with want. "I don't know where to taste you first. I want to ravish all of you and at the same time savor every little piece."

He looked up at her and, while she lost herself in his gaze, he eased his fingers between her thighs, into her sex, his thumb stroking the swollen bud at the center. She cried out, sensation coursing through her with such force she shuddered, but he gave her no relief, tasting her breasts and at the same time rubbing her slick folds with exquisite pressure. Her head fell back, her long hair another erotic pleasure as it swept over her back and heightened her awareness.

She closed her eyes and moaned, wanting him to stop and never stop, craving the climax of gratification he promised with every delicate touch of his fingers until the intense ache inside threatened to consume her. Need twisted tighter and tighter, and he sensed each tremor, feeling her thighs tremble with impatience every time he stroked back and forth, knowing she couldn't bear much more.

Until at last, with a featherlight brush of his fingertip, she cried out and bliss coursed through her body with an intensity she'd never known. Leaning into his strength, her hair fell forward in a curtain around them. She found him ready for her kiss, his embrace enveloping her as they tumbled back to the mattress together, her slippers lost to the floorboards.

THEODORE HELD LOLA AGAINST HIS CHEST, HIS heartbeat thrumming in rhythm with hers, their legs entwined. He kissed her, tasting her with slow, languid strokes though his body burned with intensity.

"I want you, Lola." Something fierce and possessive shot through him as he spoke the words. Not desire, something far more dangerous. *Far more meaningful.*

"Yes," she answered, her eyes fluttering open to meet his gaze. "I want you, Theodore."

Without effort he reversed their positions, the bedlinens tangling with the motion and promptly kicked aside. She still wore her stockings and the slide of her shapely, silk-covered legs against his body stoked his ardor, his arousal hard and insistent. Without another word, he discarded his smalls and moved over her, his erection pressed against the creamy soft smoothness of her thighs.

She wiggled beneath him, positioning herself better as he braced on his elbows. He leaned down for another kiss, the moment fraught with reverence and tenderness. His chest tightened with emotion.

She stared up at him, her eyes wide as he settled between her thighs, his length thick and hard at the seam of her legs and she opened for him, raising her hips slightly, telling him what she wanted without words. Holding her gaze, he nudged into her, slowly at first, finding her tight and hot and incredibly wet. He tried to wait, but couldn't, his desire too strong as he entered her with a swift thrust. She gasped as they joined, his hard cock perfectly sheathed within her as if they were made to complete each other. She closed her eyes and he did the same before he withdrew almost completely and thrust again, each stroke establishing a rhythm, their bodies working together in a dance of give and take. She met his movements, gasping at the exquisite friction of his thrusts, the delicious tension of their bodies together every time he pushed into her heat. A sheen of exertion covered his skin, the overwhelming sensations racing through him. Pleasure threatened to consume him, destroy him, as if nothing had any meaning except this moment in time, together with Lola.

She must have felt it too. Her whole body trembled. She clung to his arms, her body rising to meet his, her breathy gasps and sensual sighs too much for him to bear. When she tilted her hips, taking him deeper, he had to fight for clarity, burying himself within her tight body one last time. She cried out just before he withdrew and spilled himself on the sheets. Not wanting to be separated, he drew her close, holding her to his heart as their breathing slowed.

For several long minutes they stayed that way. Time ceased to have meaning. The air was heavy with emotion, unspoken words, and the scent of their lovemaking. Eventually, she turned, creating a small space between them as she wrapped herself partially in the sheets although her pale shoulders were exposed, tempting him to lean in and kiss her again. She looked beautiful, her hair fanned atop the downy counterpane like a mantle of black silk, her skin flushed pink.

"You belong in my bed," he said, reaching forward to sweep a stray piece of hair from her brow, unable to keep from touching her.

"I like being here." She caught his hand and brought it to her mouth where she kissed his knuckles. Perhaps she couldn't keep from touching him either.

"I want you to know how important you are to me," he began, unsure of his words and even less sure of her reaction. He waited, the only sound the crackling wood in the firebox. He touched her cheek gently. "How much I care about you."

Her eyes widened slightly and she didn't immediately respond. She turned beneath the sheets so she too lay on her side, able to look at him directly.

"I do," she said, her voice a soft whisper. "It makes me wish things were different. Our lives..."

She seemed at a loss to finish her sentence so he went ahead. "Our lives were meant to intersect, Lola. I'd only returned from America the day before Bow Street knocked on my door. The

Runners allowed me to accompany them because I insisted and would not be deterred. I knew I had to go to Vauxhall. Losing Fremont was a tragedy I never anticipated, but it also brought me to you."

"I am grateful for that." She reached up and placed her hand on his cheek, stroking over his jaw with tenderness. "It makes my choices in the past that much more meaningful, why I left Ipswich and found my way to London, but it doesn't change the circumstances now."

"What circumstances?" he asked. "You'll have to explain that to me."

She rolled onto her back and stared at the ceiling. "You are an earl. I am a Vauxhall performer with a sordid past. Society would never have it. If you carry on with me, it will ruin your reputation, tarnish your heritage and ultimately bring you shame and embarrassment."

She said the words matter-of-factly but he knew her well enough to hear the tremulous emotion hidden in her voice.

"No." The one word sounded loud in the room. "I don't believe it will be as damning as you predict. Society finds a new scandal to bandy about every week, if it even takes that long. I care nothing for gossip rags and idle scorn and have no one to please besides myself and *you*, Lola, you please me."

She didn't say anything and his heart lurched. The longer she stayed quiet, the faster his pulse raced. When she turned on her side to face him again, he saw tears in her eyes.

"But that's the problem." Her brow furrowed and her lips quivered as she drew a stilted breath. "There's something about me you don't know that will forever keep us apart."

He waited, but she didn't continue. A tear slid free and when she reached up to wipe it away, he caught her fingers, accomplishing the task with the pad of his thumb while keeping her hand in his, keeping them connected.

"You can tell me anything," he began, wanting her to know the depths of his emotions. He drew her to his chest and held her a minute, her damp cheek pressed against his skin. "I'll help you every way I can and we'll solve the problem together because I can't live another day knowing you carry around such pain."

She let out a long exhale and glanced up at his face, her own filled with sorrow. "When you visited Ipswich did you try to find out about my life there?"

"No. I knew you would tell me about your past when you were ready," he answered immediately. "And I respect you too much to deceive you or be dishonest. I haven't lied to you."

She bit her lower lip. "I wish you had."

"Lied to you?" he asked, his voice filled with disbelief. "Why would you say that?"

She swallowed, her eyes closing for a long blink before she answered. "Because I've lied to you, Theodore, since the first day I met you."

Twenty-Three

L ola watched Theodore's face register surprise, confusion, and then the most damning emotion, *hurt*.

"What do you mean you've lied to me since the first day?" His voice sounded different and she felt his body tense. "Is this about us or what happened to Fremont?"

"No," she answered quickly. "I didn't see anything besides a man in a black greatcoat. I mean, I saw what he did, and I saw your friend on the ground, but I was on the rope. I told you everything about that."

She realized she was talking too fast and took a deep breath, wanting to explain calmly.

"Go on," he said, his eyes watching her intensely.

"I don't know where to begin."

"At the beginning, Lola. If you want me to understand why you've lied, you'll need to tell me everything," he answered, his voice not at all like the rich, affectionate tone she'd come to love.

"My name is Lola Morgan," she said, drawing the coverlet closer to her chin. "I took the name York when I came to London."

He was staring over her shoulder at the flames in the firebox and she wondered what he was thinking. What he would think of her when she finished telling him everything.

"My parents, sister and I lived a comfortable life in a lovely cottage on the grounds of the Duke of Leinster's country seat in Ipswich. My father was a sought-after horse trainer and His Grace, an avid equestrian. The duke met my father over two decades earlier and their association was one of friendship as much as employment. Or so we all believed at the time we were invited to live on his property where my father was in charge of the extensive stables.

"Mostly, things were fine. Life was enjoyable. But His Grace had a stern hand with the horses and my father and he openly disagreed about discipline versus training. My father wouldn't tolerate abuse of any kind and His Grace knew that. They occasionally exchanged words and I suspect His Grace kept his darker habits for when no one could witness his cruelty."

She heard Theodore curse under his breath, but he didn't say more so she continued.

"One afternoon my father took delivery of a young Hanoverian the duke purchased for an ungodly sum. His Grace wanted the stallion broken immediately. He wanted him saddled so he could show the rare breed to a few noblemen he planned to visit, but my father refused, knowing the horse should become acclimated to its new home first. Father believed livestock needed to gain trust before he initiated training, but the duke objected and they argued openly. That night my father expressed his anger at the dinner table. He was frustrated and my mother encouraged him to take a long ride and clear his mind.

After dinner, I wanted to see the new horse. Hearing my father describe the stallion made me curious, but when I approached the stables, I heard a whip crack and a horse's frightened snort. Thinking back, I shouldn't have gone inside. But I did. I stayed in the shadows with my heart in my throat, however I'll never forget what I saw. His Grace whipped the stallion without cause. The horse was tied and couldn't escape. To callously injure a captive animal was one of the most brutal things I've ever seen. I couldn't help but wonder how many times the duke had done the same with no one the wiser, All that suffering..."

She'd long ago dropped her gaze to her hands where they were wrapped tight in the bedsheets, but she looked at Theodore now. At some point during her story, he'd turned to watch her, his expression unreadable.

"Eventually the duke grew tired or bored. I don't know. He left and I went to the horse to wash him down and soothe him. After he was fed, I led him outside. I took my mount and rode out with the stallion as far as the Gipping River. He'd only just arrived in Ipswich and didn't have the familiarity to return to the duke's home. I set him free and he ran for the hills."

She saw Theodore swallow whatever he was going to say. When he nodded, she continued, wanting to get it all out now.

"The next morning His Grace went to the stables earlier than usual and discovered the stallion missing. He became incensed and blamed my father for the horse's escape. When my father noticed the bloody whip in the stall, he questioned the duke and then everything became madness. His Grace accused my father of negligence and liability. Having paid an exorbitant price for the horse, he was enraged about the situation. He went to the magistrate with his claims and my father was taken into custody. No one believed my father and since he'd gone out riding, his confession sounded incriminating instead of exonerating. Nobleman have far too much power at their disposal."

She said the last sentence with quiet vehemence.

"Many of them do," Theodore commented, his expression solemn. "Then what happened?"

His body had relaxed from when she'd first begun and he stared at her now with what she hoped was understanding in his eyes.

"I couldn't allow my father to be punished for what I'd done," she explained, emotion clogging her throat. "I went to the duke and told him I was responsible, and he flew into a rage. That same morning, he cut ties with my father, evicted my family from his property and notified the authorities. I was to be brought before the magistrate the following day, but I ran away and left Ipswich that night. I didn't tell my parents I was leaving. They were understanding and loving about what I'd done and they already worried on my behalf. I thought by my leaving, at least I wouldn't cause them further shame. With me gone, the gossip would die down and things could return to normal. So, I came to London, took a new name and found my way to Vauxhall."

The room was so quiet, every crackle in the hearth sounded like a thunderbolt. She looked at Theodore, his handsome profile outlined by the firelight, knowing this would be the end. He wouldn't associate with a criminal. He couldn't possibly want to continue seeing her, knowing what she'd done. A crime against anyone was awful, but against a duke, one of the most revered noblemen in England, was unthinkable. But whether he believed she'd acted foolishly or not was a question she needed answered because his opinion mattered so much her heart ached. Swallowing emotion, she went on.

"I'm aware the world is often an ugly, unfair place, and I acted selfishly when I released that horse. He didn't belong to me and I had no right to set him free. But I cannot apologize for it, because I would do the same thing again." She took a deep breath and began to wrap the sheets around her. "You must think the worst of me, now that you've heard the truth, but you should know I took no pleasure in deceiving you. I'm sorry I lied. I had no other choice." She sat up, preparing to get dressed and leave.

"What you did was very brave," he said at last, his words causing her to pause. "I thought I understood your daring when I watched you balance on that narrow rope suspended over the grandstand, but I realize now you're far more courageous than I ever imagined."

When he didn't say more, she scooted toward the edge of the bed, anxious to dress and leave before her tears fell. She had no one to blame for her pain except herself, yet she'd rather Theodore didn't witness her crying. She gathered the sheets closer and made to stand, but he caught her arm and stopped her.

"What are you doing?" he said, his voice firm.

"I need to dress. I can't leave until I've put myself back together." When she didn't turn toward him, his grip on her arm tightened.

"You're not leaving," he said, his tone giving nothing away.

She looked at him over her shoulder. Did he mean to call the authorities immediately? Her eyes welled full of tears. She hadn't expected him to act so swiftly. She knew telling him the truth was a risk, but she'd thought he would at least allow her the chance to run. He'd said he wanted to help but that was before she'd confessed the magnitude of her crime.

"Please," she said, feeling all the more vulnerable for that one word. "I need to get dressed."

"For what reason?" he replied, his voice softer now. "I'll only have to undress you again when you come back to bed."

"What?" She couldn't stop her tears from blurring her vision.

"You're not going anywhere, at least not without me, and definitely not at this time of night." He gently hauled her across the mattress and back into his arms, tucking her against his bare chest. She instinctively nestled into his warmth.

"You're not summoning the authorities?" Her question whispered out in a mixture of worry and hope.

"To insist they arrest the Duke of Leinster?" Theodore asked, his voice hard as steel. "That would probably be a waste of time."

"Aren't you angry?" she asked, recovering her composure as she breathed in the scent of his skin against her cheek.

"I'm furious," he said, his body tensed. "Leinster should be whipped for the way he treated that horse and no doubt, countless other animals. Then he should be whipped a second time for how he treated your family. Friendship and loyalty meant nothing to him when he chose to protect his reputation above all else. Does anyone else know about this, Lola?" He stroked his fingers through her hair and she let out a deep breath, relief rushing through her.

"Only Marco and Sofia," she said, "I wish I never told him, but I trust Sofia completely."

"That explains a few of Marco's comments now that I think about it."

"I'm sorry, Theodore." She pulled away from him and sat up, the sheets still bundled around her. "I never meant to bring trouble to your doorstep."

He smiled, and it was like the first time she'd ever seen him grin, her heart beat so hard.

"You're a bit of troublesome baggage, that much is true," he said, affection in his voice. "I still wish you had told me, but I realize why you didn't."

"Thank you for understanding." She moved closer, aligning her mouth with his.

"There are things I haven't told you either," he murmured as he drew her closer. "One thing in particular."

"Really?" She whispered. "What is it?"

He unraveled the sheets she'd bundled around her body and wrapped her in his arms instead.

"Why don't I show you?" he said, as he lowered her to the mattress, skin to skin, heart to heart.

THEODORE AWOKE TO THE SOUND OF THUNDER. EASING from beneath the covers so he wouldn't disturb Lola, he pulled on his trousers and went to the hearth where he poked at the embers and stirred the fire into a heartier blaze. The clock on the mantel read half two.

Restless with his thoughts, he paced to the window and looked out at the moonless sky. Fremont's killer was still free. The Duke of Leinster went about his business with none the wiser. And yet, Lola had left her family and home behind for the sake of protecting an abused horse. A sense of protectiveness, fierce and indomitable, settled inside him.

Somehow, he would make this right.

He glanced to the bed where Lola slept, her hair like silk ribbons strewn across the white bedlinens. He hadn't told her how he felt, *that he loved her*, the evening already fraught with too many fragile emotions.

And yet he'd shown her. The way they'd made love after she'd confided in him couldn't be described as anything other than a joining of souls.

Still, there could be no future for them until her past was resolved and that wouldn't be an easy task. He'd likely already made an enemy of the Duke of Leinster when he'd outbid His Grace for the Arabian at Tattersall's.

What a tangled knot it had all become.

Another rumble of thunder shook the window glass, quickly followed by a sharp strike of lightning. There was nothing he could do to solve any of these problems now and he wasn't certain Lola wanted him to intercede. She'd deliberately concealed the information and hadn't asked for his help in any way.

Walking to his desk in the adjoined sitting room, he put on his spectacles and reached for the pile of correspondence he'd neglected. The first letter was from Margaret, inviting him to supper at Fremont House. She wanted him to meet Viscount Sidmouth as they'd previously discussed. Theodore would accept the invitation and bring Lola with him. It would be beneficial for everyone to spend time together. Margaret needed to realize he intended to keep Lola in his life as long as possible.

No.

He intended to keep Lola in his life. Period.

Together they would find a way to resolve the Duke of Leinster's charges. The matter would have to be handled delicately, but

Theodore would accept no other outcome than dismissal of the case brought forward by the duke. Lola deserved to live freely without fear after all she'd experienced.

Frustrated with his lack of solutions, he removed his spectacles and returned to the bedchamber. Lola was sitting up in bed. She looked deliciously mussed amid the pillows and covers, though as he stepped closer, he noticed her frown.

"What's the matter? Did the storm wake you?" He unbuttoned his trousers and removed them before he climbed beneath the counterpane.

"Yes, but when I reached for you, you weren't there," she said, curling up beside him once he was settled.

"I was tending the fire and reading through some mail," he said as he gathered her closer. "We've been invited to dine at Fremont House. Margaret would like me to meet her intended groom and has asked us to join her for a quiet dinner at home."

"She invited me?" Lola asked with skepticism.

"She invited me and my choice of guest," he said, amused by her cautious tone. "Which means you're invited because I choose you."

"Just the four of us?" she asked with that same note of doubt.

"Lola, we're together, aren't we?"

"Yes," she said, falling quiet right after.

He slanted a look to where she rested beside him trying to gauge her reaction. "What's wrong?"

"I don't want you to be criticized or judged for having me on your arm," she said, the words coming out in a rush. "I wouldn't ever want you to be the subject of a scandal."

"As far as I'm concerned, anyone who chooses to ridicule a person without knowing them properly reveals more of their own personality than whatever gossip they choose to pass along."

"But—"

"I'm not finished," he scolded her gently. "And it wouldn't matter if the Prince Regent told me to stop seeing you, I'd refuse, knowing he was only saying that so he could scoop you up himself."

Lola laughed a little, the sound delightful. "Are you sure?" she asked, though her voice no longer sounded tentative.

"Yes." He breathed deep, hoping she would come to realize what he already knew without a doubt. "Don't you realize how much I care about you?"

"Yes," she answered immediately and leaned up to look into his eyes. "I do. That's why I asked about visiting Margaret. Because I care about you."

"Good. That's settled. We don't need to discuss the subject again," he said knowingly. "Now that we're both awake, are you hungry? I arranged for there to be a light meal left in the kitchen in case we wanted something to eat."

"You arranged for my horse and for the house to be quiet." Her fingertips feathered through his chest hair as she spoke, a hint of humor in her voice. "And you arranged for a meal. So, I have one other question."

"What's that?" he asked, placing his hand over hers.

"If the rain continues, there'll be no need for me to go to Vauxhall today. Not for practice or a performance." She looked up at him, her brows raised in question. "Did you arrange for this weather too?"

"Very clever," he said with a smile. "Unfortunately, I don't have that kind of authority. Although, I'll never begrudge a rainy day again."

Twenty-Four

T he rain continued through mid-morning and Theodore's staff reappeared as if they'd hidden in the woodwork and simply materialized to begin their duties for the day. Fires were stoked, curtains were drawn, and an elaborate tray with delicious breakfast foods and steaming tea was delivered to the sitting room adjoining Theodore's bedchamber.

Lola looked down at the oversized banyan she'd selected from Theodore's dressing room and clenched her eyes shut with an inconvenient reality.

"I have nothing else to wear aside from my evening gown," she said, replacing her tea cup on the saucer. "I need to go home."

"I can see how that might present a problem," he murmured. "Although I have no complaint about your present attire."

"Somehow, I knew you would say that." She hummed a little sound of amusement. "What time are we expected at Margaret's this evening?"

"Dinner is at seven," he replied. "I'll have my carriage return you to your home as soon as you're ready to leave. I'm sending an additional tiger with you."

"That isn't necessary," she objected, not wanting to inconvenience anyone. "It's midday and—"

"*I* haven't forgotten that someone held a knife to your back and threatened you, even if you have. Just because it's been quiet of late doesn't mean it will stay that way and I'm not willing to take a chance with your safety," he stated firmly.

"I suppose you're right," she said as she placed her napkin on the table and stood. "I'll get dressed now."

"If you must." He smiled across the tea tray. "And I want you to know I'm already looking forward to seeing you this evening."

"You really shouldn't say things like that."

"Whyever not?" He asked.

"It causes all kinds of fluttering inside me," she confessed. "And I find I can't think straight for hours afterward."

"Then maybe you should take to bed immediately and lie down?" he said with a roguish grin.

"You're incorrigible!" She let out a playful squeal as she evaded his grasp and made for the bedchamber. "I'm getting dressed now."

"Yes, you did mention that," he called after her, matching her laughter.

When she reached the boarding house, it was still raining steadily. A part of her had wished the weather would clear. She wasn't altogether comfortable with the idea of a dinner party at Margaret's house. Yet at the same time she knew if she was going to become part of Theodore's world, she needed to meet his friends. So much had happened in the past few days, both pleasurable and elucidating, she couldn't help but feel overwhelmed by the pace of things.

She leaned against the wall and closed her eyes, recalling how they'd made love through the night. She'd never felt closer to someone, as if he understood her without words, in a far more important manner than their physical relationship.

She sighed, basking in the blissful feeling until the reality of her situation invaded once again. Unless things were resolved with the Duke of Leinster, she would never be free to love Theodore the way he deserved. She hadn't returned to Ipswich since she'd left two years ago. Perhaps it was time. But what would that accomplish? If she suddenly appeared, the magistrate would enforce the court order and take her into custody.

A light knock interrupted her thoughts and she was happy to abandon them. She unhooked the latch and opened the door to see Sofia on the other side. Her friend rushed in with a knowing smile on her face.

"I think the earl liked your new chemise. You were gone all night," Sofia said in a sing-song voice. "*Dio mio.* You're glowing."

"No, I'm not," Lola insisted, though her laughter ruined her attempt at indignation. "We did have a very nice time though."

"Nice?" Sofia scoffed. "That's not the face of someone who had a *nice* evening. Look in the mirror, *bellissima*. You are in love. Very much in love."

"I am in love with Theodore," Lola said, the words settling in her heart.

"And I'm happy for you," Sofia said. "Will he help you solve the terrible problem with the duke?"

"We didn't talk about that," Lola said solemnly and hurriedly changed the subject. "We're going to a dinner party this evening."

"That's wonderful. You'll meet his friends and they'll want to get to know you," Sofia continued, excited by the idea.

"Yes, that's what has me most worried."

"But you will have your earl beside you. You needn't bother your head about it. He will take care of you," Sofia assured her. "Besides I'm worrying enough for both of us. I did something yesterday while you were gone."

Lola looked at her friend's conflicted expression and hoped what she suspected was true. "Did you write your letter?"

"Yes," Sofia said in a careful whisper. "I did, and I sent it by post."

"Did you ask him to send his response to my address?" Lola asked, feeling encouraged Sofia had finally made a decision.

"I did." Sofia took a deep breath. "Though I suppose now all I can do is wait and time will reveal what will happen next."

"I have a good feeling about this, Sofia," Lola said. "You were the one who told me the only way to move forward was to make peace with the past."

"Did I say that? Sometimes I surprise myself," Sofia said as she stepped toward the bedroom. "Come. Let's choose what you'll wear for the dinner party later. How lucky we are that it's raining and we won't have to go to Vauxhall tonight."

THEODORE RANG FOR WYNDHAM, CURIOUS IF HIS MAN-of-all-things had learned anything in regard to Viscount Sidmouth. Tonight, Theodore would share dinner with the gentleman and he'd rather be prepared with dependable information before meeting Margaret's betrothed in person.

"Good morning, my lord." Wyndham entered the study and stood before the desk.

"Thank you for your flawless arrangements concerning my plans last night," Theodore said. "Everything went smoothly."

"Very good." Wyndham nodded. "As you requested, I inquired about Viscount Sidmouth and have information to share in his regard."

"Excellent. What have you learned?"

"According to reliable staff, Lord Sidmouth is a mild-mannered sort who keeps respectable hours, visits his parents regularly, and maintains a tidy budget. He belongs to White's though he rarely spends time there. I was told the viscount is very fond of Lady Margaret and speaks of her highly, anxiously anticipating their upcoming nuptials," Wyndham finished.

"He sounds the ideal gentleman. I sincerely hope that proves true," Theodore said, knowing Margaret would want a husband who was easily managed after her unpleasant experience with Baron Mowbray. "Thank you, Wyndham, your assistance with this matter is greatly appreciated. That will be all for now."

Wyndham left but returned not five minutes later with the Earl of Huntington on his heels.

"Essex." Huntington entered the study and greeted Theodore with a hearty handshake. "I'm glad I caught you in house."

"Good to see you too, Huntington. To what do I owe this unexpected visit?" Theodore indicated the two armchairs beside the hearth and both men sat down.

"Do you recall me speaking of my interest in a particular young lady?" Huntington asked, a gleam lighting his eyes.

"How can I forget? You were calf-eyed at the club the other evening," Theodore replied wryly. "A bit like you are now."

"Right," Huntington said with a chuckle. "And you may also remember I mentioned that if the lovely lady granted me the honor of accepting my invitation, we might all have an outing together."

"Is there a reason for this elaborate retelling? There's no need to create suspense. I remember our conversation well," Theodore commented. "I even shared your suggestion with the special lady I plan to bring along."

"Capital! Everything is falling into place nicely," Huntington said, his exuberant reply loud in the otherwise quiet room. "Except the plans have changed slightly, so I'm here with the details."

Theodore raised his brows in a gesture meant to prompt Huntington to continue.

"We're all to attend Lord Prinn's masquerade ball this Saturday evening. I had Prinn add you to the invitation list now that you've returned to London."

"A ball?" Theodore said with less enthusiasm. "I thought you mentioned a countryside drive for our outing. A chance for us to relax, become acquainted, and take in nature. I hardly think a gathering in kind to Lord Prinn's extravagant entertaining sounds ideal. It doesn't lend itself to your initial intention."

"Oddly enough, it's does, in quite the opposite manner. Hear me out." Huntington popped out of his seat and paced before the fireplace. "My lady is newly arrived to London and anxious to partake of the Season's festivities, albeit she's feeling a little nervous. She's always dreamed of attending a fancy affair and Prinn's event couldn't be grander."

"Go on," Theodore said, willing to tolerate more of Huntington's convoluted explanation if in the end it made sense of the situation.

"Since the party is a masquerade, it offers all the advantages of jovial enjoyment without any of the uncomfortable pressure one might encounter in a smaller gathering," Huntington continued. "You and your lovely lady can dance the night away and only reveal your identities if you choose to do so. No one knows if you leave early."

"Or arrive late," Theodore said mostly to himself.

Lola performed Saturday night and afterward she'd need time to get ready. Huntington sat back down and fell silent, apparently allowing Theodore a few minutes to consider the idea. It was true Prinn's gathering would provide Lola a chance to become more comfortable in a large social setting within the ton, while at the same time offering her total anonymity.

He certainly liked the idea of her dressed to the nines. She looked beautiful in whatever she wore, but he could only image how breathtaking she would be in a decadent ballgown, her long silky hair arranged in an elegant style. He would surprise her with something pretty to wear around her neck. He didn't know what gemstone she preferred, but tonight at Margaret's dinner he planned to find out.

"What do you think?"

Huntington's impatience cut into Theodore's fantasy, forcing him to focus on the conversation again. "I like the idea."

"Prinn's masquerade is one of the most sought-after invitations of the season. Everyone who is anyone will be there," Huntington continued, committed to his persuasion.

"And by your logic, since we're *somebodies* we should attend?"

"Indeed!" Huntington replied with a wag of his head.

"Then I suppose it's decided," Theodore said. "But I'll be arriving late on Saturday so let's plan to meet in the foyer at midnight. With everyone masked, it will be impossible to find you in the crush otherwise and I'd very much like you to meet the lady on my arm."

"Brilliant idea," Huntington said as he aimed for the door. "Until Saturday, Essex."

Huntington left and Theodore strode to the window, the rain reduced to a steady drizzle now. He hoped Lola would embrace the idea of attending Lord Prinn's masquerade ball. Huntington was correct in mentioning it offered both ladies a chance to experience the thrill of an extravagant event without giving a thought to witty conversation and censure by the ton.

But for now, he would focus on Margaret's dinner invitation. With any luck, Viscount Sidmouth would prove as charming as Wyndham had reported and at last, one of the concerns occupying Theodore's mind could be put to rest.

Twenty-Five

L ola grasped Theodore's hand as she exited the carriage, careful to stay beneath the umbrella Jenkins held over head. Once inside, she was relieved to see Margaret's warm smile as they were welcomed in the foyer. Lola had worried over how she'd be received, even though Theodore had assured her they would all enjoy a pleasant evening together.

Holding tight to his elbow, she walked with him into the sitting room where the window casements remained draped in black crepe and a mourning wreath hung over the fireplace. Viscount Fremont's passing was a reminder of the strange path which brought her to this moment, yet the mood inside the room was light. Introductions were made all around and while the two men shook hands Margaret scurried to Lola's side.

"Hello Miss York," Margaret said. "It's nice to see you again."

"Thank you," Lola said sincerely. "Please call me Lola. I hope we'll be able to become friends."

"I do as well," Margaret replied. "So much has happened lately, an informal visit like this is exactly what I need."

With conversation off to a smooth start, the evening proved to be as amiable as Theodore promised, and soon they were all engrossed in convivial chatter around the dinner table.

"I can't imagine balancing on a tightrope, Lola," Viscount Sidmouth said, his eyes bright with interest. "Surely there must be a trick you employ so you won't fall."

"I wish there was," she said, placing her fork on the edge of her plate. "But I've only my concentration to keep me company when I'm up there above the crowd."

"She's magnificent. You must see her," Theodore boasted. "Once it's acceptable for Margaret to return to a social schedule, we'll plan a splendid evening at Vauxhall."

The pride in Theodore's voice warmed Lola from the inside out.

"Yes," Margaret agreed cheerfully, "and Colin and I will finally be able to go ahead with our wedding plans. If only Stephen was here. Then all would be right."

"Stephen would have been proud to escort you down the aisle," Theodore said, his tone sincere. "Hopefully by next year when your wedding day has arrived, Bow Street will have apprehended the man responsible and you'll be able to carry your brother's memory with peace in your heart."

"I wish we could find Stephen's journal and hurry along the process," Margaret lamented, her irritation evident. "You searched his study and bedchambers twice. Where would he have put it?"

"A journal?" Sidmouth asked, a wary look on his face. "What are you talking about?"

Lola watched the young gentleman go pale before her eyes, but Margaret was too busy taking out her frustration on her mutton steak to notice.

"My brother kept a journal. His valet, Timmons, said Stephen wrote in it daily. Theodore and I believe that if we can find the journal and read the last few entries, perhaps—" Margaret's fork and knife clattered to her plate when she finally glanced in her betrothed's direction. "Colin! What's the matter? You look dreadful. Are you ill?"

Viscount Sidmouth shifted his attention from one person to the next before he cleared his throat, removed his napkin from his lap, and pushed his chair back from the table. He stood and took several deep breaths in a row.

"Margaret," Sidmouth's voice sounded strained.

"What is it, Colin? Just tell me already." Margaret rose now too.

Theodore reached beneath the tablecloth and squeezed Lola's hand in reassurance. They both waited silently as the scene on the other side of the table unfolded.

"I wasn't aware you were looking for your brother's journal," Sidmouth said, his voice somewhat recovered.

"I didn't mention it to you because it wasn't of your concern," Margaret replied as she walked to his side. "Do you know what happened to it?"

"I do," Sidmouth said, his brow creased with worry. "I hid it."

"What?" Margaret asked with disbelief in her voice. "You hid it?"

"What do you mean you hid it?" Theodore asked as he stood from the table now too. "You need to explain quickly, Sidmouth."

"I will." Sidmouth paused, his eyes shifting from Margaret to Theodore and back again. "The day you asked me to speak to Stephen, the night before he was killed, I went to his study and we argued. Stephen was resistant to almost every idea I presented for the wedding and said he needed to reconsider the arrangement. We had an awful row and, not only did I feel as though I'd failed you, Margaret, but I knew I had destroyed any chance at having a strong relationship with your brother."

"Go on," Margaret insisted, hardly allowing him a breath.

"Having exchanged harsh words, I felt badly after I left the room, so I returned a short time later to see if I could make it right.

Stephen was seated at his desk writing in a brown leather book, his body angled away from the door, and he didn't look up when I entered. He must have assumed I was his valet because he only gestured in the air and said *Not now, Timmons. I'll be upstairs as soon as I finish writing in my journal. Close the doors on your way out.*"

"But you left right after," Margaret interjected, visibly confused. "You told me things went terribly wrong and you apologized and said you needed to go home."

"And that's what I did." Sidmouth swallowed thoughtfully. "But I couldn't bear for you to think poorly of me, Margaret. I assumed Stephen was recording his thoughts in his journal and, were you to ask him about the discussion, it would besmirch my character. I believed your brother intended to rescind his permission for me to marry you.

"Now when I reflect on it, I may not have been thinking clearly, my logic clouded by emotion because I love you, Margaret, deeply, and I didn't want your brother's opinion to interfere with our future. At the same time, I would never purposely cause disharmony in your family."

"That's all well and good, Sidmouth, but you haven't finished explaining what happened to the journal. Did you take it and put it away somewhere?" Theodore asked sternly.

"The day after we learned of your brother's death, when I was here comforting you, I returned to the study." Sidmouth looked sheepishly at Margaret now. "I told you I needed to use the necessary, but the truth is I went back and found Stephen's leather journal on his desk. It was locked and there was no key, but I still worried you would somehow read the contents, so I hid it. It never occurred to me Stephen might have written about a threat to his person or included details concerning the situation that brought him to Vauxhall. I was only thinking of us, Margaret, and our life together."

"Did you read my brother's journal?" Margaret asked, her voice high pitched with emotion.

"No. I swear to you, on my honor, I didn't read it. It was locked and I had no desire to learn the contents. I just didn't want you to find it and discover your brother was reconsidering his approval of our marriage."

"I'm upset and hurt you deceived me this way," Margaret said, her hand laid flat over her heart, though her words lacked conviction.

Lola looked at Theodore, knowing those same words had to have been alive in him when she'd confessed her real name and the circumstances for leaving Ipswich. Unaware of her attention, Theodore kept his eyes on Sidmouth. His jaw was held tight as if he barely restrained his temper.

"You must understand." Sidmouth took up Margaret's hand and kissed her palm gently. "I intended no harm. I had no way to know you were looking for your brother's journal. I only meant to remain a gentleman in good standing in your eyes. You own my heart. Please tell me you'll forgive me."

"Of course, I forgive you, Colin." Margaret breathed deeply, the two gazing into each other's eyes. "I couldn't think poorly of you. I was the person who insisted you speak to Stephen in the first place. I would never allow anyone to interfere with our relationship and I'm certain you misinterpreted my brother's attitude. Stephen was under great duress. It's another reason we so desperately want to find his journal."

"I'm sorry to interrupt," Theodore said, the sharp tone of his impatience running through the words. "You two can discuss whatever needs to be said later. Margaret may have forgiven you already, Sidmouth, but your honor is definitely in question with me. Now, show me where you hid Stephen's journal."

. . .

THEODORE FOLLOWED SIDMOUTH DOWN THE HALL TO Stephen's study, attempting to rein in his temper. The young viscount's decision to hide the journal was unconscionable, no matter how Sidmouth explained it away.

They entered the somber room and Sidmouth didn't say a word, moving to the far wall where he crouched down and reached behind a rosewood curio cabinet situated below one of the windows. When he stood, he held a brown leather book in his hand.

"Here it is," Sidmouth said, his grave tone indicative of his remorse as he extended the journal forward. "My apologies, Essex, I never meant any harm and realize now how shortsighted I became in my effort to remain in Margaret's good graces."

Theodore didn't reply, but took the journal, noting it was still tied and locked. So much heartache had occurred already, he was more concerned with reading the entries Stephen had recorded than admonishing Sidmouth like a disobedient child. Besides, he believed the viscount was as contrite as he appeared, having had to explain his poor decision. "Let's return to the ladies before we proceed."

They found Lola and Margaret in the sitting room, a tray of tea on the table between them although neither of them had poured a cup.

"I have Stephen's journal," Theodore said as he entered. "What would you like me to do, Margaret?"

"What do you mean?" she asked, clearly agitated as she stood and hurried to Sidmouth's side. "Colin didn't know we were looking for the book."

"I realize that now," Theodore said, advancing into the room further to stand beside Lola. "But I'm asking you because I want to know if you'd like to read the contents yourself, have me read it, or turn the journal over to Bow Street. It's your decision to make."

"I haven't the constitution to read it," Margaret said, shaking her head vigorously and reaching for Colin's hand. "But I don't want to wait for you to bring it to the Runners and for them to look through it either. I think you should read it and then tell me what it says. Is it unlocked?"

"No." Theodore looked down at the journal. "But when I first searched your brother's rooms there was a bronze key in his wardrobe chest. I think it may fit."

"Then please get it," Margaret said, hurriedly. "I can't bear all this uncertainty. Colin and I are going to take a stroll in the garden. I need some fresh air."

Theodore nodded as they left through the terrace doors. He looked at Lola where she remained seated by the tea tray. This evening hardly turned out like he'd anticipated and yet when she glanced up to meet his attention, he saw compassion and concern in her eyes.

Placing the journal atop the end table, he went to her. "Thank you for understanding."

"There's no reason to thank me. Go abovestairs and get that key." She pushed gently on his arm. "If what's written in that journal resolves all of your unanswered questions about Fremont's death, you shouldn't waste another minute."

He leaned in and kissed her quickly on the cheek before he left the room. Returning not five minutes later, he opened the lock and began paging through the journal.

"I'm going to step outside so I won't distract you," Lola said. "I know you must want to be alone."

"Quite the opposite," he said as he moved to sit on the chair beside her. "If you don't mind, I'd like you to stay. I have no idea what I'm going to find inside these pages and having you here by my side, well, it makes it better."

"Of course." She offered him a slight smile.

Exhaling thoroughly, he opened the journal, the only sound in the room the crackling logs in the firebox. However, the further he read the angrier he became until he stood up, unable to stay still any longer.

"Lola, would you please ask Margaret and the viscount to come inside?" He saw his sorrow reflected in her eyes. "She'll need to have the support of her friends when she hears what I have to share."

Twenty-Six

"What does it say? Does the journal explain what happened?" Margaret rushed in on Sidmouth's arm, her words breathless as if she'd run all the way back to the house. Lola entered behind her.

"I think you should sit, Margaret. Some of this information may come as a shock," Theodore said, his tone steady.

Sidmouth quickly guided Margaret to the divan where he sat beside her. Lola reclaimed her chair from earlier and once everyone was settled, Theodore began.

"Stephen was being forced to make payments in order to protect you from scandal, Margaret. He bled the family funds dry, sold off valuables, and liquidated investments in an attempt to keep the viscountcy solvent while also meeting the demands of these payments. His financial concerns were why he seemed so disagreeable about your wedding plans. He wanted to give you the special day you'd imagined, but had already run through your dowry and most of his savings. Worse yet, he had no way to explain any of this to you.

"At first, the payments were made to protect you from a ruined reputation, but eventually there was a threat of physical harm.

That's why Stephen made plans with you on the evening of his murder. He wanted you here, safely waiting for him in the house where no one could hurt you. That same night, he went to Vauxhall to confront the man extorting him and reveal that there would be no more payments because there was no more money. Stephen had nothing left to lose and, with no other recourse, intended to go to the authorities even though it would compromise his attempt to keep your reputation from harm. I believe he shared his intention to involve Bow Street and that's what led to his violent end."

Margaret remained quiet for several minutes after Theodore finished. She drew a shuddering breath and clasped Sidmouth's hands as tears streamed down her face. "He was protecting me the whole time? From whom? Who knew something that could damage my reputation?"

Theodore hesitated adding more grief to the situation but he knew Margaret would not be satisfied until she learned every detail. "I'm sorry to tell you it was Baron Mowbray who demanded money in exchange for his silence."

"What?" Margaret exclaimed, standing up in surprise. "He's the most vile, despicable person. How dare he do such a thing? I thought I was rid of him and instead he stopped bothering me about our past relationship so he could threaten my brother."

She sank back onto the divan and began sobbing. Sidmouth wrapped an arm around her shoulders and tried to comfort her.

"This is all my fault," Margaret cried, her voice filled with anguish. "I caused Stephen's death."

"No," Lola said in a sympathetic tone. "That's not true. You shouldn't blame yourself."

"Mowbray is a reprehensible person who will be punished. To threaten to disclose the details of your personal relationship is unforgivable," Theodore added emphatically.

"Stephen paid all that money and took all those risks to

prevent scandal because of my actions in the past," Margaret insisted. "I am to blame."

"Stephen wanted to protect you in every way. I imagine that's why he didn't tell you about any of this. I'm so sorry, Margaret," Theodore said. "I will bring your brother's journal to Bow Street but you must realize the same threat to your reputation still exists."

"That might not be true," Lola interjected. "If Mowbray's taken into custody and attempts to spin a tale, the journal and house ledger will prove he'd extorted money from Lord Fremont. It will appear Mowbray is fabricating a story to escape conviction, not the opposite, and his credibility would be stained far worse than any damage to Margaret's reputation."

"I'm prepared for whatever happens," Margaret said valiantly, though her voice wavered. "I'll soon be a happily married woman. His words can no longer hurt me and I will not have my brother die in vain."

The room fell silent after that, Margaret's vow a fitting sentiment to end their conversation.

FOR TWO DAYS AFTER MARGARET'S DINNER, LOLA AND Theodore didn't see each other. With the details of Fremont's murder explained, Bow Street arrested Baron Mowbray who was reported to be in a bad way, heavily in debt, and drowning his misery in liquor.

Lola knew Theodore must be busy, but she missed him and was relieved they had plans tonight to attend Lord Prinn's masquerade. She'd purchased an elegant ballgown and new silk slippers, while Sofia had offered to arrange Lola's hair in a sophisticated style. The anticipation of seeing Theodore's expression when she joined him in fine eveningwear was near overwhelming.

Now as she stood on the tightrope platform, she cleared her mind, determined to practice before her performance later. But just as she was about to step on the rope, she heard Marco's call from below.

"Can you come down?" He asked as he shielded his eyes and stared up at her. "Morland told me what happened in the Pleasure Gardens."

She already knew what had happened, but climbed down the ladder and walked over to Marco anyway.

"You needn't worry about the man who threatened you in the crowd. You're out of danger," he said. "The Runners caught the nob who caused the problem and he isn't going to walk free and get away with the crime. Finally, there will be some justice in the world."

"That's good to hear, because it was an awful tragedy," she said. "But not all noblemen are the same."

"So now that you're keeping company with Essex your entire perspective has changed?" Marco asked in an accusatory tone. "What about your past and how easily the duke manipulated circumstances to protect himself?"

"I haven't forgotten that, but I believe the capacity to cause someone pain has nothing to do with whether or not there's a title in front of his name." She fell quiet for a moment, not wanting to argue again.

"It must be difficult balancing between both worlds," he said, studying her while he spoke. "Even harder than walking a tightrope."

"What do you mean?"

"You're here performing one night and then you go off to some fancy event the next night. We're different people and that's a different world. It's one or the other. You can't have both."

"I don't see it that way," she said, her voice just as strong as his.

"How long do you think it will last?" Marco asked. "If you don't choose, he'll ask you to make a choice or worse he'll choose for you. You realize that, right?"

"I don't know," Lola answered honestly. "But I never said I wanted to work at Vauxhall forever."

"I remember," Marco said, most of the anger gone from his voice. "You found your way here out of necessity, nothing more."

Lola offered him a tight smile. "I'm sorry we've quarreled lately. I thought we could remain friends."

"We *are* friends," Marco said, his expression softening. "But he'll hurt you. Nobs always do. And I don't want that to happen to you." He cleared his throat before he continued. "Unless you're just with Essex so he can fix your family's problems with the duke. Then you should use the earl before he uses you."

"No, Marco, it's not like that," she snapped, unsure why she'd expected him to change his attitude or understand. "I'm with Lord Essex because I want to be with him."

"Then I was wrong. You're not out of danger yet," he said before he turned and walked away.

THEODORE EXAMINED THE PARURE SET INSIDE THE velvet box he held and imagined the sapphire and diamond necklace around Lola's neck, the earbobs dangling from her dainty lobes. She lived among the stars when she balanced on the tightrope. She should have a piece of the night sky sparkling against her skin.

He'd purchased the exquisite pieces earlier that afternoon, anxiously awaiting when he would escort Lola to Prinn's masquerade ball. Only two days had passed since he'd shared her company and yet he was restless and eager, checking the time and counting the hours until he would see her again.

His carriage rolled to a stop in front of her building and he placed the velvet box on the seat beside him. As he stepped out, the house door opened and Lola came into view at the top of the stairs. She smiled at him and the sight took his breath away.

She was dressed as decadently as any sophisticated lady of the ton, her dark hair done up to expose her lithe neck, her body swathed in rich honey-colored silk, and yet she possessed something no other woman did, something he couldn't explain.

"You look beautiful." He took her gloved hand in his as she descended the stairs. "You always do, but tonight..." He stopped talking, unable to find the words for what he wanted to express.

"Shall we go?" she asked, her eyes twinkling. "I'm sorry it's so late."

"Never mind about that," he said as he handed her up into the carriage. "It's more fashionable to arrive after the crush."

They settled on opposite seats and he saw her gaze flit to the black velvet case on the bench beside him.

"Do you have our masks?" she asked.

"I do, but before we leave, I have something to give you first." He picked up the jewelry case and handed it to her.

"What's this?" she asked, her delicate brows furrowed in question.

"Something I chose especially for you," he said.

"Another gift?" she asked in a whisper. "I'm overwhelmed."

"This masquerade is our first formal night out together and a special occasion to be remembered," he replied, his voice amused. "I wanted to surprise you."

She gasped when she opened the box, her eyes wide. "I've never seen anything so beautiful."

"I have," he murmured softly. "Every time I look at you."

She smoothed her gloved fingertip over the necklace, touching the circle of gemstones reverently.

"It's not meant to stay in the box," he said as he gently reclaimed the jewelry case. "Allow me to help you."

"Thank you, Theodore." Her voice was an awed whisper. "I don't know what else to say."

"Then you like it?" he asked.

"How could I not? It's the loveliest thing I've ever seen."

"It reminded me of you walking amid the starlight, dazzling everyone against the velvet night sky."

She smiled up at him and he handed her the ear bobs before he reached forward to clasp the gems around her neck. She turned on the bench and he couldn't stop from pressing a kiss to her nape before he fastened the necklace in place. She turned back around and all he could manage was a single word. "Perfect."

She reached up and touched the necklace, her eyes never leaving his. He rapped on the roof and the carriage began to move.

"I've looked forward to seeing you all day," she said, a smile playing on her lips.

"As have I," he admitted.

"You look every part the dashing and distinguished gentleman tonight." Her eyes took him in from cravat to polished Hessians. "I shall be the envy of every lady in the ballroom. It's serendipity we'll all be masked, so they won't know me any more than I'll know them."

"At least we'll know Huntington and meet his new acquaintance. They're to find us in the foyer at midnight. He's quite enamored and shared with me that the lady on his arm is new to London and excited to attend her first formal event."

"We have that in common."

"Huntington's not the only one who's enamored," Theodore murmured as he gazed across the carriage.

"Is that so?" Lola said as her eyes met his and held. "I may have fallen victim to a similar condition myself."

No, that wasn't true. She wasn't enamored or smitten. She'd fallen head over heels in love, but that confession was locked in her heart. Because even knowing her past, Theodore spoke about the future as though their relationship would follow a natural course and that was impossible. How could she embrace that same optimism knowing she still had difficult problems to solve? Problems that would ultimately destroy their relationship. Marco was correct when he'd said there'd be a grim choice to make, except it wouldn't be whether or not to work at Vauxhall.

Not wanting to ruin the thrilling evening ahead, she silenced these misgivings. Her body hummed with anticipation at the thought of waltzing with Theodore beneath countless candlelit chandeliers, the orchestra's wistful melody in the background. She was sincerely touched by his overwhelming gift. Every time their eyes met, promises were made, not just for dancing and conversation, but for later tonight when they returned to his home. Her pulse kicked up at the idea of returning to his bed.

Fate must have taken pity on her because the carriage slowed to a crawl as it joined the procession of conveyances on the gravel drive of Lord Prinn's estate. They would exit soon and needed to prepare.

"Let's not forget our masks," she said, excitement chasing away any lingering doubt.

Theodore lifted the bench and reached inside the storage compartment hidden below to remove a small bag. He took out her disguise first, a delightful Columbina half mask decorated with gold filigree against a white silk background. The ornate detail and satin ribbons would complement her gown perfectly. His mask was of the same style and sewn from black velvet with similar trim, the two designs made to be worn together.

A sense of intimacy filled the interior as they took turns tying the ribbons for each other. She'd removed her gloves to do the task and Theodore's hair was silky soft as it brushed against her skin. Filled with desire, the night was becoming increasingly more magical.

When they stepped from the carriage, the lantern-lit walkway overflowed with guests in all variations of disguise from full mask to narrow domino with matching cloak. A prickle of awareness skittered through her; the sensation not altogether welcome. The Duke of Leinster could stand beside her during the event and she would never know. Although, her appearance would be just as much a mystery.

"Are you ready?"

Theodore's rich voice beside her ear calmed her nerves. She grasped his arm tighter and they entered the grand event. The sight before her was like nothing she'd ever experienced. When she lived in Ipswich, the Duke of Leinster didn't entertain at his country seat aside from an annual St. Michael's Day gathering which included everyone from stable hand to family member.

Here, in the foyer of Lord Prinn's estate, Lola believed she'd entered another world in all its grandeur. Large floral arrangements and swags of greenery decorated every surface from column to cornice. Candelabras and crystal lanterns reflected golden light throughout, while the beckoning melody of the orchestra could be heard just beyond the busy entryway.

"Let's dance," Theodore said, his fingers clasping hers where they rested on his elbow. "I've already waited too long to waltz with you."

He smiled down at her and her heart thudded, a flush of contentment and adoration settling soul-deep. She had to find a way to resolve her future because the thought of saying goodbye to Theodore was no longer a logical decision. She'd never survive the heartbreak of losing him. With that solitary thought, she stepped onto the dance floor and into his arms.

Twenty-Seven

Lola floated across the tiles as Theodore led her through the waltz, his mastery of the steps as accomplished and elegant as everything else she'd learned about his life. Whenever she glanced upward, he matched her gaze. The emotion she saw in his eyes made her feel as though they, alone, occupied the dance-floor. Yet the ballroom was crowded with guests, uninhibited by their masks and engrossed in flirtatious conversation as they sipped champagne.

"Would you be comfortable in this world, Lola?" Theodore swept her through another turn, the dance step adding to the dizzying perplexity of his inquiry.

As if he'd read her mind and peeked into her heart, he had asked the same question she'd considered too often.

"Yes," she said a beat later. "With you beside me, I believe I can do anything."

He smiled as the music faded, their lovely waltz at an end.

"Let's take some air. It's nearly midnight and we're due to meet Huntington soon." He offered his arm and they made their way outside through the rear doors of the ballroom.

A polished stone terrace extended around the perimeter of the estate and continued down a flight of stairs into a neatly mani-cured garden decorated with tall stem silver candelabras and an assortment of ornately shaped topiaries. Lola breathed in the refreshing air, happy to escape the noisy ballroom for a few minutes. When they paused beside a large urn overflowing with fragrant lace-cap hydrangea, she wondered if Theodore had brought her outside to steal a kiss, surprised when he reached up and untied the ribbons of her mask instead.

"What's wrong?" she asked, startled by his actions even though they stood alone.

"Nothing at all," he said as he removed his mask next and set them both atop a nearby podium. "But there's something I've wanted to tell you and I'd rather we were unmasked when I do."

A spark of panic passed through her. They'd just enjoyed the most romantic waltz. He couldn't possibly intend to share bad news.

Nevertheless, doubt crept in and, as she stared up at him, she wondered if this was the moment she'd worried about, when he reconsidered their relationship or told her he no longer saw a future for them together because they were far too different. In the span of a single heartbeat, every fear she'd worked at keeping locked away threatened to take hold.

"I've been waiting for the right moment, a perfect moment, to tell you something," he said, his voice low and serious as he touched a gloved finger beneath her chin and tilted her face higher. "But I've come to realize there is never going to be the perfect moment, because every moment I spend with you is equally as precious. They're all perfect moments."

"Oh, Theodore." She sighed, relief sweeping through her, followed by the warmth of his affection. She needed to tell him she felt the same. He should know all the love she kept in her heart.

"When I returned to London I came home, but only in the most fundamental sense of the word. At least that's how it appeared until events brought us together. Then it seemed incredibly important I was exactly where I should be. Since meeting you, my heart has insisted I take notice and when I did, my life changed. I know our relationship hasn't followed a predictable courtship, but that doesn't matter to me. I've fallen in love with you, Lola."

"Theodore..." she said in a hushed voice as she reached up and placed her hand along his jaw. "If you've spent any time wondering about my feelings, then I regret not sharing them sooner. I love you, Theodore. I want you to know. I want the whole world to know!"

He didn't say another word as he gathered her into his embrace, their kiss at first tender and reverent, then heated and passionate. When they finally broke apart, the air practically vibrated with expectation.

Still wrapped tightly in his arms, she pressed her cheek against his chest. "I can't help but—"

"No." He stopped her from saying what remained in the way of their future happiness. "We'll find a way to solve that problem. Just not tonight."

"You're right. We're here together at this wonderful event and we should enjoy every minute." She withdrew and picked up their masks. "Let's return inside. I'd like us to waltz again if it isn't too close to midnight."

"Before or after we meet with Huntington, I promise we'll dance the night away," he said as he finished tying the ribbons of her mask, his mouth lingering beside her ear. "And I also want the whole world to know about us."

So much happiness welled inside she couldn't stop smiling, her emotions as effervescent as the bubbles in her champagne glass. She finished tying the ribbons of his mask and they linked hands as they left the garden.

THEODORE ESCORTED LOLA THROUGH THE BALLROOM doors eager to dance and at the same time, wanting to hurry her to the carriage so they could return to his home and make love.

However, the choice was taken from him. The dinner chime rang signaling the midnight hour. Knowing Huntington would be waiting, Theodore maneuvered them forward while most of the other revelers moved in the opposite direction toward the dining room. Perhaps the foyer would be relatively empty making Huntington somewhat easier to find.

A few minutes later, the flow of guests in the hallway came to a standstill, the crush holding them captive. Theodore laid his hand over Lola's fingers on his arm, locking her safely to his side. Directly in front of them, a tall gentleman faced them. He too had been forced to stop. He wore a black oval mask that covered his entire face aside from two narrow eye holes. The disguise lent him a sinister appearance not at all in keeping with the jovial affair and Theodore didn't like how the man's attention was focused solely on Lola. She definitely noticed. Her body tensed beside him and he squeezed her fingers hoping to reassure her.

"Only a few more minutes, darling." His words drew her attention and she hugged his arm in response.

At last, the crowd shifted and guests moved more freely. The masked man brushed by, but Theodore knew Lola was unsettled.

"Let's not imagine things," he said as he leaned closer.

She looked up at him and gave a little nod. "Yes, there's no reason to start seeing ghosts."

They moved into the foyer and he was relieved to see only a few people lingered. Huntington was easily discerned since he gestured at them as soon as they walked forward.

"How did you know who I was?" Theodore asked as they approached the alcove where his friend waited. "We're all wearing masks that conceal our identities."

"I've waved at every couple that's come through since

midnight," Huntington replied, a note of humor in his voice. "And you're the first to walk over and join me."

Huntington's remark caused Lola to laugh but the lady beside Huntington gasped at hearing her and took a step back.

"Is something amiss?" Huntington asked his companion.

"No." The woman shook her head, her dark hair falling gently over the edges of her mask.

"Let's make haste with introductions, Essex," Huntington said. "The ladies know who we are, but they haven't been properly acquainted and there's too much fun to be had."

"Of course,," Theodore said. "My apologies. May I present the lovely Miss York."

AWARENESS PRICKLED OVER LOLA'S SKIN AS Huntington and his companion smiled in greeting.

"So very nice to meet you, Miss York," Huntington said.

"Your gown is quite beautiful," the lady added.

That same sense of revelation made Lola lean closer. "There's no reason to be so formal. Please call me—"

"Lola?"

"Anna?"

"What the devil!" Huntington exclaimed. "You know each other?"

"Yes!" Lola reached up and removed her mask. "Anna, is that you?"

"Yes!" Anna exclaimed as she did the same. "How can this be true?"

"What are you doing in London?" They both asked at the same time before they embraced each other tightly, their laughter filling the alcove where they were tucked away.

After a moment Lola pulled back to look at her sister again. "I'm shocked and surprised and so very happy to see you, Anna."

Tears clogged her throat and she pressed her hand to her chest, reeling from the shock.

"Thank goodness, you're well and safe and... you look beautiful!" Anna said, excitement in every word.

"I am well and safe," Lola said. "I live here in London now. How is it you're here?"

"Mother and Father thought it would be good for me to have a change of scenery," Anna explained. "I haven't been myself since you left."

"I'm truly sorry to have caused so much distress," Lola said in a sincere tone not wanting to go into the details. She turned to Theodore, her smile reappearing. "This is my sister, Anna. Can you believe this is happening?"

"I'm not sure I understand *what's* happening," Huntington said, his expression conflicted. "Will someone please explain?"

"My sister and I haven't seen each other since I left Ipswich two years ago. Finding her here accidently is a wonderful surprise and makes this evening all the more perfect." She glanced at Theodore again, the reference to their confession in the garden not lost as their eyes met and held.

"Lola left quite suddenly," Anna added, in hope of clarifying things for Huntington.

"But then who is Miss York?" Huntington asked. "If you're sisters and your surname is Morgan, I don't understand."

"My family name is Morgan," Lola clarified. "I took the name York when I arrived in London, but that's a rather long story better left for another day."

"I see," Huntington said, though his expression conveyed the opposite.

"I'll explain things later," Theodore said to reassure his friend.

"How are Mother and Father?" Lola asked. "Are they here in London with you?"

"No, they're not, but they're doing well. Of course, they miss you as much as I," Anna said. "I'm staying with the Dunbury family. Father recently trained a horse for Mr. Dunbury and he mentioned how his daughter wished to attend some of the Season's events. Even with her older brother serving as chaperone, he wanted his daughter to have a female companion. Things progressed rather smoothly thereafter and I arrived three weeks ago."

"Thank goodness for that," Huntington said with adoration in his voice. "Otherwise, I would have never met your delightful sister."

Lola noticed how Anna looked at Huntington with stars in her eyes. It would appear they were both equally smitten.

"Anna?" Lola said as she reached for Theodore's hand and tugged him forward. "Lord Essex and I plan to dance the night away. Would you and Lord Huntington care to join us?"

"Of course," Anna said as she gathered the ribbons of her mask. "As soon as we put each other back together, you must lead the way."

THE CLOCK ON THE MANTEL READ HALF THREE WHEN Theodore and Lola returned to his town house. They'd talked for the entire ride home reliving the excitement and joy of the evening, but now a quiet wonder held them captive. Once upstairs, Theodore tended the fire while she slipped off her shoes and walked to the large window to look out at the stars. How had so many wonderful changes happened so quickly? She'd reunited with her sister, confessed her love to a devastatingly handsome earl, and was about to climb into bed with said earl and share a passionate night of pleasure.

As if an illusion come to life, Theodore approached from behind, his reflection in the windowpane adding to the evening's enchantment. He'd removed his cravat and his shirt gaped open, a shadow of whiskers darkening his jaw. Her skin heated with a flush of desire and she brought her hand up, her fingers settling on the smooth cool gemstones where they rested at her collarbones.

"This necklace is so beautiful I don't want to take it off."

"Then don't," he suggested wickedly as he turned her and led her away from the window. "Leave the jewels on and come to bed. I want to make love to you in nothing but sapphires and diamonds."

"I love you, Theodore," she said as he diligently loosened ribbons, unfastened buttons and removed her clothing. "I never believed I could be this happy," she added, her voice hushed and dreamy.

He discarded his clothes and boots next and they kissed their way onto the covers. She laid back against the sheets, her skin hot against the cool silk. She welcomed the heated press of his body against hers as he moved over her, his weight supported on his strong arms.

Their lovemaking could have been anxious, fervent and demanding, but instead he kissed her tenderly, trailing endless caresses against her cheek, neck and breasts, teasing with his tongue and teeth, her body responding to his promise of pleasure. She could feel his hot, hard erection against her inner thigh and sensed how he struggled to restrain his desire.

When she didn't think she could wait any longer to feel him inside her, he looked into her eyes, his heart bared for her to see. With one firm stroke he entered her, sliding deep, filling her completely. She cried out, overwhelmed with pleasure, the sensation intense.

"Please, Theodore," she said, her voice a trembling rasp.

The exquisite sound of their lovemaking soon replaced the quiet as their rhythm grew feverish. She ached for him every time he withdrew, gasping with pleasure when he filled her again. Still, she yearned desperately for what seemed just beyond reach.

He stared down at her and his eyes glistened. She blinked through her own emotion as she looked up at him.

"I love you, Lola." His voice was husky, almost broken. "Tonight, and always."

She wanted to reply, to tell him the same, but pleasure rolled over her at hearing his words, the intensity too much to bear. She only managed his name as she closed her eyes and surrendered to sensual bliss.

Twenty-Eight

Theodore sat behind his desk with a pile of correspondence spread before him. Letter after letter stated a similar version of the same disappointing facts. Removing his spectacles, he rubbed his eyes before he stood up and walked to the window.

Lola planned to spend the day with her sister before performing at Vauxhall this evening so he wouldn't see her today. He'd told himself the time apart would allow him to focus on diffusing the situation with the Duke of Leinster and yet he was unable to concentrate, his thoughts at odds. He glanced over his shoulder at the papers on his desk.

He'd contacted his solicitor, a knowledgeable, trustworthy lawyer who facilitated Theodore's investments and business dealings. He'd also written to respected members within the House of Lords, an influential archbishop, two competent barristers and a magistrate known for his openminded political principles. Keeping the information as discreet as possible, Theodore had explained the dilemma and requested advisement. Each of the gentlemen had written a lengthy reply. Unfortunately, they'd all stated the same result. Lola had no recourse. The criminal charges would stand because, with the exception of the Prince Regent, Leinster's word overruled everyone else's.

Complicating the matter, Theodore had unknowingly angered the duke at Tattersall's and that likely eliminated any chance of a civil conversation were he to visit His Grace. The situation seemed impossible and yet without a resolution, Lola would always live in fear of detection. She deserved a better life than one that forced her to walk the fine line between secrecy and discovery whenever she went out in public.

"My lord?"

Theodore turned to where Wyndham stood in the door frame. "Yes?"

"Lord Huntington has arrived. I had him wait in the drawing room."

"Thank you. You may send him here to my study," Theodore said, flexing his shoulders to ease the tension tightening his muscles.

A few minutes later, his friend whisked through the door with his usual jovial greeting.

"Essex, what has you looking glum this fine morning?"

"Everything," Theodore groused. "I'm so bloody frustrated I can't think straight."

"What's wrong?" Huntington's grin disappeared and his voice became serious. "How can I help?"

"Do you remember last evening when I said I'd explain why Lola's last name differed from her sister's?"

"Of course." Huntington took a seat in front of the desk, his attention on Theodore where he remained near the window.

"I know I can trust you, but it bears reminding what I'm about to share must be kept in utmost confidence," Theodore said.

"Absolutely. You have my word," Huntington replied without pause.

After he explained the situation, Huntington appeared equally confounded.

"What are you going to do?" his friend asked once the silence became unbearable.

"I don't know." Theodore wiped his palm down his face, exhaling his frustration. "Perhaps we'll move to America. I have several thriving investment ventures there. We could create our own life away from High Society."

Huntington's sharp laugh resounded in the room until he turned in Theodore's direction.

"Good God, you're serious?" Huntington asked, his brows high with surprise. "You've just returned to London and Lola's lived without her family for two years. She's reunited with Anna now. You can't leave."

"I don't want to leave, but I'm starting to believe we have no other choice." Theodore dropped into the leather chair behind his desk. "What kind of existence will Lola have if she's always worried someone will recognize her? Worse yet, what if we attend an affair and she comes face to face with that bastard Leinster? Neither one of us wants to keep our relationship a secret. I plan on asking Lola to be my wife, but I love her too much to condemn her to a life of subterfuge once we marry."

Huntington didn't say anything for several minutes.

"Well?" Theodore asked, impatient for any guidance his friend could offer.

"I'm sorry." Huntington frowned. "I haven't a single suggestion to help you. I'm worthless in your time of need."

"I wouldn't go that far," Theodore replied. "Pour us some brandy and we'll discuss it further because I'm not giving up until I find a way to save the woman I love."

LOLA LOOPED HER ARM THROUGH HER SISTER'S AS THEY strolled along the promenade within St. James's Park. They'd chattered incessantly the entire morning, reliving the past two years and describing the events they'd experienced leading up to their unexpected reunion last night.

"My heart aches for you," Anna said sympathetically. "You've been through so much."

"It's been difficult, but I've managed," Lola said with a slight frown. "Theodore also suffered a loss."

"Yes, what happened to his friend was horrible," Anna said, her voice a concerned whisper. "There's been so much grief."

Lola drew a cleansing breath and tried to brighten their conversation. "That's true, but it did bring Theodore and me together. I would never have met him otherwise, which means I would never have attended last evening's masquerade and thereby—"

"Wouldn't be walking with *me* now," Anna finished more cheerfully. "In that way something wonderful came out of all the sadness. Not just me seeing you again, but your relationship with Lord Essex."

Lola couldn't stop the smile that spread across her face. "I love him quite completely."

"I'm thrilled you've found each other, but what will you do?" Anna asked. "I can't imagine how your life is now, always looking over your shoulder and slipping into the shadows whenever you see a fancy carriage approach."

"Actually, I didn't venture far beyond Vauxhall Gardens or my neighborhood until Theodore came into my life," Lola continued as they took a turn leading into the flower gardens. "Everything seems different now. I'm not so sure performing is what I want to do anymore. I haven't mentioned any of this to Theodore yet, but I will once I'm certain it's the right decision for my future."

"I'm still in awe that you walk a tightrope. So much has happened so quickly."

"It has, but I'm ready to focus on my future," Lola added with a sense of surety.

"I know you love Lord Essex and you want to be together, but what will you do if..." Anna's voice trailed off as if saying the unthinkable aloud would cause the worst to happen.

"I know. You don't have to say it, because I've thought about it endlessly since I realized my feelings for Theodore. The situation with the Duke of Leinster will always be an obstacle in our path. The fact I wasn't born a proper lady already created a risk to his social standing and I would never harm Theodore's reputation or tarnish his heritage. At the same time, I don't want us to conceal our relationship or live some strange restrictive life. It all weighs heavily on my heart."

"I wish I had some wise advice to share or a solution to your problems," Anna said, pausing in their walk to clasp Lola's hands in her own. "I love you and want you to be happy."

"Thank you, Anna. Seeing you after all this time lifts my heart and reminds me that unforeseen miracles can occur when we least expect them. I want to believe this will be resolved in the end. But if by chance, my being with Theodore will cause him unhappiness or scandal, I'll walk away. I love him too much to hurt him in that manner."

"Oh, Lola." Anna's voice was a sad, hushed whisper. "There has to be something we can do. What if you went to the duke and apologized? It can't look very well for him to be involved in litigation. I know you would have to swallow your pride to appease his, but if your apology convinced him to drop the charges, wouldn't it be worth it? To be able to go ahead with your future and stay with Theodore without worry of exposure?"

"The duke is a despicable person. He's arrogant, quick-tempered and unpredictable in his moods. I don't know if your idea would work. What if I went to him and instead of retracting the charges, he sent for the authorities and had me taken into custody immediately? I'd have nothing but regret then." Lola began to walk again, restless with her sister's suggestion. "Less of a future is better than no future at all."

"But what of your heartache?" Anna asked as they moved

further into the gardens. "Would you ever be able to be happy again without the earl by your side? You just told me you love him."

"With all my heart."

"Exactly," Anna said, huffing a breath of frustration. "Then we have to think of a solution to this problem. Nothing else will suffice."

THEODORE HANDED HIS CARD TO THE STOIC BUTLER who answered the door at the Duke of Leinster's residence. After talking with Huntington and settling on an idea, Theodore had decided to attempt a conversation with His Grace concerning the situation. While he couldn't outright acknowledge his relationship with Lola without inviting questions about her location, there wasn't any other course forward. Leinster possessed all the power at the moment.

"His Grace will see you shortly," the butler said when he returned to the foyer.

"Thank you," Theodore replied quickly. He'd expected to be turned away.

He was installed in the drawing room to wait where he stared at the fire and mentally reviewed his brief confrontation with the duke at Tattersall's, a predicament Leinster construed as vindictive, even though it was nothing of the kind. To ask for the duke's help as an honorable peer of the realm when the man was nothing of the sort was hypocrisy as its best.

"Lord Essex."

Leinster entered the room and advanced across the plush carpet soundlessly. He was a tall, thin man whose haughty demeanor was discernible in every aspect of his person.

"Thank you for taking time to see me, Your Grace," Theodore said. "I realize my visit is unexpected."

"Have you come to apologize for overbidding on that superior mare and ruining my afternoon at Tattersall's?" The duke stood a few strides away, his expression unreadable.

"My action wasn't meant in disrespect," Theodore said smoothly, not wanting to incite the man's temper.

"Wasn't it though?" Leinster replied. "Even though you became aware I wanted the horse, you continued to outbid me."

"Only because I, too, admire fine horseflesh."

Leinster didn't reply and cautious not to waste time, Theodore started to explain his reason for visiting.

"I'm here on behalf of a fellow gentleman and close friend, Braden Ulrich, Earl of Huntington."

"What is it Huntington needs that he's sent you instead of calling upon me directly? Such an act speaks poorly of his character," the duke said in a smug tone.

"Huntington doesn't know I've come," Theodore said, unwilling to allow Leinster to disparage his friend. If Theodore had any hope of meeting with success, every aspect of the conversation had to proceed correctly. "He's courting a young woman of whom you are acquainted. Her name is Anna Morgan."

The duke's expression hardened immediately. "I've cut ties with the Morgan family. You've wasted your time by coming here today." His Grace stepped closer, his eyes taking on a wily gleam. "Although I am interested if Anna knows the whereabouts of her sister Lola."

"I can't speak to that," Theodore answered, pleased he'd snagged the duke's interest enough to continue their conversation. "But the situation causes her family great distress."

"That is unfortunate. However, it was Lola who brought shame and hardship to her family when she released my prized stallion. She confessed to the crime and therefore should be punished, but instead in an act of cowardice, she ran away. In that, she's decided her fate. Separation from her family will have to serve as consequence for the time being."

"If the charges were dismissed, the family could reunite," Theodore stated matter-of-factly. "It would be a gracious gesture."

The duke barked a sharp laugh. "How tidy and simplistic you make it sound. Yet in life, we rarely have things happen exactly the way we'd like. For example, I would have liked to have won that auction."

Theodore swallowed thoughtfully, unsure how to continue. "I will gladly give you the horse if it changes your mind on this matter."

"A horse hardly makes amends for the situation," His Grace interrupted before Theodore finished speaking.

"It was my understanding you knew the family well and were fond of the Morgan sisters." Theodore pressed on.

"Which is what made it all the more disappointing when Lola betrayed me."

Anger, white hot and impatient, flowed through Theodore at hearing Lola's name said in the duke's bitter voice, yet he exhaled slowly, knowing the man before him measured his reaction. The duke had no intention of giving in. "What is it you want?"

"Justice, of course. Lola is a fugitive," His Grace said with a snide quirk of his mouth. "As a peer, it is my duty to oversee England's safety and withhold an upstanding reputation for the good of all people."

"You'd punish someone for a kind-hearted act? Lola meant you no harm and yet you'd ruin her life to keep up your appearance of respectability?"

"A kind-hearted act? So, at last we come to the point of this conversation," Leinster said.

"Which is?" Theodore asked, his words edged with anger.

"You care for her."

"I care about anyone who is being harmed or mistreated." The irony of that statement and how it mirrored Lola's feelings toward the horse the duke beat mercilessly bled through every syllable of his reply.

"Our conversation is over, Essex. There is nothing you can say to change my mind on the matter. You may see yourself out." Leinster strode toward the door without pause, but then he stopped and turned, gesturing in the air as if he'd just remembered something important. "Unless," he said, his head canted to the side as he looked directly straight on. "You agree to one stipulation."

"And what would that be, Your Grace?" Theodore ground out the words, struggling to keep hold of his temper.

Leinster exhaled, that same smug expression on his face as he replied. "You agree to break all ties with Lola Morgan. If you want me to retract the charges, you must give up the girl."

Twenty-Nine

L ola waited for the entire audience to file out of the grandstand before she climbed down from the tightrope platform. Spending the day with Anna had reminded her how much she missed her family, the emotional impact of her decision once again a fresh ache inside her. When she ran away and arrived in London two years ago, she'd worked diligently at burying her sadness, ignoring reminders of her previous life, but she couldn't pretend any longer. Decisions needed to be made and she had only herself to blame for their difficulty.

She'd acted foolishly, falling in love with Theodore while knowing their relationship would always be dictated by her past. Now she'd suffer the consequences for failing to protect her heart.

Struggling with these thoughts, she reached the bottom of the ladder, startled when Theodore appeared across the lawn. He was striking in the moonlight. She'd never become immune to his handsomeness.

"Theodore, what are you doing here?" she asked, her voice a mixture of excitement and confusion.

"I needed to speak to you and thought Vauxhall would be the

safest place. However ironic that sounds." He leaned in and pressed a kiss to her cheek. "I hope you're glad to see me."

"Yes, of course, I just wasn't expecting you. What do you mean by safest place?" she asked, immediately concerned. She glanced around the area but everything appeared in kind to any other evening.

"I spoke to the Duke of Leinster today."

"Oh." Her smile dropped away and she tugged on the knot of her shawl. Tonight, the shadows of her past insisted on being heard. "I wasn't expecting *that* either."

"We should walk in the Pleasure Garden. It will offer us privacy."

"It didn't go well, did it?" She grew impatient as she deciphered the emotion in his eyes. "Does he know where I am? Is he calling the authorities and that's why I'm no longer safe?"

"Slow down." He pulled her into his arms, unconcerned they stood out in the open. "I will never allow anyone or anything to harm you. I intended to speak to the duke as a fellow peer bound by the gentleman's code, but His Grace wasn't interested in decorum."

"I thought we'd already established that," she murmured as she relished the warmth of his coat against her cheek. Still her pulse raced, knowing there was more to be told.

"I'll explain everything once we're away from prying eyes and interruptions." He released her and together they moved beyond the grandstand.

A complex tangle of anger and relief settled in her stomach. She'd never asked Theodore to confront the duke because it was her problem to solve, *an impossible problem,* and yet knowing he'd initiated the discussion because he wanted to find a resolution soothed her heartache.

They entered the Pleasure Paths and walked on until they were certain they couldn't be overheard. Mentally preparing herself for whatever he was about to share, she gasped in surprise when the first thing he did was tuck her into his embrace and kiss her soundly. Her body heated from the inside out. She'd never become immune to his kisses either.

"I'm trying to find a way forward for us," he said as their kiss ended. "It's proving more difficult than I anticipated."

"That's because we've only viewed the future through our hearts," she said softly. "I knew I shouldn't fall in love with you and I did anyway. To spare you future pain, the smartest thing to do would be to leave you."

"Don't say that." He shook her gently, his voice firm.

"But it's the truth, isn't it?" she said even though the words cost her. "If we stay together, we can never go out in public because your reputation will suffer."

"I've told you before, I don't care about gossip and scandal," he scoffed. "Or the perception of narrowminded people."

"But you will when we're not welcome anywhere, when you see how people stare at us or talk poorly of me. It will anger you, because you'll want to protect me, but you won't be able to. And I'll suffer for it, not by the words they say because I also care little for gossip, but by seeing you upset. Eventually it will come between us and ruin what we have. I can't knowingly bring unpleasantness into your life. I love you too much to make that choice. How reckless of us to have ignored the truth."

He released her and strode to the other side of the path and back again. "We can travel to America."

His words held such resolute determination she almost smiled.

"And you'd give up your life here? As a peer of the realm? You've only just returned to London."

"Yes, but nothing binds me to England so much that I can't explore the world," he said without hesitation. "We can build our life in a new place. Americans are more openminded and accepting of change. They create their own traditions rather than depend on history to dictate the future."

"I take it then the duke offered no kindness."

"I didn't expect him to be kind, just reasonable," Theodore said. "But he's a vitriolic man who enjoys causing people and animals unnecessary pain. Once he realized I care for you, he took a perverse satisfaction in the knowledge. After I left, I didn't know if he'd have me watched or employ someone to follow me. That's why I came here tonight rather than the boarding house. It was a precaution in case he'd taken intrusive action. I didn't want to lead him straight to you."

"He's not to be underestimated," she said in a sad whisper. "I actually thought he'd be harsher than what you've shared."

"He was," Theodore said angrily as he pulled her back into his embrace. "Leinster offered to retract the charges, but only if I stopped seeing you."

"What?" Was there no end to the duke's cruelty? She was filled with the sickening feeling of loss and vulnerability. "What did you say?"

"I walked out. Had I stayed, his solicitor would be pursuing charges against me for assaulting *His Grace*."

She paused, but only for the slightest breath. "It doesn't matter anyway, Theodore. Now that the duke knows you and I are together, he will carry out his threat as soon as I show my face in public."

"Miss York!"

Hearing her name, Lola spun toward the darkened path behind them, surprised when Sofia appeared.

"There you are! We need to hurry. We're running out of time," her friend said quickly.

"What are you talking about?" she asked, glancing between Theodore and Sofia.

"I've been looking for you," Sofia explained with a grimace. "When I saw Lord Essex arrive, I guessed you might have come in here to meet after your performance. But I didn't dare call out your name. We need to hurry because there's trouble. Morland spoke to some men tonight. They asked about you and Morland told them everything, where you live and when you'll be at Vauxhall. I think there are men going to the boarding house to wait for you. It isn't safe for you to go home."

"She'll come with me then." Theodore grasped her hand as if he worried she would run away.

"He'll send Bow Street to your home too, Theodore." Lola tugged her hand free and paced across the narrow width of the path. "I have to think for a minute."

"No," Sofia said. "There's no time."

"Come with me." Theodore gestured for them to follow as he moved farther into the close walks. He stopped when he came to the same place the broken branches in the hedgerow created a passage to the alleyway on the other side. The reminder of Fremont's murder added another layer of urgency to their actions.

"We can go out to Langley Lane and hail a hackney at the corner," he said calmly.

"But where will we go after that?" Lola asked. "If the duke has men here and at both our homes, nowhere is safe."

"I have an idea. I'll explain once we leave," Theodore reassured her. "Thank you, Sofia. We appreciate all your help."

They paused in front of the space in the hedgerow, but only for a moment. Theodore went first and then extended his hand backward. Lola grasped onto it tight. She met Sofia's gaze long enough to see her friend nod before Lola pushed through to the other side.

TWO HOURS LATER, THE MOURNFUL CLANG OF A FAR-OFF wherry sounded through the window glass, an appropriate echo of Lola's distraught mood. It was nearly midnight and Theodore had secured a room for them at a modest inn near the London Docks. She scanned the dreary interior, a far cry from the opulent comfort of Theodore's town house and yet he'd not uttered a single complaint, his every word an attempt to reassure her instead.

Come morning, he intended to book passage for their travel aboard any packet ship bound for America within the week. He'd already sent Wyndham a message and awaited his man-of-all-things' reply concerning the necessary documents and funds for their trip. She glanced to Theodore as he tended the fire and wondered if he experienced the same morass of complicated emotions alive within her.

"This is madness. It's never going to work," she said, her voice both nervous and adamant. "We can't do this."

"Lola." Theodore strode across the room, his expression serious. "There's no time for second thoughts. I know you're fearless, so unless your doubt arises from uncertainty concerning us—"

"No." She cut him off, unwilling to let him continue. "Our relationship is the only thing I *am* sure of, but you've only just returned from America," she said, closing her eyes as she leaned against his chest. He was strong and warm and always there to support her and yet she was forcing him to make rash decisions and hide in a dingy inn near the London Docks.

"That makes relocating all the easier. Every American I met on my recent visit will remember me and that will be helpful as we decide where to live. If you like London, you'll adore New York City. I've established business contacts and invested in a few thriving companies there."

"My sister knows nothing of what transpired tonight. I haven't said goodbye to her or my family. What about Mercury and Venus?" Her voice trembled with the threat of too much emotion.

"Wyndham will arrange for our horses and belongings to follow. Once we're settled, my solicitor will oversee all financial matters. The London house will be closed or sold if we prefer. The servants will be pensioned."

She breathed deeply, wanting to believe it would all transpire as smoothly as he detailed.

"As for your family, you haven't seen them in over two years, so you should write to them. We can post the letter in the morning."

He pressed a kiss to her forehead. "I know you've only just reunited with your sister. I'm sorry."

"No," she objected, pulling out of his embrace. "I'm sorry. I'm causing this upheaval in your life, forcing you to make difficult choices. It's wrong."

"You're not forcing me to do anything. If I have to choose between the earldom and you, I choose you every time." He pulled her forward until she was only inches from his face. "You belong with me. It doesn't matter where we are because I'd go anywhere to be with you. I love you, Lola. Do you love me and want us to be together?"

"Yes," she answered emphatically. "But—"

"Yes is the only answer necessary," he said softly. "Now, it's late and we're exhausted. Let's go to bed and fall asleep in each other's arms."

For a long moment, she couldn't breathe, her heart squeezed tight. "Thank you, Theodore."

"You don't have to thank me for helping you evade the duke's charges. He's a horrible man who beats animals and revels in other people's pain. You acted out of love and kindness when you set that horse free and it's a travesty anyone would punish you for your merciful act."

"I wasn't thanking you for that," she said as she threaded her fingers with his and tugged him toward the bed.

"Oh?" He sounded confused and paused beside the mattress while he waited for her to continue.

"Thank you for loving me so completely." She reached up and untied his cravat, dropping it to the floor before she undid the buttons of his waistcoat.

"Indeed." He began to undress her now, too. "Once we're in bed, I'll remind you just how completely I do love you."

. . .

LOLA AWOKE AT DAWN AND SLIPPED FROM THE SHEETS without waking Theodore. The fire waned in the hearth and she quietly poked at the logs to stir up the flames. After she dressed, she settled at the small table near the window and penned a letter to her family, explaining her plans. Her sister would complete the story by telling their parents of her life in London. Lola had just finished the note when Theodore stirred.

"Good morning." He propped up on his elbow. "No more second thoughts, I hope. Although I wouldn't mind *reassuring* you repeatedly for the four thousand mile trip across the Atlantic."

"I see you've slept well. Your usual charm is intact." She tried for a teasing tone and waved the letter in her hand. "I'd like to post this as soon as possible though."

"Of course." He rubbed his eyes and got out of bed, dressing as soon as he washed his face. "I expect Wyndham's delivery of the necessary documents later this morning. We'll head out now so we're here to accept the trunks he prepared for us and the paperwork needed."

"Yes, I'm ready." She tucked the letter in her pocket and picked up her shawl.

Despite the early hour, the docks were busy. Several ships were anchored along the piers and longshoremen worked industriously to unload crates of tobacco, spice, olive oil and rum, the precious cargo guarded dockside by burly crewmen who awaited its distribution. Theodore asked one such fellow where the nearest post was situated and they headed in that direction.

They'd only walked a block from the water when they heard the hawk of a newsboy who stood on a wooden box near the corner, waving a copy of the daily print in the air. Lola thought nothing of the ordinary scene she'd come to identify with the bustle of city life until they neared the lad and deciphered his call more clearly.

"Duke trampled by prized stallion!" the newsboy hailed loudly. "Read about His Grace's tragic death."

Lola and Theodore's eyes met before he hurried straight to the lad and purchased a copy of The Times.

"Let me see. What does it say?" Lola asked breathlessly as she clasped Theodore's arm and rose on tiptoe, attempting to read the paper as he moved them away from the flow of pedestrian traffic.

"Leinster's dead," Theodore exclaimed, his voice rich with disbelief as he scanned the paper. "He was thrown and trampled by his own horse!"

"That's horrible," Lola said though her voice trembled. "Is there more?"

"According to witnesses, Leinster lost his temper with his prized stallion and began whipping the horse excessively. When Leinster realized he had been seen by two attendants, he attempted to mount and leave, but the horse threw him immediately and trampled the duke in its hurry to get away."

"But what does this mean for us, Theodore?" She wouldn't jump to conclusions even though her heart pounded like thunder in her chest.

"You're free, Lola. You're free from his accusations and charges. Without the duke to pursue prosecution, you're beyond blame." He chuckled heartily and grasped her shoulders, the newsprint crinkling against her gown as he kissed her excitedly. "Not only that, but there's commentary in the article about the duke's behavior toward animals. You're mentioned as having taken heroic action."

"What? Let me see that!" Lola snatched the paper, scanning the page as tears filled her eyes and blurred her vision. "I'm exonerated?"

A wave of relief swept through her so strong she sagged against Theodore's side, unable to speak as emotion clogged her throat. But he knew. He felt her trembling, sensed her every emotion, and pulled her against his chest tightly.

"Yes, it's true, Lola. You're free to live here, anywhere, to walk with your head held high because you were brave and courageous.

Then, and today. We can build our life together without worry or fear."

"It feels wrong to be happy," she whispered, tears of relief overflowing to her cheeks. She wiped them away quickly. "But he'd become a horrid, despicable man."

"That's true."

"And we don't have to leave London. I can see my family again." She turned and looked up into his face, a whirlwind of emotions making her unsteady even though her smile emerged. "And the whole world can know how much we love each other."

"Let's go home," he said as he matched her grin and offered his hand. "Our life together awaits."

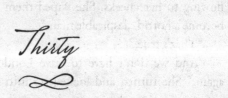

Thirty

TWO WEEKS LATER...

A shimmer of excitement spiraled through Lola as she rang a silver bell to gain everyone's attention. It was Theodore's idea to host an elegant party at his town house and announce the wonderful news of all criminal charges being nullified. Friends and family were gathered on the terrace beneath a velvet night sky filled with twinkling stars, while she stood next to the man she loved on the threshold of a future she had trouble believing was true. But this was her life now. A life of true love. Days and nights filled with happiness, hope, and possibility.

"Thank you for joining us this evening." Theodore's deep voice resounded across the marble tiles and quieted the last whispered conversations. "Lola and I have invited you here to share extraordinary news and I'll not keep you in suspense. All complaints against Lola have been dismissed. To that end, a reporter from The London Times has interviewed Lola and plans to write a story about her heroic act of compassion. With that in the past, we look to the future. Please raise your glass and join me in celebrating Lola and this very joyous occasion."

Theodore took a hearty sip of champagne and leaned down to

speak to her privately. "I know you were hesitant earlier, but would you like to say a few words?"

"I suppose I have to, don't I?" she said with a reluctant smile. She rang the bell again and looked out at the circle of guests. Her parents stood directly in front alongside her sister Anna and Lord Huntington. Sofia and her brothers were to the left, while Lady Margaret and her betrothed, Viscount Sidmouth, were on the opposite side. Marco and a few friends from Vauxhall were also present. She glanced one more time at Theodore and her heart swelled with love and gratitude. Even if she'd wished on every star in the heavens, she'd never have believed she could be this happy.

"Thank you for sharing this special evening." She began, exhaling slowly in an attempt to settle her nerves. "Life has certainly been an adventure filled with uncertainty the last few years so it means the world to me to see all of you gathered here tonight."

Anxious to speak to everyone individually, she raised her champagne glass and took another sip. She still had a lot of lost time to recover with her parents even though they'd traveled directly to London upon receiving her letter. She'd spent part of every day with them since they'd arrived and delighted in how much Theodore and her father had in common. Her mother was equally as charmed with Theodore's unwavering dedication.

She glanced to Anna and Lord Huntington who made no secret how smitten they appeared. Lola wouldn't be surprised if another exciting announcement was made in the near future. She'd never seen her sister look happier.

Squeezing Theodore's arm affectionately, she placed her glass down and walked eagerly toward Sofia.

"Tell me everything," Sofia demanded before Lola even reached her. "I haven't seen you in what feels like forever and I miss you. You spend all your time here now." Sofia's eyes widened as she indicated the town house behind them. "Not that I can blame you."

"It seemed silly, if not inconvenient, to keep returning to the boarding house," Lola said in way of explanation. "Besides, there wasn't much for me to take with me when I moved out."

"But now that you've left Vauxhall and you're not living upstairs, I'm worried I'm never going to spend time with you again."

"That's ridiculous. I'd be lost without my closest friend. Who am I going to share flavored ice with?" Lola teased. "Why don't I come by the day after tomorrow? I need to check my post and collect a few last things."

"That sounds perfect." Sofia grinned. "And it's good timing. I think your room is already rented for next month. Francesco saw the landlord shake hands with a young man on the front steps yesterday."

"A young man? Was he handsome?" Lola asked with a playful note in her voice.

"That doesn't matter," Alessandro answered from over her shoulder.

"Sofia needs to stay focused on perfecting her double somer-sault," Francesco added as he appeared as suddenly as his brother.

"*Dio mio!* Were you both listening to my conversation?" Sofia's stern tone expressed her displeasure. "You're unbearable."

"It's our responsibility to watch over you, dear sister." Alessandro softened his words with a smile before he and Francesco walked away.

"See what I'm up against?" Sofia said despairingly. "It will be a wonder if I ever find romance again."

"Don't say that." Lola clasped her friend's hand. "If love managed to find me while I was using a different name and hiding high above London on a tightrope, I know love will find you."

"I hope so, Lola," Sofia said with a slight smile. "I'll keep my eyes and heart open to be sure I'm ready."

"Good. Now, let's go talk to my parents and sister." Lola tugged on Sofia's hand. "I want them to meet you."

. . .

Sunshine filled the sky the following morning and Theodore couldn't be more pleased. After breakfast Lola had gone upstairs to change into the new riding habit he'd had delivered from his tailor. Today they intended to share a quiet day, just the two of them, riding in the park. He'd already arranged to have the horses saddled and a picnic hamper packed. Everything was in order, though he couldn't contain the pulse of restless energy that caused him to pace across the carpet in the drawing room while he awaited her return downstairs.

"I'm ready," Lola called from the hallway before she swept into the room. "What do you think?"

She looked stunning. The royal blue riding jacket with frothy lace cuffs was cropped at her waist, where a sleek skirt flowed down to meet her glossy leather boots. The impeccable fit of the ensemble hugged her curves perfectly and provoked thoughts of activities other than riding.

"What is it?" she asked, her expression alarmed. "Do I look all right?"

He eyed the petite velvet top hat set at a jaunty angle upon her head. "You are a vision."

"And you are a scoundrel," she said with a beguiling smile. "Are you ready to ride?"

"More than ready," he replied as they walked into the hall and through the house to the back of the property.

He helped her into the sidesaddle atop Venus and then mounted Mercury before they rode into the street toward Hyde Park. Once they passed through the wrought iron gates and trotted beyond the pedestrian promenade, he indicated a deep-set clearing near the bank of the Serpentine River where a patch of lush grass was surrounded by clusters of pink primrose and lily of the valley, their fragrance light on the breeze.

"This is a lovely spot."

"Almost as lovely as you." He dismounted and reached up to grasp her waist, lifting her swiftly to the ground, though he didn't immediately release her. "I can't think of anywhere I'd rather be than right here with you, Miss Morgan."

"Such flattery this morning, Lord Essex. Are you angling for a kiss?" she said in a teasing tone. "I'm happy to oblige. Kissing you is one of my favorite things to do."

"And your other favorite things?" he asked as he removed his gloves and took the liberty of removing hers. He tossed them atop the saddle and tilted her chin upward so their eyes matched.

"I'll show you the rest of my list later this evening." Mischief gleamed in her gaze before she lowered her lashes. "Besides, all my kisses are yours for free. You needn't offer compliments and work at grand gestures."

He chuckled, anticipating her objection to what he was about to say. "Well, today I do have a little surprise."

"Theodore!" She said, her voice firm yet elated. "The sapphire necklace, a beautiful horse and new riding habit—your generosity has proven overwhelming. No more presents, please."

"It's a small token. Very small actually." He cleared his throat and tried to suppress a grin.

"It's sweet of you and I appreciate your thoughtfulness but you don't have to shower me with extravagant gifts," she said sincerely, her voice going soft. "You've given me your love. There's nothing else I could ever want."

"Well, I'm hoping you'll want this one last gift," he said as he reached into his waistcoat pocket. "Especially since it's meant to last a lifetime."

Her delicate brows rose, but she didn't say another word.

"Lola, from the moment we met, you've filled my thoughts and soon after filled my heart. I love you and can't imagine my life without you. For these reasons and a million more..." He offered her the ring he held and her eyes widened in surprise. "Will you be my wife?"

"Theodore." Tears shimmered in her eyes now.

"Say you'll marry me. Say you'll spend the rest of your life with me."

"Yes!" She gasped, overcome with emotion. "Yes! Of course, my answer is yes!"

He took her hand, noticing how it trembled, and slid the glittering gold ring on her finger.

"It's so beautiful." She stared down at the brilliant diamond and watched as it caught the sunlight, glistening with all the love and hope of their future together. "Who would have ever guessed that after all we've been through, our story would end this way?"

"Lola, my darling." He drew her closer until only a whisper separated their lips. "I promise you this is only our beginning."

Epiloque

Lola climbed from the carriage and turned to thank the driver as he folded the stairs. "Please wait for me at the corner, Jenkins."

"Very good, Miss Morgan," Jenkins replied before he slapped the reins and led the team away.

Excited to see Sofia, she started across the street toward her former address. The windows in the upstairs rooms were dark. If her old room had been rented already, the new tenant wasn't home today.

"Lola! Hello!" Sofia hurried down the front steps, her smile as bright as the sun overhead. "We should take a walk around the block. The weather is fair and it's the only way we'll have privacy to talk."

"That's a good idea," Lola said, hugging her friend in greeting. "But first I want to show you something."

"Show me something?" Sofia asked. "What is it?"

Lola removed the glove on her left hand and watched as Sofia's eyes followed her every action. "I'm engaged."

"*Dio mio!*" Sofia shrieked and pulled Lola into another hug before she released her to anxiously examine the ring. "*Che bello.*

The earl has excellent taste. I've never seen a diamond that big, and look how the smaller stones dance around it in a circle. Your hand must get tired from wearing it all day."

"Not at all." Lola laughed as she slipped her glove back on. "Actually, I feel as if I'm floating on a cloud. I've never given much thought to jewelry and certainly not an engagement ring. Theodore chose such a pretty setting. The only thing more beautiful was his proposal."

Seeing Sofia's smile falter, Lola hurriedly linked arms with her so they could begin their stroll.

"I'm so happy for you. You deserve the most wonderful gifts life can offer," Sofia said after a moment. "Someday, I hope to marry too."

"And you will," Lola reassured her. "I told you, love will find you when you least expect it."

"That's good, because my expectations haven't always worked out well."

"I wish you didn't feel that way, but things may be about to change." Lola stopped and faced Sofia before she took a letter from her skirt pocket and held it out to her friend. "I visited the post earlier and this was waiting there."

"Oh, I can't believe it," Sofia said, her surprise evident in her tone. "I wonder what it says."

"I guess you'll know as soon as you read it," Lola answered lightly. "But I don't think you should open it out here while we're walking. Since you have no idea what the message says, maybe it would be better to read it when you're alone, in private, at a time when your brothers aren't home."

Lola watched as a variety of emotions passed over Sofia's face. There was no way to tell if the letter contained good or bad news. Lola knew very little about the circumstances of Sofia's past relationship, departure from Italy, and reasons for relocating in England. She'd always believed Sofia would share whatever had happened when she was ready.

To that end, the last thing Lola wanted to do was give her dearest friend something else to worry over, but she also didn't wish to instill false hope. That's why she thought reading the message should be done alone.

"You're right," Sofia said at last, tucking the letter inside her pelisse. "In many ways it seems like yesterday when I left Italy. I wish I'd had a chance to say goodbye."

"I'm sure you do," Lola said. "I hope whatever is written inside that letter helps settle your emotions once and for all."

They walked a while in silence and Lola knew better than to force conversation. Eventually, Sofia found her way to sharing her thoughts.

"Luca had a way of making me smile even when I didn't want to, but that didn't really matter because I could never stay mad at him, even when things were difficult between us."

"I'm sorry things became difficult," Lola said at a loss to understand exactly what had happened.

Sofia laughed softly, a smile of reminiscence on her face. "It was a complicated situation. Very complicated. Alessandro and Francesco were infuriated with me when they found out I was seeing Luca. They didn't want to listen to what I had to say. That's why I never had a chance to say goodbye. My brothers forbade me from meeting with him and when I tried to sneak out one last time, I was caught. The next day Francesco announced we were moving away. Since my parents' death, my brothers have watched over me and they considered what I'd done an act of disrespect. However, it wasn't like that at all. The heart wants what the heart wants and I wanted to be with Luca. I wasn't the only one who took risks and made difficult decisions. He did too. We were in love and nothing else mattered."

Sofia fell silent and Lola waited, her heart aching for her friend.

"But that's all in the past now," Sofia said, her voice a mixture of sadness and determination. "I can't allow my old feelings to become new again. I'm sure very little has changed. Luca is still in

Italy. My brothers will still become furious if he tries to speak to me. They'll still forbid me from seeing him. I just wish I could have seen Luca one last time before I left. I wrote to him and explained why I disappeared so suddenly, but I told him not to write back. I didn't want for him to make promises he couldn't keep. From the beginning we knew the situation was impossible." She fell silent for a few steps before she spoke again. "I definitely don't expect him to love me now after all this time has passed."

"Any man would be a fool not to cherish your love. I'm happy you sent that letter and I'm even happier you've received a response," Lola said, unsure how to comfort Sofia. "And there's no way to predict what has transpired in the time you've been apart."

"That's true, I suppose." Sofia sighed. "As soon as we return and I'm alone in my room, I'll read what he wrote. For better or worse."

"No matter what the letter contains, it will be good to know," Lola reassured her. "It may offer some clarity to the situation."

Sofia wrinkled her nose. "In some ways it's easier not knowing. Then I don't have to make any decisions or learn things I'd rather not. I would be a fool to invite more disappointment."

Lola squeezed Sofia's hand. "I understand. I think you should do what feels right. You'll know in your heart what choice to make."

They walked on in silence until they rounded the corner and approached the front steps of the boarding house.

"Sofia, look," Lola whispered. "I think the new tenant has arrived."

Up ahead, a tall, fair-haired man carried a large valise and set it down near the front steps of the building. Two smaller bags were also on the pavement while a hackney waited in the street. When the man turned to pay the cab fare, Sofia squeezed Lola's arm tight.

"Quanto è bello!"

"What does that mean?" Lola asked, noticing Sofia's fixed attention on the stranger.

"He's so handsome," Sofia whispered. "How can I live in the same building as this man? My brothers will become more protective than ever and I'll be worried about my appearance all the time."

"You're beautiful. You do know that, right?" Lola asked with a little laugh. "Let's say hello."

"No," Sofia objected in a hushed voice. "He hasn't noticed us and that's fine with me."

"It would be better to meet him while your brothers aren't outside, don't you think so?"

"That's true," Sofia said, taking a deep breath. "All right, I'm ready."

Lola stifled a smile at how quickly Sofia had changed her mind. Together they walked to the front stoop. The gentleman was even more handsome up close. He wore a pair of dark gray trousers, matching waistcoat and white shirt, of which he'd rolled up the sleeves to reveal strong forearms, lightly dusted with pale brown hair.

"Good morning and welcome to the neighborhood," Lola said.

The man turned from where he was busy searching through one of the bags he'd set near the bottom of the stairs.

"Hello, ladies," the stranger replied as he gave them his attention. "I've rented the upstairs room in this building but I've forgotten where I put my key. It's here somewhere." He patted his waistcoat pocket and shook his head as if frustrated.

"I'm Miss Gallo. I live downstairs with my two brothers," Sofia said cheerfully.

"It's a pleasure to meet you," the man said with a smile. "I'm Mr. Wright."

With the conversation stalled, Lola introduced herself. "I'm Miss Morgan and I lived here until recently. In the room upstairs, actually. I hope you find it as comfortable as I did."

"I'm sure I will," Mr. Wright replied quickly. He leaned down and opened the outside compartment of one of his traveling bags and then checked the other valise as well. "I know I have the key here somewhere."

Lola looked at Sofia, but her friend only shrugged.

"I suppose you should contact the landlord if you need another key. While I can unlock the door to the stairwell, I no longer have the key to the room upstairs. I returned it once Miss Morgan moved out."

"No, I understand. I would never wish to inconvenience you," Mr. Wright said. "I was running late and didn't want to miss the coach from Hampshire. I think my hands may have been moving faster than my brain," he explained with a bit of self-deprecating humor.

"Will your wife be arriving later?" Lola asked, curiously.

"Oh, no," he said with a sheepish grin. "I'm not married."

A second awkward silence ensued and Lola noticed how Sofia never took her gaze from Mr. Wright. To his credit, he possessed an easy smile that prompted the recipient to do the same. Lola wondered what Sofia was thinking and whether if for at least a few minutes, she'd forgotten about Luca's letter in her pocket.

"I really should go inside and get unpacked but that's impossible until I find my key." Mr. Wright said. He patted his waistcoat pocket again, his eyes never leaving Sofia. "Wait a minute. What's this?"

He reached toward Sofia, whose expression grew wary with his unexpected gesture. Then with a flick of his hand, he produced the key as if he'd found it inside her left ear.

It was a charming trick and Sofia's eyes twinkled from his attention.

"Why, Miss Gallo," he said in that same affable tone. "You had my key all along. What other secrets are you hiding?"

This comment seemed to give Sofia a mental shake and her expression sobered.

"It was very nice to meet you, Mr. Wright."

"Yes. Indeed, it was," Lola added. "Now I should be on my way as well. I'll see you soon, Sofia."

Sofia climbed the stairs, pausing at the top to wave goodbye before she disappeared from the entry.

Once inside, Sofia closed the door and leaned against the panel to collect her emotions. What had just happened?

She'd received a letter from Luca.

And met her handsome new neighbor.

Her heart pounded furiously in her chest.

But from which circumstance, she did not know.

She removed the letter from the pocket of her pelisse cautiously, as if by handling it she'd evoke a spell and return to the pain of the past, even though the idea was ridiculous.

What could Luca possibly have to say after all this time? He'd probably moved on with his life and established a family now. Maybe he'd forgotten everything that had transpired between them.

But she hadn't.

None of these thoughts and questions provoked the slightest glimmer of hope. She reminded herself that was a good thing. She didn't want to waste time on hope.

What if she opened the letter and experienced the same heart-breaking agony that plagued her for months after leaving Italy? What if Luca confessed he still loved her? That would be awful because the circumstances hadn't changed. They still couldn't be together. And knowing he cared for her would prevent her from ever loving someone else. She'd be tormented by the knowledge when there was absolutely nothing she could do about it.

Topolina appeared near her feet, the intuitive cat quick to offer comfort. Reaching down to scoop her up, Sofia went to her room, the letter held tight to her chest as she sat on the bed. Topolina leapt from her arms and settled on the counterpane with a sympathetic meow.

Perhaps she should put the letter away and think about it in the morning. Sleep had a way of clearing one's mind and providing perspective. Except it didn't matter how many days and nights passed. Lola was right. *Not knowing* was not the answer. Nothing would settle itself until she read Luca's letter. Not her emotions. Or her hopes. And definitely not her future.

"I'm making the right decision, Topolina," she whispered as she broke the seal on Luca's letter and unfolded the paper, "because there's no going back and changing the past. It's time for me to take control of my future."

Also by Anabelle Bryant

Anabelle Bryant Book List

Regency Rogues Series

To Love A Wicked Scoundrel

Duke of Darkness

The Midnight Rake

Regency Charms Series

Defying The Earl

Undone By His Kiss

Society's Most Scandalous Viscount

His Forbidden Debutante

-

Bastards of London

The Den of Iniquity

Into the Hall of Vice

The Last Gamble

Return to the House of Sin

-

About the Author

USA Today Bestselling author Anabelle Bryant began reading at age three and never stopped. Her passion for reading soon turned into a passion for writing and an author was born. Happy to grab her suitcase if it ensures a new adventure, Anabelle finds endless inspiration in travel; especially imaginary jaunts into romantic Regency England, a far cry from her home in New Jersey. Instead, her clever characters live out her daydreams because really, who wouldn't want to dance with a handsome duke or kiss a wicked earl?

Anabelle's books have been translated into several languages including Japanese and Russian, but writing isn't all that keeps her busy. Building miniatures, baking and photography are other favorite pastimes. Often found with her nose in a book, Anabelle is just as happy in a room full of people. She enjoys meeting readers, attending conferences and book signings. She has earned her Master's Degree and is ABD for her Doctorate Degree in education.

A firm believer in romance, Anabelle knows sometimes life doesn't provide a happily ever after, but her novels always do. Visit her website at AnabelleBryant.com.

CPSIA information can be obtained
at www.ICGtesting.com
Printed in the USA
LVHW091020280223
740499LV00005B/605